CW00860301

PROLOGUE

*L*ondon 1821

*T*he cloaked figure eyed the apples in the cart. Their bright shiny redness mesmerised it. It hadn't had apples for a very long time; after all, they were out of season back home. Yet before it lay the tantalising beauties, as if plucked out of some fairy tale and placed conveniently before it. As the figure put out a remarkably small hand to pay the seller, an elderly toothless woman who barely gave it a second glance, its stomach churned as it realised it had all been worth it. However, its joy was short-lived; out of nowhere a large hairy hand clamped over its outstretched one before the exchange of money and apple could take place. The figure jumped in shock.

A heavy gruff voice spoke into its ear. 'You *will* come with us.' The smell of sweat and an unwashed body surrounded it.

Quick as a flash the figure pushed off the heavy cloak, jumped off the stilts it walked on and began to sprint off. She knew that she had taken the men completely by surprise; they would not expect such speed and agility from her kind. They were small, heavy and looked slow – nor were they expecting a child, small but so cunning. She laughed but she was not cocky about it, she couldn't get caught.

'You idiots,' she heard a man yell. 'I told you not to surprise them. You just grab hold of them.'

Her heart raced; they had spotted her. The men had come in groups and this time they were prepared. Everything was at risk now. She began to run as fast as her tiny legs would allow but it was harder than she'd thought; she would have to duck and weave to avoid them. It was one of the tricks they had all mastered – it was the only way of ever getting out alive. The most important detail was that they could not see her disappear, she would either have to lure them away or get caught herself. She could not risk capture with the rest of the commune or they would all be killed. They were still not sure what these people wanted with them but they were not keen to find out; for whatever it was, it would be painful – probably even worse than death. As she ran through the small, filthy winding streets she did not bother to check if they were still on her trail. She could hear them so well – every sound – their cheap shoes pounding the streets and their heavy, hoarse breathing as they called out to her.

'Stop, now.'

'Stop, you vagrant.'

But she didn't stop, their words fuelling her to run faster. They couldn't catch her, she wouldn't let them.

'The magistrates just want a word.'

A wry smile crossed her lips; the magistrates wanting a word probably meant there was a higher power behind them. It indicated that these men who had been paid to protect the city would continue to pursue and hound them till they had them by the necks.

Ducking into a narrow alleyway she found herself running into the nearest door, which had just been opened. There were little screams and gasps of surprise at the sight of her as she ran through a gaudily decorated room. She knew she looked peculiar: extraordinarily small, dressed in male clothing, hair sticking out in strange pigtails, tanned leathery skin, a bulbous nose and deep blue eyes – strange features indeed. They would see a child, but she had been around much longer than any of them. Their kind did not live long. As she tore through the busy building looking for the nearest exit it took her a short while to figure out where she was. The half-dressed women squawked as she ran past, their heavily made-up faces looking on in horror. The men dashing out of the different rooms hurriedly trying to pull up their breeches and disappear into the background. A brothel. One of several in London. She had heard about them but had never been in one. She allowed herself a half-hearted laugh as she dashed under the skirts of a woman who was standing by a spiral staircase looking bewildered. The woman began to squeal and stomp around as the strange creature ran through her skirts, almost tripping her up.

Turning into a narrow hallway she paused to collect her breath wondering what to do next. They were hot on her heels; she could hear them and knew they would be flying up the stairs anytime soon. She looked up – all the doors were identical and it would be difficult to know if they had occupants. Then again it was a brothel in

London. They were always busy. They always had occupants. A frisson of fear ran through her as she tried to make a decision, not wanting to panic but at the same time not wanting to trap herself into a corner. Why make the job easy for the roguish brutes when she could make it much harder and let them know her kind were not easily captured. But there were so many doors, which to choose? The she heard a low hissing sound and turned in the direction it came from. A familiar face looked out from behind a door. It was human, but a friend. Her name was Grace. Binkers dashed to meet her, the breath almost knocked out of her as Grace grabbed her and hauled her into the room. Binkers was surprised; for such a dainty, well-mannered person she was brutally strong. She wondered what the young girl was doing in a brothel. From what Binkers recalled of this world only whores were seen in brothels – people of disrepute and poor characters – or so they said. She did not know any. She was also aware the nobility inhabited these places. She did not know any of those either.

Grace motioned to her to be silent as she shut the door behind her. Binkers took note of the room she had been dragged into. The decoration was vulgar, the furnishings smelling of cheap perfume and tobacco. Then she started; there was someone else in the room. It was a man, too well fed, who lay flat on the bed, his modesty covered by a sheet. He was fast asleep and snored loudly. Binkers thought to kick him but reconsidered. She was already being chased. Why make her hanging worse by subjecting herself to a beating first?

'Grace. How do you come to be in this place? We must leave at once. I am in grave danger,' she hissed at the girl.

Then Binkers noticed her dress and paused, recoiling in

horror. 'You? You work in this house of ill repute?' she yelped. 'I thought you were to be a milliner.'

Grace hastily clamped a hand over Binkers's mouth until she calmed down.

'Dear Binkers. Life does not always go the way we want. I found myself out of pocket and almost destitute before the lady of this house took me in. And yet you judge me harshly – after all, I have just saved your life.'

Binkers looked down, suddenly ashamed at her explosion. 'I'm sorry, Grace. It has been a terrible evening. I came up for apples. Some stupid apples, but it was a trap and here I am – about to meet my end in a brothel,' she said in dismay.

'All is not lost. They are coming. They will go from room to room but he,' she motioned to the man who lay on the bed, 'is a *sir*. He is of noble blood.'

Binkers's jaw hung.

'They will shut the door as soon as they enter for fear of embarrassing him.' Grace leaned forward conspiratorially. 'He is an important benefactor at Bow Street.'

Binkers nodded slowly, her head turning to the obese man. She turned her back in disgust. Then her eyes widened.

'I hear them.'

'Hide,' Grace whispered. 'When it's clear I will call to you and you must be ready to run, Binkers.'

She was hastily led to a cupboard and shoved in behind hanging clothes that smelt of cheap perfume. Binkers held her breath as the uproar continued through the large house. Then the door to the room was suddenly opened and there was the muffled sound of Grace shrieking in fright.

'This is Sir Bannister. Shall I wake him?' Binkers heard her ask. She grinned. No one would agree to that. There was a lull and heavy boots were heard around the room then the door was shut. A few minutes passed and the cupboard doors were suddenly yanked open.

'Now listen.' Grace bent over as though dropping to Binkers's height would help her understand better. 'Three doors to the left is a bedroom.'

'Will it not be occupied?'

'Oh, dear Binkers, do listen. It will be in use but with all the hullabaloo about the place they will not have their wits about them. I want you to run as fast as you can when you hear a commotion and dash in. There will be another door hidden behind the dresser, enter it and it leads to another stairwell.' Grace nodded. 'That is the way out and then, Binkers, I fear you must run and never look back because I know not how long I can distract them.'

Binkers nodded nervously. 'What will cause the commotion?'

Grace smiled. 'I will. I intend to draw them all to this part of the house by screaming loudly and saying I was pushed down a set of stairs round the corner.'

'That will make them very angry.'

Grace smiled. This time it did not reach her eyes. 'For a short while. I am a whore, after all.' Her voice was bitter. 'Now I will go. Once you hear the screams you know what to do.'

Binkers nodded. Her stomach felt tight as Grace inched the door open and looked round, then she ambled out, clicking it shut behind her. There were voices in the hall-way. Binkers waited nervously; the seconds felt like an eternity. The man snoring in the background did not help her nerves. Binkers turned to look at him, once more contemplating kicking him, but it would do her no good. Grace had put herself in grave danger simply by helping her and she could not repay her kindness by ruining the one chance she had of escaping. She would have been in irons by now if Grace had not intervened. The scream in the air rang out so loud and piercing that Binkers almost jumped out of her skin. The man in the bed began to stir at the commotion. Binkers inched the door open to peek out. Grace was right. Everyone had congregated at the point of her screams. The hallway was clear. She held her breath and dashed out of the room leaving the door ajar behind her. She passed the doors in a flash and ran into the third one, wondering as she did so whether Grace had meant the door after the third or the third exactly. A man sat on the bed in the middle of getting dressed; the woman who accompanied him for the evening was missing, no doubt investigating the terrified scream. The man stopped what he was doing and stared at Binkers in shock.

'What are you?' he exclaimed.

She ignored him and dived behind the dresser. Grace was right. There was a door and it did lead to a passageway. Binkers assumed it was to aid the more prestigious of their clientele to avoid embarrassing incidents if the law arrived.

Binkers headed down the nearest staircase hoping it would lead to an exit, as Grace had explained, but found herself in a dark, damp cellar and hurriedly began to try the different doors that she passed. One of them led to further stairs which, to her immense relief, led to a dark alleyway which she left behind, fearing she was even further from home than ever. But as she ran back onto the cold London streets she felt comforted; in the distance would be the covering of moss. She was almost there. Sticking to the side streets and dark corners which allowed her to hide from the public and her pursuers she headed for home.

~

The man had spotted the figure in the cloak long before his comrades and the man at the head of their party, Farringday. It was true London was in the grip of a bitter winter but there was something odd about the manner in which the figure moved: its top half was not at one with its bottom. Its movements were clumsy. He instantly knew it was one of them but said nothing. Why help Farringday when he was not good enough to lead? If this operation was botched then perhaps Farringday would be removed from his post and he, Cobbler, would take over – he would do a much better job of it. Bringing an outsider to head the runners had been a preposterous idea and badly orchestrated by the magistrates.

Cobbler stood back as an overenthusiastic man placed a hand on the figure's shoulder and it bolted.

'It must not escape,' he heard Farringday roar. He looked furious at the misjudgement. It was a lot harder to catch them once they were on the run.

Cobbler chose to remain back as the rest of the group charged into the house after the creature. The screams and shrieks that followed its appearance spoke volumes. The brothel was run by Loretta Carter and catered to the upper classes. The magistrates were favoured clients and he knew Lord Flynt and Lord Wordsworth attended with special girls reserved for them. They had their favourites in there and Cobbler knew them well: common whores born two streets away from him in just as dire circumstances, but their pale looks and ampleness had won them admirers and eventually the attentions of Miss Carter's recruiter in arms, Penelope Black.

'Come on, Cobbler,' Farringday called to him as he

charged in. Farringday was known to the brothel, not because he was any better than Cobbler but because he had gone in to report his findings to the magistrates and the lords. The likes of him would never be allowed in there as a patron – not in a thousand years – so he saw no need to go in on a chase as an employee of the magistrates.

As the mêlée continued indoors he remained outside as though none of it concerned him. Then he had a thought and moved to the stinking alleyway behind the large building, motioning to Tom Skillet who was standing guard by the door to follow him.

The younger man approached.

'What is it, Cobbler? I was told...'

Cobbler shushed him and signalled to him to wait. The two crouched in the darkness, the putrid smell of urine and vomit almost overpowering them. A drunk lay passed out, or dead, a few feet from them but they paid him no attention. As Cobbler sensed Tom about to speak his mind and break the silence, they heard the movement from a little side door as it burst open and the odd-looking vermin who had run into the main building made its escape. He gazed cockily at an open-mouthed Tom.

'Never question me again, boy. With me,' he ordered sharply.

Together Cobbler and Tom tracked the vermin to its hiding place. The man was glad the boy was sure-footed and stealthy so they attracted no attention as they skulked after it in the dark night. Those they came across paid them no attention and were mostly drunk bystanders or common whores. He was satisfied; the creature they tracked failed to notice the extra hulk to the shadows behind it. As it slunk off into the darkness, he and Tom would break away from the shadows and follow it. Cobbler grinned; these creatures were considered intelligent but he was about to prove how stupid they were. Not once had it looked behind it to ensure no one followed. For about a mile Cobbler and Tom remained close on its tail. Past the canals, the public houses, more brothels – they were determined not to lose it. Not this time anyway. Not anymore. The creatures had slipped from their grasp many a time. They watched as the little being disappeared through a conveniently hidden entrance in the ground which was cleverly obscured by a gathering of moss. Cobbler smiled to himself; after several months of hunting these creatures they finally had a result. His comrades were still tearing through the whorehouses looking for the escapee yet here it was in sight. The man refused to legitimise them by referring to them as he would a human. He would inform the magistrates straight away. His head snapped round to Tom.

'Oi, you – run off to Lincoln's Inn Fields and tell 'em, Mr Greensmith and that lot, we know where they are. They are to hasten with horses, torches, the runners and *Farringday*,' he spat.

'But, Cobbler. I ain't supposed to take orders from ya, am I? It's all supposed to be from Farringday. What if they...'

'Shut up, boy. We have found the vermin. We know where they lie. Farringday still searches the whorehouses. No – this'll be my victory and there'll be a nice cut in it for you... if you do as you're told and stop making a bleedin' fuss.'

Tom Skillet nodded. He was young – nowhere near Cobbler's age or advanced experience. He would do whatever he said. But he still looked anguished at the thought.

'It'd best go well or else...'

'Just go!' Cobbler seethed impatiently. 'And remember

to tell them it was I, Cobbler, that located the vermin.' His head turned to the patch of moss. It was an odd location, one that was out of place. Nearby were trees with the central ones forming an unwieldy arch.

Tom hurried off, disappearing into the darkness, his slight limp making a clip-clop noise on the cobbled street like a little pony would. Cobbler turned back to the gathering of moss the vermin had disappeared beneath. The vermin that tried to act as though they were some sort of advanced creatures. Farringday would have no idea where he was and he was glad of that. Farringday had stolen the attention for so long but was no better man than him. Cobbler had been in more fights, knew more of the criminal masterminds that terrorised the streets of London than Farringday would ever learn. He should have been in charge of the lot of them, but instead the role had gone to Farringday, purely because he knew how to speak to the men of power and wealth, how to make himself appear as though he had the street smarts with which to trap the vermin, the underground connections from where information could be sourced as well as the presence to stand before lords and earls. Cobbler seethed. He had worked too hard to let an upstart like Farringday take a spot which should rightfully have been his – and the upper classes wanted nothing more than to have these vermin caught. He would be the one to do it. He smiled. By the time Farringday had stopped searching the whorehouse with the rest of them the vermin would be in chains and irons and headed to the Tower.

Goodness knows how many of them exist, he thought excitedly. He wondered what he would do when he was taken before the magistrates and the lords to explain his actions and how his quick wits had led to the capture of the vermin. Cobbler had no finery, no clothing interwoven with silk, no ties. He had only ever owned one pair of shoes and they had several holes in them. His only hat was musty and smelt of mildew. He bit his lip nervously, his tobacco-stained teeth gnawing at his dried split lip; he cut through an old wound from where he had been punched a few days ago in a brawl in the Lords Tavern. Still, his fortunes were about to change; he could not let the incidents in his life as a criminal affect him. Cobbler was on the way up and he would do more than Farringday ever could. He hoped he could be some sort of a guard to one of these great men.

In the distance he heard the hooves on the streets as a party approached with lit torches; they were nearby. Then he spotted the carriage, its fine outlines silhouetted in the moonlight as four handsome horses pulled it along. A noble was approaching. That was a carriage owned by someone of great wealth and means. His heart began to pound – it was probably Lord Wordsworth, a rumoured cousin to the earl. They would be ecstatic with the news.

~

*W*alking through the large doors that led to their underground home Binkers heaved a sigh of relief. She was safe and had got away unharmed – just. That had been too close; as each day passed the runners seemed to be getting closer to them. She sometimes wondered if there was something they were missing, something right before them that they could not see, some verifiable truth that would help them understand how the runners got so close each time. As she mulled over what had just occurred she caught a glimpse of him, the older one who was never any fun, had never been any fun.

'Where have you been?' he questioned accusingly.

Binkers shifted from one foot to the other as he shuffled towards her, his dark eyes never leaving her, gruff expression never wavering. She was well aware that a restriction of some sort was in place to control their movement and keep them safe, but she was always breaking the rules. After all, she had never got caught. Binkers was young in her world (and quite old in the world above them) but was treated very much like a child down here.

'Nowhere,' she said with an impish smile, her deep blue eyes sparkling.

But the gruff one, Rufus, had clearly seen her come in through the entrance to the commune and knew she had been away.

'*Where*, Binkers?' he said in a deeper, more threatening voice.

She looked around at the crowds of passers-by who were beginning to pause, interested in why old Rufus was so agitated. She sighed with irritation. Her people were always so nosy.

'Up there,' she mumbled and added, 'trying to fetch an apple. They're not in season here for a while yet.'

Hoping her excuse would sway him she looked up at him almost meekly. However, his face had flushed, his head suddenly appearing too small beneath the wide-brimmed cocked hat he wore.

'Up there? Don't you know there is a rule?' he said with great annoyance. 'Don't you know that we are being hunted by the magistrates and their hoodlums? Don't you have any idea that there are orders?'

'There are always orders.' Binkers was determined to be defiant. 'I chose not to follow them. I knew what I was doing and I did not get caught.'

Rufus gave her a grave look. 'I understand how you feel,

but as the elder of the Unending Canal it is my duty to ensure those who live within this part of our world are kept safe. You might have just put us in harm's way with your callous disregard for our rules. We are running...' He found himself abruptly cut off as Binkers lost her temper.

'How long must we run for, Rufus? They will hunt us till we are dead anyway. Should we choose to die running or die living? I much prefer the latter.'

'You might be old up there but down here you are just a child—' Rufus broke off in shock as two others, Perry and Macintosh, who had been instructed to watch the entrance, came tearing in. Their usually tanned leathery faces had turned a peculiar shade of grey which did not suit them at all.

Without a word of explanation they began to shut the great doors. They called for their comrades to help push the large, ancient blocks of wood which acted as a stable barricade to the outside world.

Binkers's insides were suddenly hollow. Her hands shook. She had never seen the two door guardians act in such a manner before.

'Good gracious. What is it?' Rufus exclaimed.

'Something has happened,' Binkers said, although she already knew the answer.

'Rufus, I don't know how but they are coming. They know exactly where to find us,' Perry said.

'They have torches, horses, and I am certain unless my eyes deceive me this cold night that there is a lord or someone of the nobility among them.' Macintosh's words emerged in a mad rush; his face was red and flushed with sweat, the deep purple of his eyes deepening.

'They come for us,' Perry chimed as though the end was about to come.

At their words a wave of fevered activity began to run through the square by the entrance, the fear palpable in the air.

'Run for the Black Forest!'

Mass hysteria broke out among them but Binkers and Rufus stood stock still in the midst of the mayhem as their brethren ran around them for cover. Binkers felt the heat and anger from Rufus's gaze never leaving hers.

'Rufus. It is impossible...' she began.

'You were followed,' he hissed at her with a look on his face that left her cold. 'You have damned us all, Binkers,' he spat as a group went to join them at the door.

Binkers stood helplessly in the square as the panic continued around her, no longer sure what to do – how to help stop this madness she had brought upon them. How could they have followed her? She had seen no one there. The runners and their benefactors had been kept at bay for several years through the wits of the elders and the gate guardians and, in a haze of foolish pride and wilful indiscretion, she had led them right to their world. Tears began to fall from her eyes as she stood there. She had failed them all and there was nothing she could do now to right her wrongs. The next few moments of their existence would be the most excruciating. She wiped at her tears and decided to be brave. Marching up to where Rufus, Perry, Macintosh and a few others were mobilising by the doors she braced herself.

'I can help.'

The look Rufus gave her stopped her in her tracks. 'You have led us to our doom, Binkers. You have done enough tonight,' he growled, eyes flashing in anger.

Binkers stepped back as the guilt and humiliation overcame her and she began to sob. He was right.

With great difficulty the small group ran the great slab of metal across the heavy wood of the door which would bolt it. But that would not be enough – their pursuers would find a way to get in eventually. They were great big brutes and there was little point in fleeing because there would be nowhere to run, and they would only get caught and killed further along the winding paths and alleyways of their world.

Binkers looked at the fear running around her caused by her selfish actions. The underground had been their home for several centuries, and although some in the world above had discovered that their kind existed long before, they were trusted people and their location had never been disclosed, until now. The sounds of thundering feet and yelling men made them hold their breaths in anticipation. The square stilled as the panic was replaced by a chilling fear which froze them all to the spot.

'By order of His Royal Majesty, I command you to open this door and show yourselves.'

They looked at each other in silence; frightened wide eyes filled every corner of the square as they imagined what their final hour would be like. When the orders were met with silence a loud persistent thudding began on the door as their persecutors tried to gain entry. The doors were solid and very old but even the wisest in the community knew that they would eventually gain entry. There was no amount of fortifying that would prevent them coming in through the heavy doors. Yet the largest and strongest of them remained pressed up against it as if they could prevent the inevitable – which was their slaughter in great numbers. Binkers continued to sob, her cries filling the silences between the heavy thuds. They would never forgive her now. But it did not matter as none of them would live to see the morning. All her sins would be forgotten.

As the crowd descended into panic and screaming Binkers felt an odd sensation move through her, one so slight that it should have gone unnoticed but was present and alien to her. She felt herself being displaced; a wave of dizziness overcame her and she blinked several times to counter the rippling effect around her. Something was happening but no one else seemed to have noticed. The great doors continued to be subject to thuds and bangs, and then a shouted threat came through.

'You cannot hide there forever. Today is the day you will receive some justice.'

Seconds later, Binkers realised that the men's voices which had initially drowned out their screams had grown dim, as if the men had gradually disappeared and faded into the background, almost as though whisked away by some gentle force. The loud banging suddenly ceased as if they'd vanished into thin air. Binkers found, to her confusion, that when she removed her hands from her ears there was silence from outside; the screaming, wailing and crying coming from the crowds inside had died down significantly. Others remained in complete silence but no one seemed to have noticed that the noises from outside were no longer audible.

'I think they are gone,' someone said.

'No, it's a trap,' a second voice interjected nervously.

'They want us to come out so they can have an easy victory.' Another voice in the crowd. But some were not convinced.

'Why would they want that?'

'I feel they are gone.'

'It all feels different now,' someone else from the crowd said.

Binkers was experiencing the same discombobulation her peers felt but she could not explain. She felt odd, displaced, as though subtly picked up and placed elsewhere.

'It does feel different,' she said looking up, the tears drying on her tanned cheeks. 'Something is happening.'

'Or has happened,' a voice chimed.

The confusion was spreading fast.

'Silence, all.' A stout little man in a yellow checked jacket stepped forward. 'Let us not speak our minds and show our fear lest they be listening.'

The loud talking descended into murmurs and then a heavy silence fell across the sprawling main square of the commune. And so they waited, and waited, and waited. The tension was unbearable, the game that these men played with them torturous. Was it their night to die or was it not? It seemed as though an inexplicable silence had fallen on the other side of the great doors. The man in the yellow checked jacket turned to look at the older one who stood beside him, the one who had so cruelly berated Binkers.

'Rufus. We must open this door, or—'

'Or what, Fred?' Rufus looked perplexed.

'They will make sitting ducks of us.'

'Fred,' Rufus said matter-of-factly. 'Look around you. We are sitting ducks already, my friend.'

The older dweller was adamant.

Binkers looked around the commune at the faces of different ages, shapes, and attire. They all had lives, lives deemed peculiar to those in the world above, but their lives nonetheless, and ones they wanted to go back to living without the threat of the runners hanging over their head.

They could not be made to suffer this torture much longer. Fred was right. How long could they wait like this? She stepped forward and in a strong voice spoke up.

'I will go, Fred. It was my fault. I must be made to face the consequences of my actions.'

A heavy silence met her words. No one stirred in the crowd. She moved to the door.

'I repeat. I will go. If I am caught then we know it's a trap, but they,' she motioned to the large crowd behind her, 'must be made to endure this pain no longer.'

'Binkers,' Fred began.

'No. Do not try to stop me,' she responded forcefully, shocked by the strength in her own words. 'No one can stop me. No one will stop me.'

'I will and I can.' It was Rufus. 'I will go.'

'But Rufus—'

'Do not make a victim of yourself to atone for your mistakes. I am old, Binkers. You are but a child.' He smiled and it lit his face up. 'If I am taken there is very little they can do to me. I will pass quickly.'

There were murmurs sweeping through the crowd. Binkers paused in a daze of confusion, uncertain how to respond.

'Perhaps it is best we wait, Rufus,' Fred beseeched him.

Placing a firm hand on his kinsman's shoulder Rufus gently moved him to the side. Binkers felt the tears coming to her eyes once more as she stood aside with Fred. It was not meant to end this way, not with trickery and games. If they were to die then in her opinion as many of their oppressors as possible should be taken with them. Her people were a peaceful kind, though, unused to violence and the cruel ways of the world above.

Rufus nodded at the others who still pushed back

against the door, the strain evident on their faces as they used every ounce of strength within them.

'Come now. Let us not make this difficult.'

One by one they moved to the side, albeit reluctantly, as he edged closer to the door. Rufus unlatched the large bolt, which had partially been damaged by the thudding, banging and pushing; it was now almost hanging off its hinges.

Binkers and the rest observed curiously. There was nothing, no sounds beyond the door. No sounds of horses stomping their hooves, the men of significance giving orders to the lesser men, no baying lynch mob calling out for their blood with torches at the ready. Nothing. The men could have run in if they had wanted and butchered them all, but something had stopped them. Or perhaps it was a wicked game.

She held her breath as Rufus unbolted the door, moving back as it swung open unhindered. The passageway appeared to be empty; there were no great big brutes waiting with oil lamps and clubs claiming to act in the interests of the law. She glanced at Fred who stood beside her. He looked just as confused as she felt.

Looking around Rufus motioned to the others behind him.

'Yes, something is changed.'

He stepped out. Binkers, fearing it was a cruel trap, followed.

'Binkers...' Fred started.

'I must, Fred. Why must Rufus and Rufus alone suffer for my folly?' Her eyes flashed, causing him to step back. The decision was made.

Walking away from the shrieks and cries calling for her not to go any further, she tentatively followed Rufus through the dark passage, feeling around for the little steps which would lead to the outside world. The elder was a distance in front of her and it was clear that his mind was so taken with unravelling the mystery of the disappeared men that he was unaware of her. Binkers blinked her blue eyes as they widened in the darkness. It was now pitch black, where usually there was a dull glow at the entrance to their commune. The walls of the entrance also felt different – the earth had changed. If this was a trap, it did not make much sense. The men could have killed them all moments before. Binkers gingerly walked up the rough, winding stairs to the top, wincing as she did so, expecting to hear Rufus being hauled out by his collar and killed on the spot, but it was silent. Everything looked and felt so different. She remained a distance behind Rufus as she followed, her footsteps becoming bolder as each second ticked by.

'Rufus?' she called out in a loud whisper.

He turned to glance down at her with a look of such rage she was glad she was several feet behind.

'You were instructed to wait,' he hissed. 'When will you learn?'

Binkers found her strength and walked up the stairs to meet him. 'When you learn you cannot do everything by yourself?'

Despite his words the elder looked relieved at the sight of her. She stood back and held her breath as he pushed away the covering which hid the entrance to their home. But there was nothing, no uproar, no pockmark-ridden faces waiting for them. Just silence. Rufus lifted his head. Binkers followed suit, glad the darkness hid them. The outside world was now dark, the only light coming from the moon. The mossy covering which protected the entrance to their world was now gone. All around them were trees, hedgerows, and in the distance strange sounds wailed in the air. The air smelt different. It was very silent; she knew there had been a big change.

'What is this, Rufus?' she asked. 'What strange land is this?'

'This must be – but it cannot be. It seems we are still in London, but somewhere else.'

'How is that possible?'

'I know not, child. The workings of our world are still not fully understood, even by ancients such as myself.'

There was a noise down below and they realised they had left those in the square waiting in anticipation. Some of them had followed.

'What do you see, Rufus?' someone called out.

As he turned to respond a huge black beast loomed into view, which suddenly ran past with great speed, flashing bright yellow eyes and emitting the loudest roar Binkers had ever heard. She retreated into the hole hastily, almost knocking a befuddled Rufus over. She put the covering back in place. Her heart thudded violently beneath her ribcage as she glanced at Rufus; his dark eyes were wide. What new world was this, where strange beasts existed and moved at such speed? Nothing of that nature lived near their home. The others who had trailed after them shrank back in fright at the commotion.

'Hell,' Rufus called out hoarsely to those who had been brave enough to follow them out of their refuge.

'I see hell.'

CHAPTER 1

*A*rk House School, London.

Asha sat on the wrong side of the desk, wondering how she came to be in this room when things had got so bad for her. The room was cold and uninviting, the woman on the other side harsh and austere in her grey suit, with a too-thin nose and sharp eyes. Her spindly fingers clutched at her pen as she incessantly made annoying scribbles whenever she asked a question and Asha gave some sort of an answer, however inane. Her name was Mrs Devillet and she worked for Ark House Academy. Asha was scheduled to see her once a week – to talk. This was a clause written into an agreement drawn up by the headmaster, Mr Critchley. She hated it. It made her feel like some sort of sideshow attraction, something to be gossiped about by the other pupils as they went about their perfect lives. She gazed out the window choosing not to look at the offensive woman who was making her life more unbearable than was necessary.

The rain was coming down heavily in North London and it gave her comfort. As parts of the city were deluged in water, it made her feel good to know there were others suffering chaos just as she was. As the rain fell she stared at the droplets against the window, trying to count them, but they kept moving and she could never catch them. She smiled a little. It seemed these sessions could only be made bearable by a catastrophic storm. It was a chilly November afternoon and she felt for anyone who got caught in the storm without an umbrella; they would catch their death.

'Asha?' Mrs Devillet's voice intruded on her thoughts once more.

She gazed back at her, blinking in surprise.

'What were you thinking?'

'When?' Asha preferred to be difficult about it.

'Just now when you were looking out of the window?' her psychiatrist asked pointedly.

Asha wondered if she was allowed to snap at her. At what point would the taciturn Mrs Devillet decide enough was enough and finally yell at her? After all, they had got nowhere since these sessions had started. Did these professionals ever lose their cool when faced with difficult patients? In that case Mrs Devillet was headed for a tough time – Asha was not prepared to relinquish the silent world she inhabited.

'Nothing.' She smiled impishly.

Mrs Devillet took her reading glasses off the bridge of her too-thin nose and massaged her temple. She placed them back on. Asha wondered how they stayed in place.

'You were glancing out of the window just now and you smiled. You must have been thinking of something.' She smiled herself. Her face changed in an instant: she was warmer, her pointed, sharp features became softer.

Asha shifted uncomfortably in her seat. Mrs Devillet was trying to draw her out by showing kindness to her. It seemed she was a long way from losing her cool and asking Asha to leave.

'I was hoping I'd be able to go home.'

'But you know, Asha, your father is concerned about you, which was why he was hoping you would participate more openly and honestly in these sessions,' Mrs Devillet parried.

Asha's eyes narrowed. The woman was putting up a good calm fight. Her father had signed up to the agreement, meaning he wanted Asha here just as much as anyone else. Why would she be welcome at home if she was not doing what he wanted?

Just then a noise from the waiting room got their attention. It was loud and raucous. Asha had an idea who it might be – Sweeney Brown, a fifth form boy who was in danger of being permanently excluded. She felt for him, she really did, but this was just what she needed.

Mrs Devillet got to her feet, mumbling under her breath with irritation, and walked out of the room to investigate the source of the noise. She would be gone at least a few minutes.

Asha turned her head back to the window, watching the droplets cascading downwards, trying to find their way by whichever route was possible. Then she saw it on the table. She shivered in trepidation and her hands trembled. Mrs Devillet had left her precious notebook on the table lying open. It was next to a file with Asha's name on it. Asha did not think they were supposed to do that. It was all supposed to be strictly confidential, even to the client. Perhaps Mrs

Devillet wanted her to take a peek and let Asha know what she really thought of her – and how useless her incessant scribblings were.

Asha got to her feet and stood over the table. She opened the manila envelope with her patient number across it – 73608. She grinned; it sounded like something macabre from a Victorian lunatic asylum. As she cast her eyes over the paperwork she caught her breath.

Asha Saunders chooses to remain isolated and does not associate with her peers, maintaining an alarming silence which her school, Ark House, finds disturbing. Several of her fellow students and their parents have expressed discomfort at the determined silence, with some stating it is causing them undue stress.

Perhaps her background could shed some light on this. Miss Saunders's adoptive mother, Esther Saunders, passed away of stage three breast cancer nine months ago. Since then she has only spoken when spoken to, otherwise she maintains a staunch silence. Although her school work is exemplary, she refuses to participate in activities or group sports. However, she still plays piano and practises daily in the music rooms. She will be competing in the upcoming music competition at Robert Hall. Ark House is willing to keep her on as long as she maintains her records and her weekly assessments.

'Miss Saunders – what on earth do you think you are doing?'

Asha looked up, shocked. Mrs Devillet was standing in the doorway and her previous cheery disposition had been replaced by greyness.

'I've got to go,' she mumbled, dashing out of the door, her face burning with tears.

.   .   .

*T*oday was Asha's birthday.

Asha had been told that time would heal all wounds but she was finding that nine months after the death of her adoptive mother the wounds were failing to heal. The pain was still too raw. Some days she cried herself to sleep, wondering what was happening to her. Her father did not understand – or did not seem to want to. It didn't help that she had never felt connected to him or his side of the family, who all seemed uncomfortable around her. She had found a perfectly adequate way to deal with the pain of her mother's death, retreating as much as possible into herself. Overhearing a rather loud telephone conversation between her father and the indomitable Aunt Grace from the drawing room had not helped their relationship in the slightest.

'She is a beautiful girl, Patrick, but this self-imposed solitude is not healthy. Esther died over nine months ago so her behaviour cannot stem from that – and goodness knows the therapy isn't working.' Her voice dropped to a whisper. 'You don't have your child seeing *one of them* unless something is really wrong. Trust me, Patrick, you do not want this following her around as she gets older. It's not right.'

'I know.' Her father sounded despondent. Asha could hear papers being shuffled and tried to work out if it was her dad carrying on with his work or Aunt Grace with the morning paper.

Her aunt carried on. 'It is certainly strange to mourn for so long and, let's face the fact, Patrick, Esther wasn't even her biological mother. It pains me to say it but the bond between natural mother and child is a strong one.' She took a deep breath and Asha instantly knew what was coming next. 'Why you didn't just adopt a healthy child in England is beyond me – none of these mood swings and long silences. The Belgrade has a perfectly respectable adoption service. They can take requirements for eye colour, hair colour... I mean, I know you and Esther were enthralled with Mozambique but it didn't mean you had to bring a baby back.'

Her father had gone quiet. Asha was not sure if it was due to shock or just plain defeat – or whether he was elsewhere in his mind.

'Just the other day I was speaking to Dorothy and her nephew. Remember David from your rugby tournaments at Plummer's? Well, he is considering,' she paused for a quick breath, 'adopting a child.'

She let her words sink in for effect before adding sharply, 'From the same background, mind. None of that multi-cultural business. It just looks odd, to be frank.'

Asha, deciding she had heard enough, replaced the handset as quietly as she could. It was difficult as her hands were shaking. What had caused her sudden instability? Whether it was anger, shame or betrayal she had no idea, but what was certain in Asha's mind was that her father had done nothing to defend her. That had marked the beginning of the end of their relationship in her mind. She had pushed it to the back of her mind and carried on, but his disloyalty had stung her and she knew she could never forget it or forgive him.

❧

*J*onathan Stapleton tried to lead his dog in another direction, pulling at its lead with as much determination and authority as he could muster, but it seemed this was not enough. Dax the

Labrador pulled back, adamant he wanted to go in the other direction. Walking him was no easy feat; he weighed a ton and only seemed to get heavier and more insolent as the years passed, as though he realised he had won his way into their hearts and they could never let him go. Jonathan sighed; it was not purely the Labrador's fault. The seven-year-old had been down this road so many times since the Stapletons had owned him that it was only normal for him to want to head in this direction. He paused as he observed the quiet wide street with the large imposing houses on either side; he could almost see her house from where he stood. He wondered what the chances were of her emerging at that point. It was a bitterly cold November night, so absolutely zero. It was also her birthday, so she would either be moping in her bedroom or avoiding any attempts at cordiality, as she had done for so long. Also, she didn't own the street and he was free to come and go as he pleased. If he saw her on her way home or on her way out he would just ignore her. But then, Asha Saunders had lived like a hermit for the past year so the chances of her emerging at that time of the evening were low.

Holding his head high and letting Dax lead the way with his nose to the ground, he walked down the street, pausing to let the dog sniff around and inspect the odd lamp post. Why on earth he had chosen to come such a long distance with the dog? He had crossed the boundary into Primrose Hill several minutes before but he lived a mile away in Hampstead, just a few minutes' walk from the sprawling Heath. So why he had chosen to do the twenty-minute walk over here on the coldest night of the year was a mystery. Ducking his head further into the warm collar of his coat he was thankful his mother had reminded him to use a scarf. It was so bitterly cold that black ice was forming on the pavement and he found himself skidding slightly across the surface, cursing himself for walking so far. However, he was grateful for the long walk; it gave him the chance to clear his head and avoid his father who was around for the day. As Dax paused once more to inspect something else Jonathan jerked on his lead impatiently; they were close to the house now, too close. He could see the driveway, the outline of her father's car, the illuminated windows showing someone was home. He was trying his best not to look or even seem at all interested just in case she was watching from her bedroom window. Everything was completely still, so he took a chance and began to walk past the house, trying to pull Dax along.

'Jonathan?'

The voice across the street was unmistakable. It seemed the odds of her emerging from her home on the coldest of nights were very high indeed, confirmed hermit or other-wise. Stiffening his shoulders he turned to look at his old friend of sixteen years, Asha Saunders. She looked the same as she had done in school earlier that day; her hair which she usually wore in long plaits was in a high ponytail. As one of the few black students at the very small private Ark House School it was difficult for Asha to blend in – she was so unique looking. It was a Monday evening so he would no doubt see her tomorrow wandering through the halls avoiding all social contact, which she had been doing for the past year.

'Hello, Asha.' He realised how formal he sounded, conversing with her as though she were a stranger and not one of his best friends, but they had barely spoken in nine months; friends did not do that. He and Sarah spoke almost every day. Asha looked slightly uncomfortable at the sight of him.

'What're you doing here?' she asked.

He thought she sounded somewhat hopeful but he was now so cold he was certain his mind was playing tricks on him. Sniffling, he yanked impatiently on Dax's lead as the dog continued sniffing incessantly at something on the ground, threatening to topple him.

'Walking Dax,' he curtly responded. What did it look like he was doing? Jonathan desperately wanted to leave, the cold getting to him as it began to breach the warm layers he wore. As he racked his brain for an excuse, an odd silence settled between them.

As if on cue the Labrador began to bark ferociously at something down the road, a welcome interruption. Jonathan squinted, looking ahead of him, but nothing caught his attention. But Dax was insistent, barking and pulling on his lead to get to the source of his irritation.

'Quiet, you silly dog.'

Before Asha could say anything else he pulled Dax away, leading him in the direction of home.

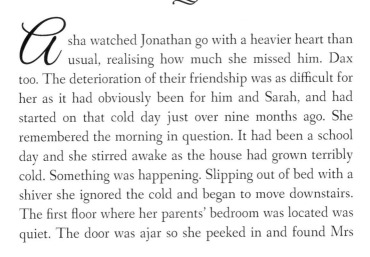

*A*sha watched Jonathan go with a heavier heart than usual, realising how much she missed him. Dax too. The deterioration of their friendship was as difficult for her as it had obviously been for him and Sarah, and had started on that cold day just over nine months ago. She remembered the morning in question. It had been a school day and she stirred awake as the house had grown terribly cold. Something was happening. Slipping out of bed with a shiver she ignored the cold and began to move downstairs. The first floor where her parents' bedroom was located was quiet. The door was ajar so she peeked in and found Mrs

Redding sobbing in the corner as she pulled the sheets from the bed. It was strange to see the housekeeper so early in the morning, she recalled, as the woman normally started her duties when Asha was at school. Her presence filled Asha with foreboding.

Noises downstairs caught her attention and she gingerly inched down the carpeted stairs, afraid of what she might find. Asha had not quite reached the bottom step but watched the scene unfold before her eyes, realising so much had been going on below her as she slept. She was shocked, watching her father sitting on the floor like a lost child, but what was even more peculiar were the people standing around him. Waking up to a house filled with people was a jolt and it took her a while to realise what was going on as myriad people in greens, blacks and whites milled around the ground floor. There was a police officer crouched before her father, speaking reassuringly in low tones as one did to a child who was upset. Then she spotted two men pushing a trolley with large wheels. On top of it was a figure covered in a white sheet which draped over its petite frame. It was a body. It looked familiar. Asha caught her breath.

The police officer attending to her father spoke to him in soft, muted tones. Asha wondered what he was saying. What could be said in that moment to make it better? Then it dawned on her – he probably wanted him to move so he did not have to see his wife being taken out of her home that way. It was a difficult feat and her father initially resisted, but eventually after much persuading he got to his feet and moved into the dining room with the police officer who sat with him. Asha was not so lucky – she saw it all. As the men who wheeled her mother out disappeared through the doorway and into the icy cold she remained frozen on that last step. Before she knew it she found herself tipping forward; her last memory of that moment was a paramedic rushing to catch her before she hit her head on the tiled entrance hallway floor. After she came to, Asha had remained silent for the rest of that day, not crying, not grieving – just existing. Her father had tried to engage her in some sort of conversation and, as family members poured in and the living and dining rooms were filled with condolence cards and flowers, she found the intrusion even more upsetting and her silence continued unchecked. Her silence soothed her and she carried on with it for a few more days and nights. Soon, however, her father and Mrs Redding tried to draw her out of it, but it was too late. Asha Saunders had permanently retreated from the world. When asked about the funeral a few weeks later Asha found she had no memory of the day; her mind was a complete blank. That had been nine months ago and Asha, although now more responsive as time went on and would answer a question when asked, chose to avoid contact with friends and family.

Sighing heavily she returned to reality as the cold in the street became unbearable. As she turned to cross over something caught her eye just a few feet away. It was cream coloured and moving around in the hedgerow. Curiosity got the better of her and she bent over, sticking her head in to get a better look, and started in shock as she came face to face with a puppy. A bulldog puppy. She was taken aback. It was an odd place to leave a puppy and on such a cold night. She wondered whether it had been abandoned, and let out a shiver when she tried to imagine anyone being callous enough to do that to a defenceless creature.

'Look at you,' she said, reaching out to pick it up and hoping it did not chose to move further into the bushes. Her arms got caught in the criss-cross branches and bramble and some of the sharper bits got caught in her jumper, but she forced her way through to reach it. She almost lost her grip as the puppy squirmed. It had no collar or tags of any sort, but rather than signs of suffering from the cold or hunger it was plump and looked healthy and well looked after.

Someone is definitely going to be looking for you, she thought, wondering how such a handsome puppy had come to be outdoors in the prickliest of bushes on a night like this. Someone must have put it there. She wondered if it was what Dax had been barking at. She looked around the street for any sign of an owner or someone frenziedly searching for a missing dog but the street was silent.

Holding it tight she looked in both directions before crossing over to let herself into her home. The house was warm and the scent of apple pie still clung to the air. She put the puppy under her coat, hoping to get upstairs to her room and out of the way of any intolerable conversation.

A voice called out from the study. 'Asha? Is that you?' It was her father. He sounded anxious.

Asha cursed inwardly, her hopes for a silent evening dashed.

'Yes, it is me.' Who else could it be? Mrs Redding had left for the day.

'Have you had some dinner? I had mine earlier and had to eat alone – I couldn't find you.'

'I've eaten,' she replied shortly. After listening in on that conversation between him and Aunt Grace she had been unable to see her father in a good light, and thought the force of her anger would erupt if she spent any time with him.

'I'm going out for a few hours. Would you like anything?'

Just to be left alone, she thought.

'Asha, it's your seventeenth birthday. We really should

celebrate, sweetheart. It's a time for...' He trailed off hopelessly, obviously searching for the right words.

'No, thank you. I've got a lot to do.' She remained calm. There was no point attracting any further attention by being churlish.

'Well, I'll be going to the high street as soon as I finish reading the paper.' He paused to look at her as though expecting a change of heart; his dark brown eyes were mournful. An uncomfortable silence passed between them.

Asha, worried she would be found out and her precious cargo discovered, rushed up the stairs, desperate to avoid his searching eyes and prying questions as the puppy squirmed under the warmth of her coat.

～

ogsley and Fred crouched silently in the bushes and watched the man leave the house, his head ducked down into his jacket to protect him from the cold. He paused at the door of his car and looked around as though sensing something in the air. Then he got into the driver's seat and drove down the road, his lights disappearing from view as he turned a corner. The twosome looked up at the large house and felt a chill go through them after the events of the last twenty minutes. It was normally a silent street, which was why they chose it for cutting through back to their home. They had waited patiently in the hedges as the boy with the large dastardly dog had walked ever so slowly down the street, almost uncertainly; it was a cold night and they would have expected his pace to be more rapid. At first they thought it was because of his dog – perhaps he slowed him down – then it became apparent he was avoiding the large house, number 19, The

Vale. The boy's actions worried them; they wondered if there was something to be frightened of.

'I wonder if she really is a witch,' Bogsley whispered to Fred, 'the girl who resides at number nineteen.'

It could not be possible. Could it? Then the girl had appeared out of nowhere, very dark and tall, and startled the boy and his dog. However, rather than the wrath they were expecting there was an uncomfortable conversation between the two. Then the dog had sniffed them out in the bushes and begun growling and snapping menacingly. Luckily for the pair the boy, like most of his kind, was too stupid to realise the dog was warning him that there was something amiss and he had yanked angrily on his lead and hurried down the street. Bogsley expected the girl to disappear as quickly as she had appeared but she remained on the cold street looking after the boy, almost regretful. Then she had spotted a movement in the bushes and crouched lower. They froze, thinking she would see them, but instead she had seen Hiller, the puppy, in the bushes and taken him with her. It had been on the tip of their tongues to cry out and perhaps launch some sort of ferocious attack, but they were not sure who else would be watching and their kind were not aggressive. There was the added fact that there was always a man and an older woman present in the house in which the girl lived. They were a strange collection of people.

'She cannot be a witch,' Fred insisted, his eyes not leaving the house.

'How do you know?' Bogsley asked, tired of Fred pretending he knew everything.

'Because if she were a witch she would have sensed we were in hiding,' Fred snapped impatiently.

'What *is* she then?'

'My guess is an ordinary human. One of *them*.'

'Fascinating. She showed affection for Hiller though.'

'So. That means nothing. We know of their kind, remember. Just because she shows affection for a wee pup does not mean she is likely to show us friendship. Do not be fooled,' Fred responded waspishly.

Bogsley cringed as he realised Fred was angry with him, a truth that was confirmed moments later when he turned to him, face half shadowed in the darkness.

'See what you have gone and caused,' Fred seethed.

'I did nothing wrong. Hiller doesn't like the rope and it's not right to put it on him.'

'Well if you had been paying attention you would have been able to keep hold of him. I blame you. The poor creature thinks he's been abandoned.'

'We cannot be certain of that – it's sure to be warm and toasty in that house. He will probably have his own quarters with his own fire and everything.'

'They no longer use fires in this time. You know that. And don't be a fool. He is not staying there. I –' Fred paused to look menacingly at Bogsley, '– *we* will just have to get him back.'

'We... we can't interfere with them, remember. That's what got us into this mess and Binkers in so much trouble. Rufus gave us orders.'

'We will not have to interfere with them. The girl is sure to leave him alone at home at some point. If we are lucky she might abandon him. That's what her kind do.'

'How about the Mimes?'

'We just have to be very careful, but we are not leaving Hiller behind.'

'How are we going to get him?'

'We will find a way – we'll do it tonight.'

Bogsley was still not sure that Hiller's kidnap had been his fault; the blame for everything that went wrong seemed to lie with him these days. He definitely did not want to get hurt or captured – they were now unsure who was in league with whom. There was no telling what they would do to them.

'Wait here. I need to take these turnips back to the commune,' Fred instructed sharply.

Bogsley sighed. It was pointless. Fred would not be forgiving until they got Hiller back.

'Okay, go carefully, and for goodness sake be wary of the firework wielding maniacs.'

But Fred was already gone, disappearing into the darkness. Nestling down into the shrubbery Bogsley felt rather sorry for himself. It was a freezing night and he was fully prepared for the elements but he was so hungry. They were on their way back and had gathered turnips and other vegetables to prepare a hearty winter soup. Some of the vegetables were not available down below so they had taken the risk of emerging in public. It was November the fifth, Bonfire Night, and on occasions like this it was easier to sneak into public and get a few items they needed. Then on the way back he had let Hillier go when they spotted the boy and his dog as the puppy would not stop squirming and they didn't want to get caught. Now Fred was angry with him.

'We will get you back, Hiller. That you can count on.'

He determinedly fixed his eyes at the top of the house where he knew the girl lived. She was a striking but odd creature, unlike any he had ever seen. For the short time they had observed her she did not appear to have any friends or companions. It was always just her. He still held the notion that she might be a witch of some sort, his own idea he had to admit. Fred thought the idea was ludicrous. They had peeked in through her windows and seen nothing untoward, just a very lonely young girl spending too much time alone. She was always coming and going on her own, sometimes on her trusty bicycle. They had not expected her to emerge from her home so quickly upon seeing the boy with the dog. They had watched, expecting her to leave Hiller in the hedgerow where she had found him, but instead she had cuddled him and taken him indoors. It was the first time they had observed her show any kind of warmth to another living being. It surprised them greatly – these people knew nothing of affection or true friendship; they had lived side by side for centuries, and knew them to be a cruel race. Bogsley curled into a small ball as he sat within the bushes, his gaze intently fixed on the house, trying to ignore the rumbling of his stomach.

~

*P*eople hurriedly got out of the way as Sarah got on the bus. She gave a smug grin; this was the best bit post rugby matches – you always got some space to yourself even on the crammed buses. Although the others on the team always insisted on showering, Sarah preferred to get on with the mud caked all over her. She got a lot of satisfaction from disgusting the snobby commuters who surrounded her.

To her disappointment her schoolmate, Sandra, was still speaking. There were four of them travelling only a few stops from Ark House School and Sandra had not stopped talking since she caught up with them at the school gates.

'So if we meet at mine at six we can get to Tom's for about seven.'

'Will your dad be giving us a lift?' Tara looked at Sandra.

'God no. He absolutely hates Tom. It's torture.' Sandra rolled her eyes in the manner that Sarah had always found overly dramatic and irritating.

'Everyone hates Tom though.' Once again Sarah had spoken without thinking.

Three pairs of unblinking eyes gazed at her and she saw Tara mouth an expletive behind Sandra's back.

'What's that supposed to mean?' Sandra shot at Sarah.

Sarah groaned. Although Sandra had a lot of bark she was relatively harmless and simply a spoilt narcissistic girl who had never put in the time or effort for rugby, purely joining because she thought it would get her closer to Tom Redman, another narcissist who captained the boy's first team and in Sarah's view had a brain that was entirely constructed of cabbage leaves. As they stared back at her Sarah refused to back down.

'Well, perhaps hate is a strong word but come on – Tom is hardly going to win any awards for camaraderie, charisma or intelligence, is he?'

As Tara and Yu snorted back giggles, Sandra's lower lip quivered.

'You think you know everything, Sarah. Tom happens to be a perfect gentleman. Besides, you're rather tall and boyish yourself. Aren't you? Perhaps he just likes daintier petite girls.'

As she spoke in her high-pitched affected voice Sarah wondered how Sandra had got so far in life without being strangled. Luckily for Sarah, and perhaps Sandra, the bus was coming to the stop that she and Yu were getting off at. Sarah desperately pressed the bell several times as Sandra kept on nagging at her.

'See you tonight, Tara.'

'See you at six, Sandy,' she cheekily called out to Sandra.

Yu giggled as they stepped off the bus. Sandra hated being referred to as Sandy, always saying it was a name designed for a golden retriever.

'How on earth are we even friends?' Sarah muttered with great disbelief.

'Pretty easy. Sandra Whitman is one of those people that you can tolerate in small doses, but she is so entertainingly good at making a complete idiot of herself that it's worth it,' Yu said with a smile.

'How is it that no one has ever asked her to shut up?'

'She has a very rich father.'

'Well none of us are exactly suffering, are we?'

'Okay, I'll rephrase that. She has a rich father who lets her throw constant parties and is always out of the country. Would your parents ever let you have half the parties she does?'

'True. You do have a point,' Sarah agreed.

They had approached the driveway to her home.

'See you tonight.' Sarah waved goodbye to Yu, noting out of the corner of her eye that her mother's car was neatly parked. Feeling a slight lurch of excitement she called out for her as soon as she got in but there was no response. The kitchen was empty and cold as a window had been left open. A further search of the remaining rooms yielded nothing but Kiki, Sarah's little sister, who was sitting in her room reading a book.

'Hey, Kiki. Where's Mum?'

'Office.' She was seven and rather monosyllabic, distracted by the book on her lap.

'Mum?' Sarah walked towards the last room of the

house, her mother's home office, which she had insisted upon having after Sarah was born. She knocked gently on the closed door.

'Mum?'

Opening the door a crack she peered inside. Her mother had her phone to her ear and a look of intense concentration on her face. Sarah caught her attention and waved to her. Waving back her mother motioned towards the phone as she turned towards the papers on her desk, *umming* and *ahhing* in the process. With a feeling of slight disappointment which she tried to push aside Sarah walked into the living room, threw herself onto a large chair and shut her eyes. She could still hear her mother a few doors away talking sharply into the phone. It sounded like business but with Mrs Collidge it always was.

The phone began to ring and she groaned inwardly, wishing her father was around to pick it up.

'Hello.'

Putting on her most dissatisfied voice was the surest way of getting rid of unwanted callers.

'Hey. It's me.'

'Oh, hi Jonathan.' She was surprised to hear from him since she had seen him a short while ago at school. 'Are you coming to Tom's tonight?'

'Yes.' He did not sound too excited at the prospect even though they both played on the same team.

'Are you sure?'

'No.' He sighed. 'I had another argument with Dad as soon as I got back so I might just stay home tonight.'

'Oh, come on, Jon...' He was always very tiresome when he got into a sulk.

'You know I saw Asha this evening whilst walking Dax...'

'That's unfortunate. We see her every day at school though, don't we?' Sarah's voice had gone dry. She wondered what he was getting at. It was not the type of conversation she wanted to have.

'I know. I just remembered the good old days when I could just go over to hers or come over to yours and we could talk before she went weird. Things were simpler back then.' He sounded muffled. 'What happened to us exactly?'

'She had a breakdown after her mum's death.' Sarah was past the drama surrounding Asha but the obvious confusion Jonathan still felt upset her slightly. She had felt the same at first but it seemed like a lifetime ago and she was no longer interested in talking about it.

'It's water under the bridge, Jon,' she reiterated as though trying to convince herself. 'Come tonight. I'll come and get you in a few hours and then we can head over to Sandra's.'

'Oh lord, I'm not feeling that bad. I'll just see you at Tom's. Charlie and I will walk over.'

Sarah stifled a giggle at his reluctance to engage with Sandra beyond the school walls.

'Okay. Bye.'

Picking up her rugby kit she headed to her bedroom. Sarah had lost interest in Asha months ago but Jonathan getting emotional over her was upsetting. What sort of a friend chose to shut others out even after a traumatic death? Yes, Asha had suffered but so had everyone else. When Sarah's grandmother had passed away just five months ago *she* had been inconsolable. It had been right in the middle of the summer holidays. The two weeks before the funeral were tense for Sarah. Any time the phone in the Collidge household had rung Sarah had run for it, hoping, wishing, and praying it was Asha but it never was. The morning of the funeral Patrick Saunders, Asha's father, had shown up at their door to offer help prior to the church service. Asha, it seemed, had not had the decency to come with him. Jonathan had been there for Sarah. Yu had been there for her. Asha had not. That said a lot. She no longer cared what happened to her.

CHAPTER 2

*A*sha lay in bed half asleep. The party at Tom's would be almost over now. Although she had been discreetly left off the guest list she had heard most of the sixth formers talking about it. It was now just past two in the morning, but having the puppy in her bed next to her made her want to stay awake. He was fast asleep beside her, snoring loudly as she stroked him idly. She had always wanted a dog but her parents had told her that she would have to assume full responsibility for it, which had put paid to her wishes. Between schoolwork, friendships and music there was not much time for much else. Now friendships were gone and it seemed she did have time on her hands. Her father had failed to notice there was a puppy in the house even when it gave little yaps. She wondered if there would be anyone looking for it – could she try to keep it? But then she remembered her plan to leave home as soon as school was over. Having a puppy on her hands would certainly prove difficult. She resigned herself to finding local shelters in the morning.

Her curtains were open, letting the glow from the moon

cast some light into her room. She shut her eyes, willing herself to sleep, ignoring the tree branches that brushed against the window. She felt herself beginning to drift off but woke up with a start. She didn't know what had woken her but it had been the tiniest noise coupled with the awareness that the house had become cold.

As she lay in bed with her eyes open she held her breath and listened, hoping it was just her imagination. The house was silent with occasional sounds from the outside world – the wail of sirens in the distance echoing around Regent's Park, the odd car on the road. But Asha felt uneasy, there was something wrong. She sat up in her bed and, taking care not to disturb the puppy, slipped her cold feet into her bedroom slippers and padded across to her window. The street below was silent. She opened her bedroom door; the little squeak it emitted as it swung open sounded extremely loud in the quiet room. Asha knew she would not be disturbing her father – his room was on the next floor down and he slept like a log. She walked to the top of the stairs and went down them one at a time, trying to avoid the steps she knew would creak whilst looking around her. The house was big and had its fair share of rooms on each floor. Asha's room was in the attic and had been converted into a large bedroom so she could have her own privacy as she got older. Her old bedroom had become a guest room. Her father's door was firmly shut and she smiled a little as she heard his loud snoring. The doors to the other rooms were shut too apart from one which she peeked into. It was a bedroom which was now used as a dumping ground for items they did not want to deal with. The old rocking horse Asha had been given at age six was sitting in the corner, the moonlight shining onto its beady eyes. But the room was warm, which meant whatever was causing the cold draught was downstairs causing it to push right up the stairs. The temperature in the house had definitely dropped and as Asha exhaled her breath formed plumes of steam around her. She hoped someone had left a window ajar but her father usually checked and she knew it would not have slipped his mind.

The cold draught led her to the kitchen, her bedroom slippers making no sound on the floor. She stopped at the door when she heard whispers. Burglars! Her heart began to race as she tried to think. She could walk to the living room and make a quick call but she had no idea how many of them there were. The realisation that some of them could be in the living room suddenly struck her. She instinctively grabbed the empty vase which stood on the table in the hallway; it was heavy and she knew it would cause some damage if she made a dash for it. Peering into the dark kitchen her eyes tried to adjust to the darkness. The whispers began again, and a sudden gust of wind caused the voices to remark on how chilly it was. She lowered the vase slightly as she listened. Something was not right; they spoke strangely and seemed to be having some sort of argument.

'Hoist your other leg up then.'

'I can't. My trouser leg's stuck on something outside.'

There was panic in their voices. They sounded terrified at the prospect of being caught and were in a hurry – hardly the menacing behaviour that Asha would expect from burglars.

'Oh no, Bogsley. We've managed to get in – I just want my little Hiller back.' The voice sounded desperate. 'He does not belong with these vile beings.'

She wondered who Hiller was. Then with a shock she realised that it was probably the bulldog puppy asleep on her bed. Her fear was quickly replaced with immense curiosity and she switched on the lights without thinking, flooding the kitchen with illumination. Everyone blinked in the bright light, then there were gasps all round as they observed each other. The burglars were two men, at least she thought they were men, although little people was a more apt description. They did not appear to be dwarves; they were no more than three feet tall and dressed very strangely. They looked as if they were in period fancy dress with their coats and elaborate hats and trousers. Their faces were very tanned and leathery – and showing immense frustration; the one that had been stuck still hung on to the window ledge with one leg in and one leg out. They both remained completely still as if hoping Asha would not spot them if they didn't move. She put her palms up in a friendly manner.

'Hello?' she ventured, not really knowing what to say.

They were still frozen in fright.

'Fred. What do we do?' the one who was hanging on to the windowsill asked.

'We must make a run for it, Bogsley.'

The little person whom she now knew to be Fred who had successfully gained entry pushed the other back out of the window before scrambling violently out himself and landing with a heavy thud on the ground. The sudden movement caught Asha by surprise, they looked so slow and heavy.

'I just want to talk—'

She ran to the window and watched them pick themselves off the ground before running down the driveway. They disappeared round the corner into the darkness. Asha ran out to the hallway, flinging the door open, which to her disbelief set off the alarm, and then ran out into the freezing November night. She could hear them running onto the street and followed, hardly feeling the paralysing cold through her thin nightshirt or the frost beneath her bedroom slippers. She chased them, slipping slightly on the frosty ground, all the way to the corner of Elm Row where they slowed down. Asha had the advantage due to her height and long legs. She called out to them, trying to catch her breath as she did so.

'Wait. Please. I believe I have your puppy.'

The one in the yellow checked coat slowed down even more.

'I just want to give him back.'

But the other grabbed him by his collar.

'Don't listen, Fred. It's a trick. There are dark forces at work.'

These words seemed to strike fear into the first, who began to increase his pace once again.

'Wait, please.' Asha was starting to feel the cold in the eeriness of the night.

'They wish to trick us, Fred. Keep running – we're almost there.'

They ran to the end of the road then disappeared from sight. Asha's run had slowed to a tired jog. She paused at the end of the road but there was no one in sight.

'Hello...' she called in desperation, but her voice echoed into the night.

She wanted to keep looking but the sound of sirens in the distance and her sudden departure from the house reminded her that she had left the front door wide open and was not properly dressed. The walk back home was a dejected one. Thoughts were whirring through her head. Who were they? What had they wanted? Who was Hiller? She assumed the puppy she had found the evening before was the answer to the mystery. But she did not think she would see them again – she had frightened them well enough. She jogged the rest of the way as she was beginning to feel the cold, her feet slowing to a halt at the sight of police cars outside her home. Breaking into a run, she ran up the drive and in through the front door which was wide open.

'Dad?' she yelled.

The lights were all on.

'Asha!' Her father came out of the dining room and grabbed her by the shoulders. 'Where did you go? I heard yelling outside, the alarms went off and you were gone.'

There were suddenly six police officers standing around them. Asha felt very small as the realisation of what had occurred dawned on her.

'There were two men in the kitchen and I ran after them.'

'Are you out of your mind?' His grip tightened on her shoulders. 'How could you do such a thing?'

'I'm sorry – they ran off.' She paused for breath. 'I wasn't thinking so I just took off after them.'

Her father hugged her tightly, almost squeezing the last bit of breath out of her. Four of the police officers walked outside, one of them speaking into his radio to say Asha had been found. The two that stayed behind got their notepads out.

'We would like to ask your daughter a few questions, Mr Saunders. We need to get descriptions of these men and other details.'

'Of course.' Her father looked drained as he walked past to shut the front door.

'Okay. Asha, is it?'

'Yes.'

'Can you please tell us what happened?' The officer had started scribbling.

'Well, err...' She was not sure how to begin.

'Go on, sweetheart.' Her father had returned; he put a supportive hand around her shoulder and squeezed it reassuringly.

'Well, there were two of them. I had been upstairs trying to fall asleep and I heard a noise – I wasn't sure whether it had come from the house or outside so I went to check.'

'Okay.'

'I walked down the stairs and heard whispers from the kitchen. Some people were climbing in through the window.' She paused. 'I turned the lights on and there were two men there – they spoke strangely.'

'What do you mean, strangely?'

'Err... accents?'

'Foreign accents?' the other probed.

'Not exactly.'

'What do you mean strangely, then?'

'Well, almost like old English gentlemen, like they were from the olden days.'

'What were they wearing?' the first officer asked.

'Normal trousers, dark brown I think, one had a shirt and waistcoat, the other had a full jacket on. They referred to themselves as Fred and Bogsley – or Bosley? They both looked really strange, like they were from another world, another time.' The officer's pens had begun to slow down.

'Anything else?' The officer who looked at her had a glint in his eye.

'They were short – like they would have come up to here.' She pathetically raised a hand to her hip level, then awkwardly raised it slightly higher, then as an afterthought lowered it again. 'Or perhaps here?'

The police officer's pen had ground to a halt. The one with the steely glint in his eye had stopped writing a few seconds ago and an uncomfortable silence filled the hallway.

'You definitely saw this?' the officer asked with a wry look on his face.

'I definitely did. I'm not lying. Why on earth would I make this up?' Her mouth had gone dry. The officer sighed.

'Can I have a quick word with your father, Asha?'

The three men stood around in a circle whilst Asha wandered into the next room. She knew they would be discussing the plausibility of her story but they would have to believe her.

'Okay, we'll file a report about the incident and someone will be in touch.'

She knew they would not be back to the household again. That was the end of the incident as far as Asha was concerned and she knew the more she tried to convince them the more insane they would think she sounded. The officers both walked out the door mumbling goodnight to her father. The words 'troubled' and 'obviously' filtered through from the driveway as they discussed what they assumed her plight was. She felt herself flushing with shame; her cheeks were burning and she could feel the tears coming. Her father returned from the drive and shut the door behind him. Without looking at or speaking to her he began turning the lights off.

'You don't believe me, do you?'

'Hey, it doesn't matter what I believe, I'm just glad you're home safe and unharmed.'

'Don't patronise me, Dad.'

'Don't use words you don't understand, Asha. You just told a group of police officers who rushed down here on a Friday night thinking something had happened that we were almost burgled by Victorian era dwarves. They probably think you fancy yourself as Snow White. I doubt they will do much, if anything, about what happened and we can only be so lucky, because if they did do you know what they would find?' He began punching the code into the alarm.

'A reclusive seventeen-year-old who has been in therapy for the past year, shuns her closest friends, doesn't speak to her own father and spends all her time alone. That would be the only abnormal thing about this entire situation.' Her father was still not looking at her as he began to climb the stairs.

'Dad, I swear that is what really happened. Why would I make things up? I'm not a child.'

He turned on the stairs to look at her.

'Maybe if you opened up more people would be inclined to believe you, but right now you just seem delusional. Hell, if you opened up more and had a life perhaps you wouldn't need to create a fantasy life.' With those words her father turned around and stalked up the stairs.

CHAPTER 3

The man evidently found the results wholly unsatisfactory. He glanced dispiritedly at the windows of the dark room, the lack of any sunlight making the outdoors appear as if evening had dawned already. The large iron gates that ensured the privacy of the house denied him a glimpse to the outside world, a distraction he clearly would have found useful to rid him of his annoyance. The boy desperately wished he could give him some good news, anything, but there was none and he somehow felt he was to blame.

'How on earth did you manage to lose them? They are short, stumpy creatures – certainly not the fastest runners.' The man's voice, a deep baritone, was occasionally tinged with a northern accent when he got angry. However, his anger was never a violent rage; it was always controlled, quiet, well thought out, but that was what made him dangerous.

'Please explain how you managed to cock it all up.' His voice had become dangerously low, his last words emerging as a snarl.

There was an audible gulp in the large room as the boy swallowed nervously. He desperately wanted to defend himself but he had to think carefully. He had to be cautious about what he said.

'I have helped you all – all of you. I have plucked you all from the depths of your own filth and yet you fail me time and time again. Why do you do it? Do you think that is what I deserve?' The man lifted his head and gazed at the boy, who shuddered at the cold detached look on his face.

'I'm sorry, sir. I w-won't fail you again.' He found himself stuttering again, an affliction from childhood he thought he was well rid of. He never stuttered unless he was deathly afraid and the man terrified him.

'N-none of-of us will f-f-fail you.' He licked his lips nervously, eyes still closed.

The immense house was silent. The boy had come to realise that he never heard the sound of other voices or human movement in it. The only noise was the ticking of the grandfather clock, timely and consistent, and the sound of the man's voice; even the outside world did not intrude on them. The boy always simply pushed the large side door open and walked through the halls into this private study a few doors down. The initial written instructions had been clear on that: he was to go in through the side door and never open any other door or look at anything else. The man's instructions to him had always been to leave the others outside. He did not want them in the house, yet did not want anyone to know they were around. Everything was to be shrouded in absolute secrecy.

'What did you say they had with them?'

'A puppy, sir – a v-v-very small puppy – then they almost seemed to sense us and disappear.'

'A puppy?'

His face was once again hidden in the dark shadows of the study.

'How sickeningly sweet. It seems our little vermin are determined to appear as human as possible.'

There was a pause and a long, protracted silence as the boy stood as still as possible lest he invoke the man's anger.

'Very well. Go, and don't fail again. I'm very disappointed at the moment – you do not want to make me angry.'

'Yes, sir.' The boy nodded, relieved that the man sounded almost bemused by the thought of the puppy. Maybe he did have a sense of humour, however macabre it might be.

'Don't forget that I have done a lot for you and your family and there is a lot more to come.'

'Thank you, sir. I won't forget. I'm very grateful.' The stutter was gone, his confidence restored.

'Goodbye.' The dismissive tone caught the boy unawares, especially since he could no longer see the man's face, just the dark outline of his figure.

'Goodbye, sir!'

The boy backed out of the door as quietly as he could, uncertain as to what the man would find disturbing. He walked out into the cold hallway, treading gently on the polished oak floorboards. The silence always gave him a sense of foreboding, as though the house held a secret. One of the others had joked that perhaps the man might keep the dead bodies of those who had wronged him deep within the property. Shuddering, he let himself out through his designated door; it didn't make a sound as it swung open which always spooked him. The house was clearly designed to be as silent as possible so any entry or exit could be effected undetected. There wasn't a single squeak of door hinges, bedsprings, or even the settling of wood. He had done some odd jobs in a few of these big houses in North West London and he knew something was not right here. It was not his job to question, though, that was not what he was getting paid for – and he was getting paid a lot more than he had ever dreamed possible for honest work. He was simply spying and reporting and he did not have to do anything that would land him in the police cells. His friends who were doing the runs on his estate for the larger criminal gangs would baulk at the wages he was receiving, he knew, because they had had to do some very horrible things for less money. They were constantly at risk of being grassed up or getting a knock on their front door from the Metropolitan Police murder investigation teams, whilst his biggest worry was the possibility of suffering from exposure after following these little people around. It was not a difficult decision to make, although he had to admit that the dwarves were quite strange. He had never seen anything like them before but he was happy to oblige, the instructions were simple enough to follow and there were no risks to take.

The afternoon air was chilly in the large garden; the tall trees surrounding the house kept any prying eyes out. The man had gone to a lot of trouble to preserve his privacy in as tranquil a setting as possible. The flower-strewn garden was in stark contrast to the estate that the young man had grown up on and still lived in. The small fountain nearby had a cherub on it with a constant stream of water flowing out of its finger as it pointed westwards. Not many people could afford luxuries of this sort. This garden had a romantic feel, almost as if it had been specially made with a lot of love; the young man's estate in comparison was cold and barren, cement and tarmac marking the areas where grass or flowers ought to be. The council had to be realistic; after all, flower beds and plants weren't a necessity, and took up vital inner-city space. He simply had to be successful with this task he had been set and he could move his family far away from their grim reality; he just had to remain focused. The dwarves were getting awfully careless and they had tracked them to within a popular park in North London, where they hoped in the next few days or weeks to locate them. His instructions after that were simple: let the man know of their exact location and the rest would be handled. He would have no business with the dwarves or the man after that and would be paid handsomely for his troubles. The man was not fibbing – he had already allocated approximately half the promised amount and the rest would come at the end. The boy did not doubt his words; the man seemed intent on finding the dwarves. For what purpose he did not know but he didn't have it in him to ask. He had long since realised you didn't gain anything from asking questions that did not concern you.

Leaving the garden behind he passed through the small iron side gate hidden in the wall. The man did not want anyone knowing he was having visitors – or, in the young man's view, did not want his neighbours to see the type of guests he was entertaining. He closed the gate behind him and stepped out into the serenity of the Regent's Park inner circle. The road was quiet as usual with few cars and hardly any pedestrians, the street immaculately clean. He inhaled contentedly; if wealth meant peace of mind and a street free of wrappers, cans and plastic bags then he was all for it. He crossed the street and walked to the small enclosed park where he knew they would be waiting. He had been gone for half an hour, leaving them in the bitter cold, but they were unlike any others he had ever met. They had great tenacity, were very patient, and could spend hours waiting if they had a true purpose. They had been recruited by the man. He was not sure where the man had discovered them but the boy found that they scared him; although he had met dysfunctional youths before, these particular ones had an insane hunger within them that was almost subhuman. The man had definitely picked the right people for this job.

Ensuring no one was around he pursed his lips and gave the signal: a low-pitched whistle that he knew they would not ignore. They did not use any names to identify each other because they had been instructed not to, but the man knew who they all were. He had their records, knew their faces and their histories. The pale faces began to appear from the various corners of the park – a lot of them dressed in their standard uniforms of black and grey tracksuits, jeans and hoodies. When they had all emerged he ensured he had their attention and began to speak; as he spoke they listened intently.

~

The London air was stinging cold with just a hint of damp as Asha walked home from school that evening. It was only four o'clock but already very dark. A heavily coiffured lady covered in mink walked past with a little dog in her arms, giving Asha a strange look which made her grin. Her thoughts turned briefly to the two little people. She had not caught sight of them again in the last few days, but occasionally woke up in the dead of night thinking she heard a noise, then realising it was just her imagination. She realised she wanted them to come back – after all, they had dared to return for Hiller so they deserved to have him. Asha knew she couldn't keep him. She had managed to get away with leaving him in the house to amuse himself but once he began to grow it would be torture for him with his boundless energy. He could not be sent to an animal home if there were people looking for him.

The sound of quiet footsteps walking behind her made her quicken her pace. She glanced behind her; it was a group of girls from a local school. They stopped when they realised she had caught sight of them, giggling maniacally to themselves. She turned back and kept her pace, suddenly feeling unsafe on the lonely street. They did not go to her school and she did not know much about them but their uniforms were a giveaway.

'Excuse me.'

She pretended she did not hear and kept on walking straight ahead. She only had to turn the corner in a few steps and she would be on her street.

'Excuse me.'

The voice was more insistent this time and she was nervous. More giggles filled the air. She felt vulnerable.

'Have you got the time?'

Her heart rate quickened. Something about the girls made her uncomfortable; they were too persistent and easily keeping pace with her long strides. They moved as a pack did. She knew they did not really want to know the time but wanted her to stop and engage with them in whatever game they were playing. She suddenly wished her two closest friends were around.

'Excuse me.'

This time they caught up and moved in front of her, blocking her path. She looked around. There were four of them. There was no one else on the street.

'Yes.' Asha looked at the one she assumed was the leader. Although she was in uniform she was unkempt – her tie was loosened around her neck, a button was missing from her white shirt, her school skirt had started to pucker; she was all straggly long extensions, bright long nails and too-heavy make-up. They would never have got away with dressing like that at Ark House. They were all from a local girls' school a few miles away, which rumour had it was on the verge of shutting down.

'We just wanted a word with ya.'

'I'm sorry, I don't have the time. I've got to get home quickly – my dad's waiting.' She tried to walk past the girl.

'You think you're the only one with a dad and places to go?' the girl asked.

'She thinks she's too good to hang out with the likes of us.'

'Silly cow.'

The recriminations came fast.

Asha had no idea what was prompting this spate of interrogation. 'That's not what I said,' she said, confused. Realising they were just looking for trouble she tried to skirt past them but was stopped by another girl who looked remarkably like a weasel.

'Oh no you don't,' she said, hurriedly grabbing Asha's wrist, catching her by surprise.

'Don't grab me!' Asha yelped, trying to shake her off.

'You go to that fancy school, don't ya.'

'Yeah. Lil princess here thinks she's all that.'

'Get off,' Asha wailed as the feral group of four circled her.

But she realised the more she tried to shake off the grip the stronger it became. She looked at them.

'What do you want?' she asked, fearing the worst. If she could stall them long enough perhaps someone would come round the corner to help.

'Well, we just wanted to be friends.'

'You know – have a little talk.'

'But you've offended us now, see.'

They laughed in unison.

'I'm sorry but I don't know you and my dad is waiting.' Asha tried again, feeling like a trapped animal being toyed with by voracious predators.

The girl did not let her arm go, grinning at her as though it was particularly funny, her partially obscured face making her grin look like a wolf snarl. Asha, perhaps foolishly, decided to make a dash for it and gave the girl a swift sharp kick in the knee. As she let her go with a surprised scream Asha realised they had been joined by two others who were attacking the girls from behind with sticks. It was the two little men from the other night – Fred and Bogsley – the ones who had come for the bulldog puppy. Fred had jumped onto a girl's back and pulled her hat over her eyes whilst Bogsley pummelled another as the girl howled in surprise. Asha went for the leader, whacking her with her bag which was heavy with books, and the fourth looked on no doubt wondering if this was a fight she was willing to get involved in. Before she had the chance to make a decision an overexcited Bogsley had sprayed a lot of dirt and sand in her face. She started to yelp and retreated down the street like a wounded animal, trying to get the dirt out of her eyes and hair. The other three must have decided they were not prepared for a long fight and raced after their friend.

Fred and Bogsley looked at each other as though what they had just done was dawning on them. Asha sensed what was on their minds.

'Please. Don't run away. I'm the last person to cause you any trouble.'

They regarded her with great suspicion.

'I'm Asha.' She enunciated her name.

Silence.

'Who are you? Are you dwarves?'

'How dare—' the first began, apparently insulted at being referred to as a dwarf.

'I didn't mean to be rude.'

'We are the dwellers,' the second one replied. He was an odd-looking creature, short, squat with a bulbous nose and the most tanned skin she had ever seen – apart from that of his friend. 'I am Fred and my companion is Bogsley.'

'Where do you live?'

'Beneath the arches—' Bogsley began, but was silenced by a look from Fred.

'Believe me, I'm the last person to cause you any harm.'

They still observed her warily, their wide eyes showing distrust.

Asha looked around skittishly, an act that caused them to shrink back in fright.

'I'm sorry – I don't want to alarm you, but those girls might return with reinforcements. They're from a really rough school a few miles away. I don't know why they've come this far.'

'Thieving,' came Fred's glib reply.

'What? How would you know that?'

'We see a lot,' Bogsley responded as though she was daft.

'They steal from the trinket shop,' Fred added, his eyes widening further, which made Asha take a step back.

'So you won't tell me where you're from or anything about yourselves?' Asha asked.

A silence fell on the party as the temperature plunged. She realised she had to make a decision for the sake of their health.

'For people who have gone to great lengths to get their puppy back you're both being very reserved.'

Not a word.

'Look.' She heaved a sigh. 'Meet me at my front door in a few minutes and I'll have Hiller waiting. If you choose not to come then there is nothing more I can do for you.' She thought it was best to add a clause just in case they chose to run away again. 'Just to let you know I can't take care of him because I'm in school and my dad works. He says if I don't find the owners within a few days it's down to the shelter for him.'

Bogsley gave her a dirty look as Fred gasped in horror. With those words she walked off leaving the pair standing on the street corner but expecting to see them shortly.

Asha waited in her room with Hiller in her lap. He was fast asleep, bundled in some sweatshirts to keep him warm. She walked to her sash windows; there was no sign of anyone down below and all was quiet. The two dwellers were nowhere to be seen but she knew they would be there – they were obviously accustomed to keeping themselves hidden. She remained a while in her room to give them the chance to find a good hiding place. She prised her door open and listened for any signs of her father but he didn't seem to be nearby. Gingerly navigating the stairs as she held on to Hiller she listened outside his bedroom but there were no sounds; there was no sign of him in the other rooms either. Then she heard the familiar tone of his voice coming from his study. He sounded angry and would be too distracted to hear anything. She moved quickly to the front door and gritted her teeth. She opened it quickly paying no attention to the cold as she stepped out into the frosty air and shut the door behind her. There was no one in sight;

she walked to the edge of the driveway which was partially hidden from the view of the front door.

'Fred! Bogsley! Are you there?' she whispered. 'I have Hiller here.'

Nothing. Asha was bemused as she stood there waiting with the squirming puppy who wanted to be let onto the ground.

'I know you want to keep yourselves and your existence a secret and you can trust me to do that,' she continued. 'I also want to thank you for coming to my aid – no one else would have done it. But I have to give Hiller back to you – I can't keep him.'

There was a slight movement just behind her. She turned slowly to find it was Bogsley who had emerged from behind her father's car. He stood there watching Asha. She wondered how such short squat creatures could be so light on their feet.

'Do you really mean that?'

She jumped slightly as Fred emerged from the bushes across from her.

'Yes, of course I do.'

Fred's gaze was fixed upon the bundle in Asha's arms. He warily reached out for Hiller as Asha bent to hand the excitable puppy over.

'I've missed you, my boy,' he sobbed as he buried his face in Hiller's fat little body.

'Who are you?' Asha asked the question that had plagued her for the last two days. 'I know you're the dwellers, but how did you come to be here?'

The two dwellers looked at each other.

'It is a long story.'

'Well, I'm not doing anything for the rest of the evening,' she said with a little laugh.

CHAPTER 3 | 67

Fred and Bogsley retreated deeper into the bushes, their larges eyes widening suddenly.

'We must remain hidden – we have enemies,' Fred said with a serious look.

'Why don't you come in?' she asked.

'How do we know we can trust you?' Fred said.

'We've been hunted for so long...' Bogsley chimed in.

Asha was chilled by the ominous words but didn't show how affected she was.

'You have to trust me. If I wanted to hurt you I would have done so by now. I could also have hurt Hiller but I didn't. I think you realise that, which is why you came to my aid. Please come in for some tea. My father will never know you are in the house, it's quite big.'

The two little men looked at each other with surprise in their eyes.

'It's been over two hundred and fifty years since we were invited to tea.' Fred looked at Bogsley excitedly.

Bogsley looked just as thrilled at the invitation to tea.

'We must be wary, though. They are everywhere.'

Their words went through Asha like a cold knife and she wrapped her jumper tightly around her, keen to get indoors.

≈

The boy was having a harder winter than normal. It was a lot colder, and the cold seemed to be reaching parts of him that he didn't know were so sensitive. The cheap body warmer he had on wasn't doing the trick; the freezing evening almost made him wish he'd taken part in the store raids a few days before with the rest of the boys from his estate. He could at least have picked up some decent winter clothing. Then he remembered the police presence on the estate that morning as doors were rammed in and some of those who took part in the raids were hauled from their beds. There was no pride in being dragged out of your home like that and embarrassed before family. He would just have to get another cheap jacket, perhaps a bundle. They would warm him eventually. He had made a solemn promise to himself for the sake of his sister that he would stay away from the law.

Although he had been paid more money than he had ever seen in his life by the man, he was hesitant to spend it. That was what the others on the estate did when they got their huge payouts from their dodgy dealings – they went on spending sprees, lavishing money on dubious girlfriends, expensive trinkets, dodgy cars – but they were always still poor. Their circumstances changed but the mentality remained the same. They never left the crime-ridden sink-holes they had been born into, were never far away from the scenes of their numerous crimes, and were always seen with the same friends. Before anyone knew it, they had spent a fortune and had nothing to show for it, returning to the crime lords who would pay them handsomely for their misdeeds. Then the police would return for them. It was a vicious circle. Nothing changed. The boy was determined to be different, deciding to save the money in a bank account – his very first.

As he caught himself shivering once more he decided to circle around the block on his bicycle to warm up; by the time he got round perhaps they would be here. He was still upset that they were not able to meet elsewhere. This was too close to home. His mother and sister were just a few metres away. He knew they were aware of this, which was exactly why they had decided on that location. He was the most vulnerable, the one who had the most to lose, the only sane one; he knew that even if they did not.

As he pedalled slowly he noted the lack of cars around at that time of the night. The angry daytime traffic that passed through on the way to the industrial estate nearby was gone, replaced by the occasional loud violent voice, a blaring television when a door was opened, an out-of-control dog in the distance, a screaming baby – in addition to the harsh sounds of mopeds being driven at dangerous speeds around the block. These would be followed a few minutes later by sirens: a chase, perhaps. It was all normal to him. He had taken a lot of ribbing for choosing to go round on a bicycle, but he had his reasons; it served a purpose so he had put up with it. He had a lot to lose; his concern was always for his sister – he tried to ensure this life they lived would not always be theirs, tried to make everything as easy as possible for her. The problem, which he had come to realise early on, was that he was too naive, a trait which he had definitely not inherited from either of his parents. His uncomplicated character had not done him much good except keep him away from the police and the custody rooms. He had never been attracted to the flashy lifestyle of the older criminals. What was the point of all that money when you were always on the wrong side of the law? It made no sense to him. It seemed easier to remain on good terms with the police and the courts so you were free. The other boys his age made money; he never asked how – the less he knew the better. He did not want to risk prison. He had always had an aversion to it after visiting his father there in his childhood; besides, his mother and sister would not be able to cope without him. He loved them too much to risk it.

He was not sure what the *others'* circumstances were

like, but he could guess that they were all from similar backgrounds – broken homes, broken lives and broken hearts. There were some with broken minds – quite a few of them disappeared early on in the task, there one day and gone the next. He chose not to ask questions, instead choosing to keep his wits about him.

His thoughts wandered back to the close proximity of this location to his home; the very thought of the others knowing where he lived chilled him. He had looked into their eyes and seen a wickedness. The man, their benefactor, had probably seen it too which was why he had put the boy in charge, not realising that he was terrified of them. Their instructions were to stay beneath the radar: the law would never become involved, no one would ever be alerted to their presence or their deeds.

Exhaling, he took a quick look at his watch and grimaced. They were not even late; he was just extraordinarily early. The thought of them catching a glimpse of him emerging from his tower block was just too horrifying to imagine, so he always ensured he was prepared thirty minutes ahead of their meeting time. The street lights were dimly lit, giving the estate a depressing air. As the boy pedalled around he noticed the figures in the shadows waiting, tense furtive glances all around them for anyone in uniform. Then another shadowy figure caught his attention. This one was calm, almost mechanical in its movements, and very self-assured. It was the girl; he could feel it even though he could not see her features. Like him, she had been recruited by the man. The boy had no idea where she had been acquired from but there was an air to her, a disturbing temperament he had been unable to shake off. As if sensing him, she turned around; the dark hood that cloaked her features did not hide her lips. He inhaled deeply then swallowed nervously before speaking.

'Where are the others?'

She did not reply, which got on his nerves. He tried to steady his voice and made an effort to gain control.

'Come on then. They should be on Church Row now. It's almost five past seven.' He tried to inject an air of authority into his voice. 'Let's go.'

She rode off slowly on her bike and disappeared around the corner. He followed, wishing once again he could have got some other form of gainful employment, but knowing he would never get paid as much for doing menial work. He rode a short distance behind her till he saw the faces of some of the others. They were all dressed appropriately, all with bicycles at the ready.

There were the three of them who always remained cloaked and then there was Tamara, a young North Londoner whom he affectionately referred to as Tammy. He was concerned to see her with them. She was also a recruit of the man but there was something about her that was innocent and precious – as though she did not know what she was doing half the time. Although she came from a violent background she lacked the killer instinct of the others. After their last exploration he had urged her to keep away; this life was not for her. 'You'll be better off at home safe with your family,' he told her, but here she was. He sighed dismally – he could not fight her battles for her and had to keep his own wits about him.

Straightening up the boy resumed control – he was in charge. He could not look weak or soft. They knew what they had to do. He stopped and cleared his throat to get their attention.

'Remember, we can't arouse any suspicion. We ride as a group.' He paused for any interjections. 'Let's go.'

They rode close together as a pack, avoiding the main roads and going down the quiet side streets. Their lights remained off and they moved as one into the night, disappearing into the dark corners. It was early winter and the nights were longer; London was in darkness for much of the day so it was the perfect time for them to hunt.

~

S arah and Yu had decided to take a long walk after school, not content to go and sit at home with their respective families. Excitement was sweeping through Ark House Academy, not just about the approaching festive season but also the end of year celebrations and the New Year.

'I can't believe there's absolutely nothing to do tonight.' Yu dispiritedly fingered a button on her coat.

'Well, everyone is pretty shattered after the party last weekend. Not to mention parties are pretty much banned in every house until the Christmas holidays.' Sarah had to admit that she was still feeling the effects of being awake for most of the weekend.

'Yeah, I know – that was pretty hilarious last week when hockey came dressed in tomato costumes. I wish the rugby teams had done something.'

They both laughed out loud at the image in their minds. They crossed the street giving a quick glance both ways. Sarah kept talking as she stepped onto the pavement.

'I feel pretty on edge about the final classics essay,' she mused.

'That is going to be a deciding f—'

Yu was cut off violently as a force slammed into her, knocking her to the ground. Sarah looked around in confusion as her friend crumbled to the ground in front of her.

'Are you all right, Yu?' She bent over to look at her. Yu looked shocked and shaken; a bruise was forming on her face where she had hit the pavement. Spinning around fast Sarah faced the wrongdoers.

'Hey – what on earth are you doing? Why don't you watch where the hell you're going?' she yelled angrily.

The words were out – nothing could stop her when she got angry. There were quite a few of them, all on bicycles – one with a dog on a leash – but there was an air about them that made her pause. Out of the corner of her eye she noticed Yu looking up from the ground. She felt the worry emanating from her friend.

'Leave it, Sarah. I'm good.' Yu sprang to her feet in a show of bravado, trying to defuse the situation. Putting her hand to her head she once more bent over in apparent agony.

'They almost ran us over.' Sarah was not quite done. The anger coursed through her.

'It's illegal to ride on the pavement, you know. People have been injured and worse.' Sarah was rarely sensitive but her mood had been getting worse of late. 'We should be calling the police. Take those bloody hoods off for starters so people can see what you look like – and perhaps you could also see where you were going,' she added snidely.

'Sarah. Shut up!' Yu grabbed her by the arm and dragged her off roughly.

The group had stopped in their tracks and stared at the twosome as if they were aliens. Their hoods cloaked their identities well. They were perfectly still as they scrutinised the two girls. Sarah swallowed nervously. She noted their numbers – they were five strong plus a dog, and it was just her and Yu. There was a change in mood and she suddenly did not feel safe. They stared intently at her as she held her breath.

'Oh no. What have you done, Sarah?' Yu whispered, looking around them for any signs of help.

But the streets were deserted for so early on a Friday evening. Then they heard a familiar cheery 'Hello'. They turned in confusion and heaved anxious sighs. It was Dolapo, a fellow Ark House Academy pupil and a neighbour of Jonathan's. Beneath his heavy coat Sarah got a glimpse of his Ark House uniform, which meant he was avoiding going home too.

'Help us, Dolapo,' Yu said.

'These people just ran Yu over.'

Sarah turned to point at them but her words faltered on her lips. Where the group had stood moments before was an empty pavement. It seemed they had disappeared as quickly as they had appeared.

'What? Someone ran you over?' Dolapo looked Yu up and down, concern written over his dark features.

'I'll live. I might not be doing any swimming for a while though,' she said grimly as she rubbed her face.

'There's a nasty bruise forming below your eye,' he said, leading her beneath the glow of a street light.

Sarah was not listening. She was looking around, wondering where the group had gone.

'How could they just disappear?' she whispered to herself. 'They were right there.' She shivered as a taxi went down the eerily silent street.

Sarah did not recall ever having seen a group like that on bicycles. In her part of North London most of the older teens were known to each other and attended one of two secondary schools – Ark House Academy or Downe School, otherwise they were shipped off to boarding schools – but she did not remember ever seeing those people and for some reason their presence disturbed her. Their cold disregard for Yu, their emotionless response as they stilled in unison when she challenged them – all except one who was in discord to the rest of the group and seemed separate.

'Oh, Sarah. You're not still worrying about them, are you?' Dolapo interrupted her thoughts. 'They're probably just a bunch of prats cycling around acting tough with a dog on a leash. The neighbourhood watch will catch up with them soon enough.'

'Probably just as well that they're gone. I found them a bit scary.' Sarah shuddered, pulling her coat around her. She turned to Dolapo. 'Where are you off to?'

'Trying to clear my head and do some thinking. My parents flew in yesterday and are driving me insane. They expect to ask you about your university choices one night and then hope you mysteriously come up with the answers the next morning.'

The two girls laughed. Yu winced in pain.

'We need to get home and get Yu's face seen to before it swells up,' Sarah said urgently. She looked in the direction they had been going, which was the same way the bicycles must have gone, but she did not want to risk seeing them again.

Dolapo glanced at her. 'Okay – if you want to get home quickly why don't we cut through the park? I'll walk with you – we should be fine as a group of three.'

'Yeah, three Ark House Academy kids,' Yu joked. 'Real threatening.' The bruising was getting worse.

Dolapo chipped in, trying to elevate her mood. 'Sarah plays rugby. She can terrify anyone on or off the pitch.'

Sarah was forced to laugh at her friend's disparaging joke. She looked backwards in the direction of the empty street. It was still empty. Yu linked hands with Dolapo and moved along in the direction of the park. Sarah despondently followed, now unsettled.

～

The excitement coursed through Asha as she sped through the narrow streets on her bicycle, narrowly colliding with a crossing pedestrian who carried myriad shopping bags with him. It was the Christmas shopping season and the local high street was filled with busy shoppers hypnotised by the deals and displays available in the little boutiques. She seethed in frustration as she dodged another unwary shopper who crossed right in front of her. If she was not careful she would end up either on a car bonnet or with a passer-by sitting in her basket.

'Sorry,' she yelled. It was not her fault – well, not entirely. During her period of self-isolation she had failed to realise how much she missed human company. Then she had invited the two dwellers, who she counted as human, into her home and they had talked for hours in the darkness of her bedroom lest they arouse her father's suspicions. Everything they had told her now appeared far-fetched in the harsh light of day, even though darkness had already set in that early November evening. Afterwards she had made sure the exit from her home was clear and her father was asleep. Fred and Bogsley departed with their beloved Hiller, but not before extending an invitation to her to come and visit their world. Asha had woken up wondering if it was all an elaborate dream until she noticed the used cups of tea on the little table in the middle of the room and the bedding laid down so the exhausted Hiller could go to sleep.

So the next day, after school was over, curiosity had got the better of her and she found herself cycling to the huge park, only half a mile from her home, where they claimed their abode was. If the distrusting creatures had been telling the truth – and she knew they would have no reason to lie to her; after all, if they could not trust her who could they trust – there was a particular group of trees that they had described to her which she knew well. The arches, they called them. They had been given that name because their thick heavy branches had intertwined through their lifetime to form an unwieldy arch close to a red phone box of which only three existed in that particular park.

As Asha arrived she noticed that the park was not busy, it being a very cold and dark November evening. Taking advantage of the darkness she cycled in, an act which was strictly prohibited. Although the tall lamps overhead gave some light they were few and far between in the dark park, and it would be shutting at 5 p.m. – less than hour – so she had very little time to find the arches. They would be in the furthest point of the park from what she recalled; the dwellers had gone to a lot of trouble to keep themselves hidden. Pedalling furiously, glad to see the pathways were clear, she got deep into the park before getting off her bicycle and looking around her. The part of the park where the arches and the phone box were located was in a separate enclosure only accessible by foot. The arches were only a few metres walk away, right behind some dense bushes which she half expected the two dwellers to pop out of, mid-argument. They were extremely private and guarded their existence fiercely from those who they claimed hounded them; she was very curious to find out more about them and, more importantly, if she could help.

'Hello,' she called out softly, wondering how anyone could live underground in London and go undetected for so long. Her voice fell flat in the heavy winter silence.

'Hello.' Her voice was stronger this time but she was scared of attracting any unwanted attention.

The silence that met her efforts was disheartening and suddenly she recalled her recent trip to the therapist hired by Ark House Academy. What had she said about retreating so far within oneself that a fantasy world filled with fantasy friends was created? Asha tried to remember her exact words. She suddenly experienced a twinge of fear – was she going mad? Had she dreamed up that encounter the other night with the girls attacking her and the two dwellers saving her? Her mind flashed back to the night that of the presumed break-in when she had given chase to the two. Had it all been imagined? How could it have been?

'Don't just stand there,' a sharp voice instructed.

She whirled around, eyes darting suddenly to the voice with no face.

'She's not used to our ways, Fred. She knows not what to do.'

There was a slight movement in the bushes and Bogsley's head popped out with a cautious smile on his face.

'Hello there.' He looked around, his sharp eyes searching cautiously.

Asha was relieved. Now she knew she was not going mad. She gave herself a pinch to make sure.

'Hello, Bogsley.' She kept calm; there was little point in revealing she thought she had been losing her mind. She knew he would disappear in a flash if he became suspicious.

'Pop your bicycle somewhere and come in here.'

'This is a clean coat and I'll be too big to fit—'

'Don't you worry, love, it's nice and hollow in here. It's also quite warm.' Another voice could be heard from the bush. It was Fred.

Asha rested her bicycle against the low black gate at the edge of the enclosure where she would have a perfect view of it from the bushes. Squirming as she got onto her hands and knees she climbed into the bush. Fred was right – it was hollow inside, but the bush was deceptively large, giving her space to sit comfortably on a little bench they had in there.

'What's going on?' She looked around, surprised that something so small to the human eye could hold a space so large from within.

'Ah.' Fred leant over to explain. 'This is a hollow bush,' he repeated.

'How on earth do you make it—'

'We have our ways,' Bogsley said, with more mystery than was required.

'This is our lookout point. So far it is undiscovered,' Fred explained, holding Hiller who had begun whimpering at the sight of Asha.

'Hiller!' She reached for him.

'Shh!' they both hissed at her, looking immensely fearful. 'We must keep our voices to a whisper. Even now I can feel them. They are always around.'

'Okay,' she whispered grudgingly as she played with Hiller.

Her father and Mrs Redding, the housekeeper, had enquired about the absent puppy, but Asha had simply said she had found its owner and the matter had been settled.

'Why don't you get a dog of your own?' Fred asked her, possessively reaching for his pet.

'I could have got one when I was younger but my

mother just seemed too busy to be running after a puppy *and* a child.'

'Oh?' Fred looked sad. 'Where is she now? You talk of her like she is gone.'

'Yes. She is. She died about a year ago.' The words caught in her throat.

There was a silence and she sensed what question was coming next.

'How did she die?' Bogsley asked inquisitively.

The question pierced the thick air in the same manner that it pierced her heart, and she realised the pain was still very raw. There was a slight yelp from Bogsley as Fred gave him a sharp kick.

'Hush. Do you not think at all, man?'

'What?' Bogsley snapped back.

'It's very rude to ask such questions.'

'Oh, you even think releasing a bit of gas is impolite.'

As the pair bickered in violent whispers Asha, who was still in a daze, spoke.

'She passed away just under ten months ago.' The dwellers went quiet. 'It all came as a bit of a shock. I knew she was very ill but I didn't know quite how ill. She kept it very quiet and had begun to put her affairs in order. She and my dad had done the legal stuff months before so they knew it was coming. I didn't. They just couldn't tell me. I had already lost one set of parents...' As she felt the emotion rising in her throat she reached for the locket around her neck. It was a dainty gift her mother had given her a few months before her death. She flipped it open and passed it to Bogsley who gently took it.

'She doesn't look like you.'

'No. I was adopted as a newborn. You see, I was born in Mozambique and the country had just descended into civil war. I guess I was orphaned. My mother, who was actually white Zimbabwean, was working as a nurse and about to flee with my dad when she saw me in her hospital. Both my natural parents had been killed days before. They were apparently local activists fighting the government. I was supposed to be sent to safety to an orphanage in Kenya. The rest is history.' She smiled wistfully as she recalled the story her mother had told her. 'Apparently she saw this cherubic, fat, happy baby and could not let me go. She said that in the midst of all that destruction I just kept laughing happily to myself. Well, anyway, she had encouraged me to play the piano, which was her first love from a very young age, and I had played in a school recital. It all went well...' Asha swallowed painfully as she watched Bogsley fingering the locket. 'She was smiling and happy. We went home and she seemed very tired so Dad put her to bed.'

The mood in the bush was tense as Fred and Bogsley sat there with the former shooting the latter evil looks, but Bogsley was too enamoured by the picture to notice.

'I came down the next morning. It was only a month or two after Christmas. I remember the house was freezing, which was very unusual, then I realised the front door had been left open. I could hear voices downstairs. Dad was sitting on the floor, which is not the most comfortable place, there were a few people standing around in black and green and there was all this commotion. They were carrying something out. When I looked at Dad I knew...' Asha had never told the events of that morning to anyone, even her therapist. There was a short silence as Fred analysed the photograph. 'I didn't know the doctor who diagnosed her had given her weeks. I thought it was years.'

'She was very beautiful,' Fred said. Bogsley nodded mutely.

'I'm... we are very sorry.' They both looked very earnest.

'We know what it is like to lose—' Bogsley began to talk once more but Fred gave him a sharp dig in his side, making him jump.

This time there was no argument and they both sat there looking forlorn.

'You can tell me,' she said. 'I've just told you something very private I've never told anyone. Not even my oldest friends – well, ex-friends. Surely you can trust me...' She wiped her eyes with the sleeves of her coat.

The dwellers looked at each other and, as though a silent agreement had been made, Fred began.

'Well, you know how we told you about being hunted?'

'Yes.' They had mentioned it briefly, but the dwellers had not been willing to divulge all the details. She had guessed the rest would come with time.

'We left our time in 1821 when we were being pursued by rogues known as the runners—'

'The runners?' Asha interrupted curiously.

Fred glared at her, clearly not appreciative of being disrupted mid-speech.

'Yes, the runners operating out of Bow Street – they were known as the Bow Street Runners. A fearsome group of tyrants who would stop at nothing.'

'Common thief takers and hoodlums parading as men operating under the orders of the Bow Street Magistrates,' Bogsley chimed in.

'What did the runners do?'

'They tormented us,' Fred said as Bogsley nodded.

'They found our dwellings one night and came after us, pounding and hammering on our door claiming they were acting under orders, and that was when the transference occurred.'

'Yes, yes, most peculiar,' Bogsley said.

'Well, not that peculiar. It has always been under-stood that whenever the dwellers are in trouble – in times of strife, when we face mortal danger – the commune within which our entire world lies will be split into three distinct parts: the Unending Canal, the Rose Wood, and Kee's Corner. When the runners came after us that night, the transference we'd always heard about happened. The runners were on our heels – they were at the entrance to the doors that would lead to the commune – and then their yells and the incessant banging suddenly ceased. We thought it was a game they played with us, some form of torture, but the silence went on so Rufus, the oldest of us, went out to see what was happening and we emerged to find ourselves in your time.'

Asha was dumbfounded by the story. 'What part of your world are you from?'

'We are from the Unending Canal,' Bogsley announced proudly.

'Kee's Corner and the Rose Wood are still missing,' Fred said with dismay.

'Surely it must be easy to find them. What are the rules in a transference?'

'That two parts of our world move in time while the other remains.'

'What does that mean?'

'Either the Rose Wood or Kee's Corner would be left back in our time in 1821 while we would be moved to a safer time.'

'So what protects you?' Asha asked.

'Magic. The commune has always been protected from those that have tried to harm us. Many have tried and failed, but the lords and earls, they are hungry for our blood and are relentless in their pursuit of us.'

'Can you sense one another?' Asha ventured. 'It would make sense to assume you would know if the others of your world had moved with you.'

'We did at first, but then something happened. They went missing—'

'Not just missing,' Bogsley interrupted, 'I know something terrible happened to them.'

'How do you know? You're no clairvoyant,' Fred snapped.

It was obviously a bone of contention between the two.

'Why don't I help you find them? I know modern London a lot better than you two do.' Asha was confident that people who lived like the dwellers would be easy to locate.

'It is not that simple. We are supposed to stay hidden so we're not targets.'

'Who's after you? Is it these people you say are hunting you?' Asha asked with a quizzical look.

'Yes. It is a group. They are relentless,' Bogsley began.

'They appear in the park at night looking for us,' Fred said.

'We see them first, though, since we have hiding places,' Bogsley added.

Hiller suddenly stiffened and growled. They all went quiet as they listened carefully, but there was no sound from the outside. Asha looked to where she had securely placed her bicycle; it was still there but no one was nearby.

'There's no one h—' She stopped suddenly; Fred and Bogsley's faces had turned a ghostly white as they looked at her.

'Never ignore the warnings of a pup. They sense evil,' Fred hissed, eyes widening.

'They are here,' Bogsley whispered nervously.

Asha was confused.

'Who? The people chasing you? There's no one out there.'

It was dark; the temperature had dropped to below freezing. Their deep breathing sent out hot air that showed in the glow from the moon. Fred held on to Hiller so tightly it looked as if he would squeeze the life out of the wriggling puppy.

'The Mimes,' Fred whispered.

'Our tormentors. They follow us. They sense us now like we do them. They will never let us be free,' Bogsley muttered.

He looked half crazed as he spoke. Asha was concerned for them and confused at the change in their moods.

'Whatever may befall us in the next few minutes, Asha, you do as we say,' Fred instructed sharply.

She merely gazed at them in a daze of confusion thinking they had gone mad.

'Do you hear me?' he spat at her, bringing his face a few inches from hers. She shrank back in fright.

'Yes, I hear you, but I'm telling you there's no one there. Look for yourselves. See what I see.'

She turned around to look past the bushes behind her. The park was silent and clear; nothing stirred. A light frost was forming on the iron railings right by her bicycle as the city began to freeze.

'There is no one here,' she whispered looking back at them. But suddenly she felt what they and Hiller must have felt moments before: a cold fear in the pit of her stomach; it crept over her slowly until it became an icy chill. She turned to look out of the opening and saw it. A large white face with dark eyes was staring back at her through the gap. It was a mime mask. Although simple in construction, with human features, what terrified Asha were the eyes staring blankly at her from the polished alabaster white. The slightly upturned lips showed the hint of a twisted smile. She screamed and in her panic instinctively pushed into the grinning face that blocked her path as she tried to get out of the bushes, catching it by surprise. Fred and Bogsley scrambled out after her as her eyes tried to adjust to the dimness of the park. There were a few of the masked people around, scouring the park on bicycles, coming out from behind trees and bushes. One of them had a dog that growled menacingly, straining against its chain leash. They all had the eerie white masks, which covered their faces entirely. She felt as if she had entered the scene of some macabre horror story.

'What is this?' she asked. 'What's going on?'

They stood in shock for a mere second. The strangers seemed equally surprised to see them. The person she had just pushed to the ground lay flat on the ground staring at her. Those eyes – the emotionless, intense gaze penetrated her. She was afraid and looked to the dwellers for guidance.

'The Mimes,' Fred hissed. He and Bogsley sucked in their breaths as though preparing for the worst.

'Follow us,' Bogsley ordered. 'Whatever you do, do not look back.'

As Bogsley and Fred began to run, Asha fleetingly considered running home but knew she would not get far. The park was now freezing and she would only get disoriented further on. Sprinting after the two she turned around to see how close the strangers were but they simply stood there staring back at them.

'They aren't coming.'

She narrowly avoided being hit by a branch.

'Do not look back,' Fred yelled as they ran.

'They're surprised to see you – you are one of them, after all.'

'Do not be fooled. They like the chase, the hunt, just like wild beasts,' Bogsley said.

But Asha in her blind panic failed to heed their words and turned around once more, instantly regretting her decision when she noticed they were over their shock and were beginning to assemble for the chase; they all began to cycle in different directions. Then she heard the whirring of the bicycles and realised they were catching up to them. They had run deeper into the park, close to the small pond.

'They're coming,' she squealed in terror.

Asha wished she had heeded Bogsley's warning not to look back, because the two dwellers had run around a corner and then vanished. She stopped and looked around, panic overtaking her senses. There was so much there. Had they disappeared into another hollow bush, shimmied up a tree, crouched at the base of a flower bed? But they had vanished into thin air. She looked around in fright; the bushes all remained perfectly still and undisturbed.

'Fred, Bogsley!' she cried out fearfully, wishing she had listened. It was the one thing they had told her to do, and now she was trapped in a dark park with nowhere to go from these maniacs in masks. She glanced backwards in the hopes that she had lost them, but as the hairs on the back of her neck went up she knew one of them was behind her. Asha began to run but it was futile; the figure had no trouble keeping up with her as it cycled alongside her, its unrelenting gaze fixed on her.

'Get away from me,' she screamed, but she found herself forcefully plunged to the ground as it kicked her with such force that she hit her head hard and everything went black.

~

Sarah, Yu and Dolapo had ventured much deeper into the park than they had planned. After the initial scare of the evening the longer walk around the colossal park seemed the way to go to calm Sarah's nerves, and the cold appeared to be soothing the swelling on Yu's face – or so they thought. Sarah's mother would probably have had dinner at work and wouldn't be home yet. Kiki and her father would no doubt have had dinner together. She would not be missed.

Now cold, tired and hungry they were eager to get home. Then screams and mayhem reached their ears and they froze.

'What was that?' Sarah whispered in fright. Yu clung to her tightly.

'A fox,' Dolapo ventured. He sounded hopeful but that did not ease Sarah's concern.

'That is *not* a fox,' she said with a shudder. 'That's a human scream.'

'I want to get out of this park as soon as possible.' Yu was beginning to panic. Sarah wondered if she might be concussed.

'No worries,' Dolapo said hastily. 'If we hurry that way we can follow that path and the row of lights – it leads to Poets Lane from what I recall. The totally opposite direction to home and slightly longer but I suppose we'll be out of the park.'

They nodded and hurried along, with Dolapo leading the way as the chaos continued. There were more screams and shouts before silence descended. Sarah looked at the surrounding darkness which seemed to be staring back at her. She felt it reaching out to her and, suddenly frightened, she snapped back.

'What's happening? It's getting darker. It's coming,' she screeched. She hadn't realised how eerie the park was at night.

'It's the park lights – they're dimming them.' Dolapo grabbed her by the shoulder and pointed upwards.

He was right; as they stared at the eleven-foot cast-iron Victorian lamp posts she saw the lights dampen and the darkness grew around them.

The park was closing for the night.

'We can't be trapped here,' Yu said, beginning to panic.

'We can go over the gates,' Dolapo said reassuringly.

'The gates are extremely high. We'll never make it.' Sarah was now unnerved by the darkness and cold.

'If foxes can get in and out I'm certain we can find a way – we're even smarter.' Dolapo tried to maintain calm. 'Besides, those gates – however tall and overwhelming – are nothing a few fit and nimble teenagers can't handle. We'll scale them easily. We might have a few damaged uniforms and ripped coats but it'll be fine.' He seemed to be trying to convince himself.

Sarah gazed at her friend's outline in the dark, wondering if he was beginning to regret bumping into them that evening. The journey home was never-ending.

Then the park went dark as the lights went out. Somewhere in the distance an owl hooted. Sarah could see plumes of white as their hot breath mingled with the cold air.

'Let's go,' Dolapo urged before they lost their wits. They

followed closely behind him, using what little light they could from the moon to see their way through.

Then Sarah noticed Dolapo pause, his body visible stiffening.

'What the—'

He crouched down behind some bushes, motioning to them to the same. Sarah and Yu followed his lead. They were now so cold their concentration was wavering. Sarah turned to Dolapo who was perfectly still and looking straight ahead, his eyes fixed on something in the distance. Sarah's eyes carefully followed his line of vision and she paused at the sight that met her eyes. They were not alone in the park but they appeared to be the only visitors keen to leave on that bitterly cold night. Just ahead of them, past the trees and bushes, was a large group of hooded figures methodically going through the bushes, trees and foliage, clearly searching for something – or someone. With a start she realised they were the same people who had knocked Yu over. The same group whose emotionless gazes had made her go cold.

'Those are the same people on bicycles from earlier. What are they doing?' she whispered to Dolapo.

'Looking for something. I don't know. There's something a bit weird going on here. We need to leave.' He cautiously peered through the bushes.

'I wonder if we should call the police,' Yu muttered.

'For what? Teenagers searching the park?' Dolapo sounded uncertain. 'You were almost assaulted. In fact you *were* assaulted, Yu. Besides, what have they got hidden in the royal parks? Alcohol, drugs, stolen goods...' He was muttering to himself.

'What's going on?' Sarah asked him.

'I don't know and I don't wish to find out,' he said decisively.

'Look – let's just go in a different direction. Or better yet, go home. I'm getting cold and extremely hungry. My head is throbbing.' Yu made to move.

'Wait.' Dolapo placed a firm hand on her arm. 'You're not thinking straight. We need to make sure there aren't more of them.'

Two of the group looked up as though sensing them in the darkness; the time that passed seemed to go on forever but they looked right through them.

'Okay,' Dolapo whispered. 'Something is wrong here. We're going to avoid anything that will attract attention to ourselves and just get the hell out of this park.'

Sarah had never seen him so guarded before. She felt the tension coming from him as his jaw set determinedly.

He looked back. 'How many did you see this evening?'

'See?' Yu hissed indignantly. 'I was totally blindsided. I saw stars. Ask Sarah.'

Sarah racked her brain as she went through the incident in her mind. 'Four,' she said, recalling the two who seemed almost identical, their mannerisms, height and movements the same, and the other two with long hair peeking out of their hoods who she thought were female – one with dark, straight hair, the other's bright red with a bit of a wave. She remembered vividly because the red hair was in contrast to the dark clothing they wore. Then a fifth came to mind who stood apart from them, not in distance but in spirit.

'No. Five,' she whispered with certainty. 'Five.'

Dolapo watched, his eyes darting to and fro as he tried to make the numbers. 'I see only four.' He looked back at them. 'There'll be a fifth nearby so we need to stick together and be prepared to run.'

Sarah and Yu nodded mutely.

Dolapo hunched over and stealthily began heading north. Yu followed him closely. But Sarah lingered for a while longer. She watched the group as they searched the bushes: tall, dark figures, desperate to keep their identity a secret but so resolute in their task that they were willing to search acres of land on a cold winter's evening. There were just the four of them. Where was the fifth? She turned to find her friends and seeing they were almost out of sight ran to catch up with them, suddenly anxious to get home, her heartbeat drumming out any other sound. The peculiarities of the night were too confounding to comprehend.

In Sarah's mind there was a new evil in the world and it was very close to home. It worried her. She wished there was someone she could speak to. Jonathan was one of her closest friends but he was having such a hard time with his parents at that moment and would not think it was anything serious if she told him that teenagers on bikes were in the neighbourhood or scouring the local park. And Asha, well, their friendship had disintegrated, and because of that Sarah felt alone, confused and scared. The two people she desperately wanted to confer with she could not.

Then she did something she instantly regretted: she looked back. She caught her breath. The fifth figure, the one Dolapo had not been able to locate, was watching them leave. It stood stock still a distance from the others and calmly observed them. Something obstructed its face and as she moved blindly ahead she realised it was a mask.

CHAPTER 4

There was a strange sweet smell engulfing Asha; it assailed her nostrils, filling her air passages until it became sickly sweet and overpowering. She began to gag and tried to shift herself away from it but her body hurt too much, her head throbbed, and she felt an ache running through her. Then the whispers began, the speakers clearly trying to keep their voices low and inconspicuous, but she heard them nonetheless. Groaning, she opened one eye and then the other, trying to remember why she was so sore. She lay still, staring at a ceiling that was certainly not hers and not one she had ever seen before. It dawned on her that she was not in her bedroom at home – she was far away from home. The ceiling resembled some type of structure found underground in a cave or warren. It was very low and there was a dull glow lighting it up. Then it all came flooding back: her trip to the arches, the hollow bush, the white grotesque masks, the chase, the dwellers. The Mimes. The room was dimly lit by candles, which helped to soothe her aching head and tired eyes. She tried to raise her head to get a closer look at the ceiling, her fascination overcoming her.

'Fairy dust.'

The voice that spoke seemed to be that of a child. She turned her head, ignoring the twinges of pain, and opened her eyes wide, shrinking back in fright as she caught sight of some people who looked similar to Fred and Bogsley. The dwellers! They all had the same leathery tanned skin, bulbous noses and peculiar clothing of a time past, with the same aged look to them. The voice that had spoken belonged to a young girl who looked very odd in men's clothing, a top hat and a single-breasted waistcoat, and pigtails that stuck out in the air. She also had the greenest eyes Asha had ever seen.

'Hello?' Asha ventured warily.

They all stared at her, silent and unblinking. The room she had been put in was a bedroom which was too small for her, in a bed that she was too large for; her legs hung over the end of it, but it felt comfortable. The room was cosy; a few books lined a bookcase in the corner, a small fire crackled in the fireplace by her bed, and on a side table was a pot of what she assumed to be tea. Asha gazed, mesmerised, at the fire, wondering how it functioned without a proper chimney in place.

'How does that work?' she asked.

'Our ways are different.' The same young dweller responded to Asha and the others maintained their silence. Her voice was gruff and she lacked the warmth of Fred or Bogsley.

'Do you know where Fred and Bogsley are, and how I happened to be brought down here?' There was a silence; these dwellers did not seem as chatty as the other two. 'You know, they look similar to you, always together with a little bulldog puppy,' she said. 'Very cute. I meant Hiller the puppy not Fr—'

'We know who they are,' another dweller responded. He was just as gruff as the young girl and even more peculiarly dressed in checked trousers, a jacket and a cravat, all in clashing colours which somehow added to Asha's throbbing headache.

'I will fetch them. They don't know you're awake yet.' The girl who had spoken previously left the room.

Asha looked them over in as they did her. There was a long uncomfortable silence; she gave up on any attempt at conversation whilst the others maintained their stance of not speaking but without breaking their gaze. Asha moved to sit up and a palpable wave of anxiety ran through the room. She eyed them all.

'There's no need to panic. I just want to sit up.'

She studied the room in more detail; the furniture looked old, very old. She tried to get to her feet to inspect the books on the shelves. They all seemed to be hardcovers, which she liked, but her head still throbbed. She clutched at her temple and fell back onto the bed.

'You should rest, that was a nasty hit you took,' another dweller said.

'I think that was a brave thing you did – we all do,' said someone else.

Asha was not sure what she had done that was so brave, apart from getting kicked to the ground, but there were general murmurs of agreement and nods across the small room. The girl with startling green eyes and pigtails had returned but didn't join in with the observations.

'Asha!' Fred and Bogsley came into the room with Hiller in tow.

'How do you feel?' Fred asked her, wringing his hat in his hand and looking distressed.

'Fine, Fred. Don't you worry.' She said this with a lot more conviction than she felt.

'But we need to worry, Miss Asha.' The gruff dweller in the clashing colours spoke again, looking agitated this time. 'These people, these creatures of the night. They have become more persistent in their pursuit, they are hounding us—'

'We should allow Miss Asha rest a while with Fred and Bogsley, Rufus, she has had a very harrowing evening. They will explain everything.'

They began to pour out the door mumbling to themselves and looking disgruntled, some anxious. The door shut behind them with a small thud. Asha looked at her two friends.

'Where exactly am I?'

The twosome exchanged a glance.

'Deep...'

'You mean...' Asha said incredulously.

'Deep beneath London.' Bogsley's voice seemed to echo through the room. 'In our world.'

'It is more daunting than it seems,' Fred said with a wan smile. 'But we had to bring you down here. It was the safest place to go in a hurry.'

'What happened? They got me, didn't they?'

'We were safe in the commune entrance but we saw you were no longer with us. Nanette had attacked you so we returned for you.'

'What? I thought you said they were dangerous. Why would you come back?'

'They are extremely fast but we are wily. Never try to outrun a dweller,' Bogsley said proudly with a glint in his eye.

'Bogsley and I distracted them by running around whilst Rufus, Badger and Macintosh carried you in.'

'Thank you.' She was humbled that those who had no reason to care for her had returned to save her life – especially when there was so much going on in theirs. Something else Fred said had caught her attention.

'Nanette?' Asha asked.

'Yes, Nanette!' they both said.

'How do you know their names?' she asked curiously. 'You always refer to them as the Mimes. Now you're on a first-name basis with them.'

'We only know of Nanette.'

'You see, we know of her because she...' Bogsley was pulling at his waistcoat and beginning to pace.

'What?' Asha probed.

'That autumn evening all those years ago—' he began.

'Hush, Bogsley, you fool,' Fred said with such anger that he startled them both.

'What did she do?' Asha's curiosity was now heightened.

'That is a topic which we do not wish to discuss.' Fred's voice was cold. 'What you must heed is that Nanette is probably the most dangerous of them all. Do not be distracted by the fact that she is female and of slight build.'

'Who *are* they?'

'We refer to them as the Mimes because of those hideous ghoulish masks they wear to cloak their faces so they cannot be identified.' Fred explained.

A shudder went through her at the memory of the white faces waiting for them as they emerged from the hollow bush. The image of the lone one peering into the bush made her suddenly feel uneasy. It was the dead eyes. Emotionless, cold, dead, brown eyes. She wondered if that was Nanette.

'They have been chasing after us for so long.'

'But why?'

'We do not know,' Bogsley confessed, anguish written all over his features.

'How can you not know? You must have done something to deserve all this attention.' The disbelief in Asha's voice must have been apparent to them. 'Perhaps they want to reveal your location and identities.'

'But that would be of no use to them.'

'What do you think they want with you? You must have some idea.'

'They are trying to destroy us.' Bogsley had a wild look in his eye. 'The same way the hoodlums were trying to in our time.'

It was unsettling to see how troubled they were by the Mimes – as they had been by the runners. Two distinct groups with seemingly nothing in common. Asha wondered if the twosome were being forthright with her about not knowing the reason behind the intense interest in them through the ages.

'He's right.' Fred's voice was matter of fact. Bogsley settled himself in a chair.

'Well, perhaps I can talk to them and find out what they want,' Asha suggested simply.

'No, Asha. That will not do. They attacked you when they could not get to us – or do you forget so quickly?' Fred's eyes were as large as saucers, the whites suddenly brighter than ever.

'Okay. How about if we tell the police?'

'The police?' Bogsley looked confused by the word.

'The police are the men of the law in this time,' Asha explained, hoping they would understand. 'They catch criminals and bad people.'

The two dwellers looked at each other and there was an uneasy air.

'The runners were after us in our time and they were supposed to be men of the law,' Fred mumbled. He looked at Asha with distrust. 'They were recruited by the magistrates to maintain law and order in the city but they pursued us relentlessly.'

'Yes, but it's different now,' Asha said.

'It will never be different, Miss Asha. You know you are the first of your kind to be allowed into our world. We have never been able to trust a human,' Fred remarked solemnly.

'These Mimes will not let anyone get in the way of finding us. There is just too much for them to lose.' Bogsley had slumped down onto the floor pathetically, clutching his hat and looking as if he was on the verge of tears.

'What we dare not do, however, is involve the law,' Fred continued, ignoring the distressed Bogsley. His gaze remained on Asha as he moved towards her. 'We have put our trust in you enough to bring you into our world where we hold our deepest secrets, so we must ask that you do not reveal what we have told you to anyone else – however well meaning your intentions.'

Asha nodded, astonished by the Fred's intensity. There was one more option, but she wondered how best to say it.

'I know... perhaps I know others who can help and they aren't involved with the law in anyway.' She put a hand up to reassure them.

The fire crackled in the fireplace as Fred stood before it. Bogsley got off the floor.

'Are they to be trusted?' he asked hopefully.

'Yes – they are the most trustworthy and loyal people I have ever met,' she said with a lump in her throat.

'Then request their aid so we may be removed from this

hell,' Fred announced, his shadow cast by the fire making him look like a giant.

Asha lay back against the warm wall, thoughts whirring around in her head as she gazed at the fairy lights up above. She felt excitement, nervousness and rejuvenation at this new challenge – a purpose had reawakened the fire within her. But the first thing she would have to do if she was to help the dwellers would be to put old demons to rest.

~

*J*onathan hurried to the café off the high street close to the park. He was almost out of breath after running the distance from his home but Sarah's message had sounded frantic. His friend was normally unflappable so it was a surprise to receive such a message when he got home that afternoon. His mother was in the kitchen; she came out to meet him in the hallway as soon as he walked in from rugby practice, tired and out of breath.

'It's Sarah, dear. She wants you to meet her at the tea rooms just off the high street at one o'clock. Apparently there's been some sort of emergency. You must hurry, there isn't much time.' His mother gave him a worried look.

Jonathan had glanced at the clock and groaned. It was almost fifteen minutes to the hour but it was a most unusual message, especially from Sarah, so he had taken it seriously and changed out of his muddy clothes and dashed out of the house before he could be cornered by his father whom he knew was around.

He walked in and duly saw Sarah sitting at one of the tables reading a book. There was a calm, unhurried air about her. He was baffled; the message she had left with his mother had sounded urgent, prompting his mother to look worried and rush him out of the house to meet her. He did think it strange that she had asked him to meet in a public tea room – an odd location to meet, especially since they were neighbours, their respective homes a few minutes' walk from each other. He did recall, though, that she had been acting strangely over the last few days – jittery and nervous – leaving school as soon as the bell rung and heading straight home without waiting for anyone and, on the rare occasion that she did wait, wanting to go the long way round and avoid the park. As he approached the table she looked up at him.

'What's up? My dad said you sounded troubled,' she queried with a worried smile. 'I tried to call you back to find out what was wrong but you weren't home.'

He sank into the chair opposite her in an exhausted heap looking perplexed.

'No... *you* wanted to meet me, right?' He cocked his head at her, slight confusion on his face.

Sarah shook her head. 'No. You called and asked to meet me—'

The café was not very busy that Saturday afternoon and the sound of the door opening caught their attention. Sarah, who was facing the entrance, looked to the door. Jonathan watched her full lips press into a thin line and her demeanour change: back stiffened, shoulders squared as she sat up to her full height. She was bracing herself, clearly preparing herself for a fight. He had seen that look – usually when she was involved in a game of rugby and someone on the pitch was causing irritation. He turned around and gawped. In the doorway stood Asha who looked at them uncertainly. She paused and then, as though making up her mind, walked in towards them with her arms raised.

'Look – I know things got a bit strange between us…'

Jonathan winced, wondering if Asha had practised her speech before luring them both there. She sounded as though she was trying to shift the blame for her absence onto them.

'They didn't get strange, Asha. You dumped us, remember?' Sarah said through clenched teeth.

Jonathan exhaled tiredly. The exhaustion he felt from an hour of hard practice was about to be exacerbated by Sarah's rage. He wished he had somehow missed his mother as he came in the door.

'I didn't dump you, Sarah. I was going through a difficult time and needed to be on my own,' Asha began explaining.

Jonathan interjected before it descended into an argument. 'What do you want, Asha?' He had not meant his voice to sound so impatient.

She sighed. 'I need help.' She paused dramatically. 'Well, not me personally. Some people I've met need help and you're the only people I know who are… who can help them.'

Jonathan and Sarah glanced at each other. It sounded to him like she was trying to flatter them. He wondered how Sarah would react.

'New friends of yours, I suppose?' Sarah snapped.

'What sort of help?' he asked, wishing Sarah would remain calm and listen to what Asha had to say. He was curious.

But Sarah had clearly heard enough. She got to her feet. 'I can't help you, Asha. Perhaps Jonathan can but I refuse to have anything to do with you anymore.' She brushed past her former friend.

'Sarah, stop, you're being boorish,' Jonathan called out after her, getting to his feet in pursuit.

Leaving Asha standing in the middle of the tea room, the few patrons shooting them curious glances, he ran out after Sarah. She was still fuming when he caught up with her.

'The nerve of the girl, to come here and act like everything is all right,' she seethed between clenched teeth.

Jonathan walked next to her, his dark head down, thinking. All three of them had been extremely close friends, and they had practically grown up together. He knew Asha had acted inappropriately but his interest was piqued. What was this dilemma she found herself in that caused her to reach out to them? She had mentioned 'people' who needed help, but she had barely spoken to anyone in the past year. Asha's vow of silence was now part of the school politics. It was almost expected. Sarah was still fuming and he tried to pick an appropriate point at which to cut in and calm her down. He paused and looked into her eyes.

'Aren't you even a little bit curious to find out what has caused her to abandon her silence after nine months?' He knew he was.

Sarah blinked in comprehension but it was obvious the stubborn side of her refused to cede to Jonathan's rationality.

'No. I don't care, not if Asha or any of her friends, who I doubt she has by the way, are in trouble.'

'Why are you so mad at Asha, Sarah?'

Jonathan knew she did not want to admit it but Asha's rejection over the past year had affected her more than she had thought possible, yet he felt there was something else that made Asha unforgivable in Sarah's eyes.

'She ignored us for nine months.'

'There has got to be something else. You almost despise her. Her mother died and she went into her silence just after – she was really depressed, as was explained to us. I know you're compassionate, so her ignoring us alone would—'

'She never got in contact when Grammy died.'

That was it. Sarah's words hit him harder than he expected. He had almost forgotten about Grammy Collidge's death six months ago, or perhaps he had simply pushed it to the back of his mind.

'I can never forgive her for that.' Sarah stubbornly lifted her chin, and her lower lip trembled with emotion.

'Hey,' Jonathan said, putting a gentle hand on her shoulder, 'she had so many issues of her own too. Remember she missed over a month of school.'

'Maybe, but I still feel all this anger inside. She wasn't there to support me in my time of need and we were always there for her.'

'Yes, but sometimes we have to be there for others even if they have not willingly been there for us – it seems terribly unfair but I think we come out on top and stronger in the end.'

'Aren't you the little philosopher?' She sniggered but he knew he was appealing to her rational side.

'Think about it. Something is going on and she needs our help so desperately that she was willing to call our individual homes pretending to be the other just to get us to meet her after nine months of unbroken silence. I'd say that's a distress call.'

She looked up at him, curiosity taking over. 'How much trouble do you think she's in?'

'We'll never know if we don't speak to her,' he responded sensibly.

'I don't know, Jonathan. Grammy was always so good to her and she chose to ignore me at one of the most difficult points of my life.'

Jonathan did not dare suggest to his friend that perhaps things had been so fractious in the Saunders household that Asha had not been told about Grammy Collidge's death.

≈

*A*sha had been left standing in the middle of the tea room feeling somewhat foolish. A few curious glances had been thrown her away and she decided to take the long way home, tears beginning to fall, her friend's harsh rejection burning deep into her. She wanted to avoid anyone who might cause her trouble – the girls Bogsley and Fred had saved her from were still at large and would be searching for her the first chance they got. Her detour home took longer than expected and when she got back to the house at four o'clock it was lying dark and empty. She realised her father was still at work and Mrs Redding had the day off.

She would have to manage it all on her own and she was not sure if she could. Suddenly Asha felt weary. Her father was curious about her movements and what she was up to; he noticed the late times she returned home. It was only a matter of time before he curtailed her movements, something her mother had successfully done but which he was unaccustomed to. The thought of her mother and the security she had offered made Asha sob hopelessly as she let herself in. Her mother was dead, her old friends did not want to know her, the two dwellers she was trying to help did not trust her enough to tell her the entire truth, and Hiller who had been a source of comfort was gone.

Asha was sitting alone in the cold dark kitchen dejectedly staring into space when she heard the doorbell ring. The peephole did not reveal the identity of the visitor. It was pitch black; the porch light appeared to have gone out.

'Who is it?'

Silence. She flung the door open, wanting to vent her frustration at being disturbed, but no one was there. There was nothing posted through the letter box either. She walked out onto the driveway but it was empty. Her presence activated the porch light; she turned to inspect the peephole and saw it was filled with dirt. Cursing under her breath, she began to scratch at it with her nail to get it clear but as she pieced the sequence of events together in her mind she froze and looked around her. A sudden flashback to the group of girls who had stopped her just days before made her dash back in, slam the door and slide the chain onto its latch. The large house suddenly felt too exposed and quiet. Her father would not be back home for a few hours yet; his working day had suddenly seemed to double in length since her mother had passed away, including Saturdays. Asha walked back up the stairs looking around, her arms wrapped tightly around her. The sound of the doorbell ringing again made her jump, her heart leaping in her chest and thudding loudly. She remained at the top of the stairs uncertainly, wondering what was the best thing to do. She had no friends to call for help or support. She briefly thought about calling her father but she hated the thought of seeming helpless in front of him once more. Steadily walking down the stairs, she looked around for something she could use as a weapon. Since the break-in her father had removed the vase and the tall pedestal it had been placed on. The only other time it had been moved was when her mother had passed away and they had needed to make some space. As she approached the door she held her breath, fervently hoping whoever it was had gone. But an impatient shuffle on the other side of the door caught her ear before the doorbell rang again, louder and more insistent this time. Standing right in front of the door she tried to put on as brave a voice as she could.

'Go away. The police are on their way.'

There was silence.

'I repeat, I have called the police.' Her voice did not betray the terror she felt.

'Asha?' It was a male voice on the other side of the door.

'Who is it?' she queried sharply, trying to sound as challenging as possible.

'Jonathan and Sarah.' This time it was a female voice with a sarcastic undertone.

Asha looked through the dirty peephole and saw them both standing there looking slightly bemused, Sarah's bewilderment mixed with irritation.

She slowly opened the door a crack in case it was some trick and her friends were not really there. Peeking round the heavy door she spotted Sarah's annoyed face glancing at her, Jonathan standing beside her looking concerned.

'Oh – you scared me to death. You pressed the bell and disappeared the first time.' She pulled the door open to greet them, relieved, suddenly feeling shy at the sight of her oldest friends.

'No, we pressed the doorbell just now when we arrived.' Jonathan was gazing at her with such worry she felt she was losing her mind.

'Oh. You mean you didn't press the doorbell and then run away?' she asked worriedly as Sarah brushed past her.

'No, because we're not nine years old, Asha.' Sarah motioned sarcastically between herself and Jonathan.

'Do you mind if I come in?' Jonathan asked uncertainly.

'Yes, of course. Sorry, I'm just a bit tired. You didn't see anyone on the doorstep or hanging around, did you?'

'Nope,' Jonathan said flatly, clearly tiring of her line of questioning. He joined Sarah in the hall.

Asha gazed outside for any hint of the mischievous doorbell pusher but all was quiet. She wondered if it was the group of girls from that night, then shrugged; there were more important things to worry about now. Shutting the door behind her she turned to her friends who were giving her a curious look.

'I didn't think you would come.' She gestured for them to follow her to the kitchen. 'I mean, you were so angry earlier on.'

Sarah, who was still stony faced, harrumphed but remained silent.

'I talked her round in case you were in some serious trouble,' Jonathan said.

'And clearly you are,' Sarah muttered with an eye roll. 'Talking about phantom visitors and gazing out into nothing like some fruit loop.'

'Sarah.' Jonathan put his hand up for peace.

'Asha, we've been friends since we were in those god-awful baby jumpers together. There's too much history between us all, even though Sarah is still very angry with you, but sometimes it takes time to sort these problems out. It will never happen overnight,' he said.

'Yes, I suppose.' Sarah's voice was begrudging. Asha knew it would take a lot more than an apology to win her around. 'We just don't leave friends behind when we feel like it.'

Asha ignored the slight; she did deserve it after all.

Jonathan sat at the coffee table. 'So – what's this problem you had that you needed help with?' he asked.

Sarah was sitting on the counter and looked up with interest. That had always been her favourite spot when she had come round in the past and she seemed to remember it.

Asha cleared her throat as she tried to compose her thoughts. 'What I am about to tell you will come across as strange to say the very least, but a lot has happened in the last few days.'

They leaned forward with interest.

'A few nights ago I was attacked, but before anything could come of it I was helped by these friends. On a visit to them a few days later I was attacked yet again...'

'What?' Sarah looked disbelieving.

'You've been attacked twice in the last few days. Do the police know about it? Have you told your father?' Jonathan was dumbfounded.

'No.' Asha wrung her hands in distress, realising she had been through rather a lot.

'Where did these attacks happen?' Sarah asked.

Asha hesitated. 'Well, the first one was just two streets away from here – that was where I first met the people who needed help when they came to my aid.' She realised she was unable to explain much without giving anything away. 'The second attack happened in the park when I went to meet these friends and we were chased.'

Sarah visibly froze. 'What night was this?'

Asha closed her eyes as she racked her brain. It had been on the same day of her second meeting with the thera-pist – the one in which they were supposed to make a break-through. She could never forget that.

'Two nights ago,' she recalled enthusiastically.

Sarah started to her feet, appearing to shiver. Asha and Jonathan gave her odd stares.

'What is it, Sarah?' Jonathan asked. They could both feel the heightened tension in the room.

'I think I was there.'

'What?'

'Yu and I were walking home from school – we decided to delay going home so we walked along the high street. We were walking along the north end of the park, Alberts Road, when out of nowhere these *people* emerged on bikes and knocked Yu over. She was badly hurt. Then Dolapo showed up and escorted us through the park as it closed. Then that's where it got strange. The park closed shortly after and we were trapped but these people were in there and they were combing the bushes and ground for something.'

'What were they looking for?' Jonathan looked baffled.

'Me,' Asha said, deciding it was too soon to reveal it was really *us*.

'Why would they be looking for you, Asha? What have you done?' he asked. 'And are the two incidents linked – you being attacked twice?'

'No, they aren't. I get the feeling the people that Sarah and I saw that night in the park are entirely different to the girls who attacked me on my way back from school. If we were in the park on that same night, the people who kicked me to the ground are the dangerous ones.' She wondered if Sarah had seen any masks.

'So was this the problem you approached us about? Errant schoolkids our age running riot can easily be stopped by the police,' Jonathan said, gently squeezing Sarah by the arm to calm her down.

'No,' Sarah responded violently. 'These were not people like us. They were different.' Asha knew then she had seen the mask and felt the same chill she had, the one that had to be experienced to be understood and could not be explained.

'Well – let's tell the police then.'

'No. Not yet, anyway. I made a promise.' Asha hesitated as she recalled Fred's face when he had spoken of not wanting any police involvement. If she broke her promise they would never trust her again, even if the police believed her.

'We can't have people terrorising our neighbourhood, Asha.'

'That's not the problem – it's a little more delicate than that. I will tell you but it has to be in complete confidence,' she began, then paused and looked at them with a mischievous twinkle in her eye. It was probably the most alive they had seen her in a long time and her expression caused them to pull back. 'Actually, perhaps it's best if I show you.'

～

*H*alf an hour later Jonathan found himself standing with Sarah in freezing temperatures, wondering what he was doing in the middle of the cold dark park at night. Even worse – the park had been shut when they arrived. However, Asha had known of a convenient entry point – a hole in the brick wall – that was obviously used by foxes or some other stinky animal, and had made them crawl through it on their hands and knees. His hands were horribly damp and cold and, after making them both walk twenty minutes into the park without as much as an explanation, Asha had disappeared. He was beginning to regret talking Sarah into coming with him. Asha had taken them to a location that appeared to have been selected at random and instructed them to wait, to Sarah's irritation and his incredulity.

Now they stood there awkwardly, looking around and still waiting. There was not much to see as it was dark and there was no moon that night. The park was particularly damp and he half hoped Asha had not brought them on a wild goose chase on a whim. She had been particularly fragile these last few months; what if she was more fragile than he had originally assumed? What if Asha had suffered a breakdown and no one had known it?

'Asha!' he snapped. He was growing increasingly hungry.

'Perhaps she really had no choice about speaking to us these last few months?' Sarah suggested cautiously, grabbing onto the trim of Jonathan's coat and looking around in the dark.

'Asha? This is not funny any more,' Jonathan said, his nerves and the cold getting the better of him.

'What are we doing here, Jonathan? The park is closed and it's freezing,' Sarah hissed, wrapping her arms around herself. 'What if Asha is, well, you know, not *all right*?'

Just as Jonathan was beginning to believe that Sarah might be right they heard a little movement in a dark clump of bushes. Asha suddenly emerged, looking around carefully. There was a glow behind her and a source of light appeared.

'What are you doing in the bushes?' Jonathan asked. 'I thought you went that way.' He gestured behind them.

'Yes, but there are several entrances and exits, you see.'

'Stop being so damned cryptic.' He had never spoken to her that way before but he had never been this cold, hungry and tired.

'Have you seen anyone?' she asked, looking around.

'No, Asha. We are the *only* people in the park at this time and in this weather. It's cold. Why would there be anyone else in here?' Sarah asked, observing her friend worriedly.

'For the same reason we're here. The same reason you got spooked when you saw those people searching the park that night.'

Jonathan felt Sarah shiver beside him.

'Stop it, Asha. You're scaring us.' He did not mind admitting himself to be scared. It was an odd situation and his old friend was acting very strangely.

'I'm sorry.' Asha stepped forward till they were only a few inches apart and whispered. 'I want you to promise me that whatever you see tonight you will keep it a secret – even if you decide not to help.'

'Asha, what's this about?' Jonathan was tired of her antics and wishing himself in bed.

'We promise,' Sarah said, clearly feeling the same anguish as Asha and understanding the gravity of the situation.

'Thank you.' Asha was wearing a broad grin that looked slightly deranged in the moonlight. It caught her friends unawares; they had not seen her smile in so long, never mind looking so unhinged. She stepped aside and Jonathan and Sarah gasped. There was a small man standing right behind her; his dress was odd. He held a lantern in his left hand.

'Hello. I'm Fred. Would you like to follow me? We must remain hidden, you see. We have enemies that seek to destroy us.' His large eyes widened even more in the darkness, the whites almost glowing in the dark, causing a very nervous Sarah and Jonathan to step backwards.

～

*S*arah took a little sip from the cup she had been given. It was so small that her hands swamped it. Jonathan, ever fascinated by reading material and history, was going through the rows of books that filled the bookcase.

'This is amazing – some of these are first editions,' he exclaimed as he gingerly picked up a book. 'They even have author inscriptions.'

The others sat by the fire in Bogsley's slightly unkempt cottage. There was a commotion outside as the rest of the community pressed up their noses against the little glass window to catch a glimpse of the visitors.

'So how many of you exist in the Unending Canal?' Sarah asked.

'We are plentiful in number,' Fred responded. 'In the thousands, we believe. The Unending Canal carries on for many, many miles, you see, hence it is...'

'Unending,' Sarah finished flatly.

'There is another commune out there but we do not where they are hiding. When we were transported, you see, the dweller world was split,' a dweller called Emily chipped as she picked up the kettle from Bogsley's fireplace and made fresh cups of tea.

Sarah had never drunk so much tea in her life but the tension of the day, from Asha's shock appearance back in their lives to being several feet below London, had taken its toll on her and she needed something warm and soothing. Tea always helped her think, no matter how small the cups were.

'Kee's Corner is missing. We have not heard from them in near seven years,' Fred said.

'The Rose Wood is back in our time,' Bogsley added.

'Won't they be in danger?' Asha looked puzzled.

Sarah was still trying to understand what it all meant, all these different worlds with different characters.

'Not necessarily. There are different entrances into our world, you see. The Rose Wood had its own separate entryway.'

'How can you tell Kee's Corner is here?' Sarah asked.

'We know – we feel it.' Bogsley said this with such assuredness that she felt it must be true.

'Why would it have been split?' Jonathan asked, moving back to sit with them.

Fred and Bogsley looked at one another. 'We think it would have been to ensure our survival. We are primed to survive, it seems, in every possible situation, and with all these people hunting us, splitting the communes ensured the continued existence of the dwellers.'

'What do these people want with you?'

No one appeared to have an answer to Sarah's question and stared at her forlornly.

'How come none of the books mention you, even the mythical books? Surely someone must have had a sighting of you.' Jonathan, ever the bibliophile, was showing greater interest in their history than the very real danger they were in. He got up and walked back to the bookcase, stepping over Hiller who lay on the floor wrestling with what looked suspiciously like a dead mouse. Sarah felt like snapping at him to sit still and leave the books alone.

'No, we won't be in any of your books, pleasant though they may be. We believe we were driven underground centuries ago because we were so different. One day our worlds became separate entities,' Fred explained. 'As long as we exist and are different there will always be someone somewhere wanting to find us to line their own pockets.' His voice was filled with disdain.

'In 1821, we suppose it was, we were being pursued and then we were brought to your time at that precise moment.' Bogsley stated.

'In our time some humans wanted us for experiments in their laboratories and medical schools,' Bogsley began nodding so furiously that Sarah thought his head would fall off. He excitedly got out of his chair and spoke in a whisper, clutching Hiller too tightly, 'some paid a lot of money to get us so they could perform all kinds of experiments to see what we were, why we were the way we were, lived the way we did and how we could survive underground.'

'Even though they promised to pay us handsomely we knew we would never come out of there alive or intact. We saw what they did to their own people, so why would they treat us any better? How could they?' Emily said, swinging the kettle around in her hand right by a horrified Asha's head.

'They became increasingly upset because we refused to comply and we began to be viewed as a menace as they felt more threatened by us.' Bogsley's voice got louder.

The room went quiet, the only sound was Hiller's excited scuffling on the floor.

'And now you're being pursued again, you say?' Sarah asked. She shuddered as she recalled the group in the park that night. They were slow, meticulous and driven. The deliberation with which they combed through the bushes, the intention behind every movement they made signalled minds that could survive on bare bones, would not hesitate to strike and could lie in wait for any enemy, even on a cold night such as tonight. 'I only got a brief glimpse.' She swallowed. 'What do these masks look like?'

'Oh, Sarah. They are horrible,' Asha burst out. 'Alabaster white – the lips have been drawn on in a grotesque fashion and the eyes are always black. The other day when they came after us they were like an army.'

'How many of them were there?' Jonathan asked.

'Seven,' was Fred's guess. Asha and Bogsley looked uncertain.

'I counted five.' Sarah caught herself shivering. Emily came over to offer more tea, perhaps thinking her cold, but the room was warm.

'Their numbers change rather often, you see,' a voice added from the doorway.

They looked to see who had joined them. He was introduced to Sarah as Rufus. He had just pushed through the crowd outside and walked in.

'Their numbers are weakened now but soon they will be replenished.'

'Do you know their names?' Sarah was not sure she wanted to know.

Silence came over the room again and Sarah felt the fear Fred and Bogsley were feeling; it was that same trepidation that had stopped Asha revealing what she knew about the dwellers. It was a fear born out of the experience of being hunted.

'Just one – Nanette,' Fred said hesitantly.

'Nanette?' Sarah repeated dumbly.

Sarah mulled the name over in her mind. She had never met a Nanette, nor did she know of any that existed in their school, Ark House. It was such a normal sounding name. *Nanette*, she thought. The name would be forever etched in her mind.

'How did you come to know her?' Jonathan asked.

'Don't bother,' Asha said. 'They won't even tell me.'

'If you want us to help you then you are going to have to trust us,' Jonathan said, looking straight at them. 'There's no reason to distrust us.'

There was a long silence. Rufus, Fred and Bogsley avoided eye contact with them and Emily made a point of fiddling with the kettle.

'Look – if you don't want to, it's fine,' Sarah said. 'But you're going to have to trust us soon – after all, you're asking for our help.'

The silence continued unabated. Sarah exchanged a little glance with Asha and Jonathan. Asha discreetly shook her head. Sarah understood. The dwellers did not trust them enough, yet, so it was best to not badger them. They'd have to wait till they had earned their trust.

'Okay – here's what we do.' The homemade brew had sufficiently calmed Sarah who got to her feet and paced the small room slowly. 'Asha and I will search for a place that sells these masks. There can't be that many around North London, whilst Jonathan will try to find out if there have been any other sightings of the rest of you.'

Fred and Bogsley nodded. They looked uncertain. 'Are you saying you will help us?'

Sarah knew Asha was in agreement so she glanced at Jonathan, who nodded enthusiastically. She knew he did not take her and Asha's encounters with the group seriously. He still considered them to be unruly teenagers who were running wild in the park but he had not seen them that night – she had. He had not been kicked so viciously to the ground that he blacked out – Asha had.

The dwellers who remained outside had overheard the conversation and suddenly spilled into the cottage. 'Blessings to you all.'

'We are so very grateful to you for taking it upon your-selves to help us.'

'We cannot wait to return to our time.'

'Modern-day London is terrible.'

But Rufus, who remained seated as pandemonium broke out around him, was the first to utter words of doom.

'This is not going to end well, Fred. I can feel it in my bones.'

'Oh, Rufus, you doomsayer.'

The others obviously did not share his sentiments as a feeling of excitement flushed through the room, excitement that someone else was joining their struggle and would be watching over them from above. As the crowd erupted into cheers Sarah stared at Rufus, who dejectedly barged his way to the doorway looking mean spirited and dissatisfied. He caught her gaze and with a snarl swept out of the over-crowded room and disappeared into the dimly lit passage tunnels.

Asha had noticed Rufus's gruffness as well.

'What do you think is wrong with him?' she whispered to Sarah.

'I don't know. He seems pretty miserable.'

'Oh, don't mind old Rufus. He's always a bit gruff with strangers.' Another dweller had walked up to them.

'Has he always been like that?' Asha asked.

'No. He was much happier once but he changed, you see.'

Bogsley, in a vain attempt to clear his cottage, began to usher out those who had entered uninvited. The happy crowd of dwellers returned to their duties in their under-ground world.

'We must be leaving now, Bogsley, Fred. It's getting

pretty late and we have a hole to crawl through,' Jonathan explained and Asha cringed.

Sarah burst out laughing.

'I will walk you out.' Bogsley beamed.

As they emerged from his cottage Sarah realised that although they referred to the separate parts of their world as communes, it was too simple a word to explain what they were. The Unending Canal was so called not only because it was unending but because it had a long dark canal running through the middle of it with picturesque cottages on either side. Sarah had never seen waters so dark and still before. Her reflection perfect in the still water, she bent over to dip a finger in. It was nice and cool but she barely caused a ripple. It was not a normal canal.

'Has anyone tried to get to the end of the Unending Canal?' she asked. Sarah was not being impertinent but thought it had to run somewhere, or at least end in a larger body of water.

'No – several have tried and there have been expeditions but no success.' Bogsley shrugged.

'What has been the longest expedition to get to the end of it?' Asha asked.

'Over six years,' Bogsley answered matter-of-factly. 'Taken on by Rufus's older cousin Fuller.'

Sarah did not think it possible, but if that was correct it meant that this world, although assumedly below London, both ancient and modern, was enchanted and subject to its own rules.

'So... magic?' Jonathan muttered in her ear as Bogsley and Asha chatted on.

'It must be,' she whispered.

She noticed someone sitting down by the canal with a

fishing rod in his hand. He appeared to be talking to himself.

'That's Biddy. He likes to pretend he's fishing but never actually catches anything. They say he's a bit mad but I don't think he is, he just likes his own company,' Bogsley explained with a slight shrug.

Sarah found the most fascinating feature about the dwellers lives was how they lived quietly and harmoniously even though they were all so different. As they came to understand it, Hogey always stuck to the rules and was very careful of the outside world but not so careful that he was boring, Bogsley was a lot more earnest and trusting of humans and, unlike the older dwellers, seemed to get into the most trouble, and Fred was steady, always torn between his responsibilities to protect the commune and the mischief of his best friend, Bogsley. The trio were still unsure about Rufus; there was something very dark within him.

The group slowed as some children ran across their path, their little shoes making clopping noises on the cobbled streets. The flames flickering in lamps lining the pathway and canal routes gave it an iridescent glow and cast their light onto the still waters of the canal. A few metres down a little woman scrubbed clothes in the waters of the canal.

'We are supposedly below London but it doesn't feel like we are in London anymore,' Sarah whispered to Jonathan as she looked around, narrowly avoiding the children who were running past them again.

'Our commune exists independently of your world,' Bogsley explained. 'We have almost everything we need down here in our world and can remain here for a very long time without surfacing.'

'How did you come to be discovered all those years ago then?'

'No one is really sure. Rumour has it that a drunk lord discovered us one evening when heading out of a Covent Garden brothel after some entertainment. Something of that nature.' Bogsley's voice was light.

The small boats that lined the canal were all of delicate colours like the lights, silently bobbing up and down on the water, their oars organised neatly alongside them.

'How long have you lived like this?'

'Many centuries.'

'You're very quiet – surely hardly anyone must know you exist,' Jonathan said.

'But the Mimes are a determined group, Jonathan. They're not just hunting them for fun, there's a purpose behind it and I don't think it's scientific experiments or over-ambitious medical students this time,' Asha said.

'On a cold winter's night – I don't think so,' Sarah said.

'But they chased us with such ferocity – I know they'll be back and I'm not sure how long we can keep them off.' Asha was apparently getting worried again.

Sarah ignored Asha and paused to join Jonathan pressing her nose up against a window like a toddler gazing into a sweet shop. Inside were children sitting by a fire, watching in a captivated silence as a man who looked just like Fred, though not as serious, played on a little flute. The children ceased their listening to look at the strangers, giggling at their faces pressed up against the glass. Sarah gave a little wave and they waved back. The flautist resumed play and the children their listening.

'Asha, it is simply a case of finding out who these people are and reporting them to the relevant authorities. It will be fine,' Jonathan said airily as he trudged along behind Bogsley.

Sarah was always the confident one but this time she felt the state of affairs was a lot more complicated than they believed and they had to tread carefully. Jonathan was being dismissive of what she and Asha had been through. Her friend had not been there when she had glanced into their eyes and seen nothing: no emotion, no anger, just a blank expression – except the fifth one who seemed removed from the others.

They walked on and Bogsley regaled them with stories of the world below until they finally reached the same entrance they had come through where an alert Perry sat, a large cup of tea in his hands. Bogsley turned to them.

'I must leave you here and bid you goodnight. Macintosh will be stationed outside in a hollow bush but you will not see him. Asha knows the way out of the park. Please be careful,' he urged.

'Goodnight, Bogsley.'

Perry opened the vast wooden doors for them and they exited the commune, following the narrow pathway and spiralling stairs that would lead back to the park above.

∼

The fire had burned low in Bogsley's cottage but still gave out a warmth. It was late and most of the residents of the Unending Canal had retired for the night after the exciting happenings of the evening. The canal rippled dark and silent as the lights around it were dimmed. However, not all was calm down below; four dwellers remained awake sitting around the long table in deep discussion. The mood was dark and foreboding. All around Bogsley they brooded. The other occupants were Emily, Rufus, and Fred, with Hiller in tow. They were the oldest residents of the Unending Canal bar Blackworth, who never wished to be disturbed and had normally retired to his cottage and was in bed by the time the lights were dimmed. Bogsley was aware of what kept their eyes from closing. What had transpired that evening was a shock. Humans had traversed their world and they were not the unpleasant folk they thought them to be. Instead they were willing to help and offer their hand in the search for Kee's Corner – and for that Bogsley was grateful. However, there was one verifiable truth.

'We lied to them.' He spoke aloud to the room.

'We didn't lie, really,' Fred said. 'What we did was more a hiding of the truth. What is this truth that you speak of, anyway? How will it help them in the search for Kee's Corner? Why must they know?'

'Are they not to be our friends?' Bogsley now considered them companions. He was a firm believer in trust, in holding nothing back.

'If they are to help us and stake their own lives, I feel we must be forthright with them,' Bogsley said.

Rufus groaned at the innocence of his words. 'Oh, Bogsley, you fool. They are not our friends. Because they come down here, sit among us and pretend to help us you call them friends. I promise you that in a very short time when they know what sideshow attractions we are, they will see us as a means of lining their pockets. That is what happened to us back then – they turned on us.'

'No, they never turned on us, Rufus,' Bogsley argued. 'We had friends in their world who were steadfast and loyal.'

'We were never betrayed.' A fifth voice emerged.

Bogsley looked to his doorway. It was Binkers. He idly wondered if he would get any sleep that night. The more of them who drifted into his cottage the more awake he would become. He thought Binkers would have resigned herself to sleep like the others but she was just as disturbed by the events of the night as they were.

'I was the one who ended us.'

'Oh, Binkers, we are not ended,' Rufus gruffly responded. 'We could not continue to live the way we were, always hiding, always running.'

But his words did nothing to quell her anger. Binkers had remained angry for seven years since the shift. Bogsley observed it in her mood, her mannerisms. The younger dweller had transformed herself before his eyes, shifting from a most entertaining and adventurous young dweller to a sullen and angry one, blaming herself for their displacement, but Bogsley did not bear her ill will after that night. His anger would be misdirected – after all, they would have been shifted if their lives were in danger at any time. It was written that way.

'We have no secrets to tell.'

They lapsed into a dull silence as the fire flickered, its flames lowering as it died from within. Bogsley, in a vain attempt to distract himself, got to his feet to tend to the fire.

'There is little point, Bogsley. We shall all be retiring soon,' the ever-prudent Fred insisted, holding on to Hiller who was fast asleep on his lap and snoring contentedly.

'I shall not retire. I fear they shall return with pitchforks and lanterns.'

'Oh, Binkers, you terrify us all with your talk. We shall have sleepless nights now.'

'Sleepless nights. You brought humans into our midst. Even when the runners were after us, when I led them to our home they never entered. Yet these people did with no question.' Her deep blue eyes flashed.

'Yes, because they mean us no harm,' Fred insisted.

'It might change,' Binkers continued, her voice beginning to rise. 'What if, like Rufus says, they realise something is amiss about the way we live – like Lord Wordsworth did?' Binkers countered.

Emily and Rufus remained silent as though defeated. Bogsley, realising none of them were going to get any sleep that night, placed the kettle on the fire and as he gazed at it plumes of steam began to rise as the water heated up. Soon they would all be sipping calming cups of tea.

'What a good idea, Bogsley,' Emily said. 'Any biscuits to go with that?'

Bogsley nodded gruffly. 'I'll fetch us some. I have some squirrelled away for an evening such as this one.' He moved to his larder as the debate raged on, glad to be occupying himself. He heard Binkers's voice rising again and furrowed his brow. She was being most extreme and he feared would wake the others, and then they would have a time on their hands.

Hastening back to the front room he placed a wooden plate on the table.

'Binkers, you shall join us and you shall be calm,' he instructed. 'They will do us no harm.'

Still Rufus was not convinced. 'You heard what he said. The boy, Jonathan.' He spat out his name like it was bile. 'He insists we will have to tell them and trust them with what we know.'

'Then tell them we shall.'

'If we tell them what we know of that house, of those people, you do know it will endanger them?'

'We might as well be leading them to their deaths.' Emily's voice was mournful.

Fred leaned forward hoping to alleviate their fears and feelings of guilt. 'We have not requested that they stop the Mimes. They agreed to help us to find Kee's Corner so that we may reunite with our brethren and return to our time. This is what we have been unable to do for these past seven years because the Mimes are watching and waiting.'

'Really?' Emily looked doubtful.

'That is all we need to return. We find Kee's Corner and return to 1821 where we reunite with the Rose Wood and our world shall be complete once more.' His eyes darted to Bogsley. 'Do you not missing travelling to Rose Wood to see what fruit and vegetables they have in season?'

'Terribly. I do not relish the prospect of scurrying above like a rat in the night to pinch turnips from above. I fear I will be captured,' Bogsley avowed.

'Exactly.' Fred said. He turned to Emily who was wide eyed, her lower lip trembling.

'And do you not miss the markets in the Rose Wood? The hustle and bustle, the colourful stalls, the tea shops?'

Emily's eyes shone excitedly at his words. 'Why yes, of course I do.' She sounded wistful.

They watched Fred with growing excitement as he turned to Rufus and Binkers who were close to him. 'I know that you miss fishing in the Graine Lakes very much, Binkers. I did hear you rather crossly berating the Unending Canal fish as being too wily to take the bait. You also miss the wild forests that we have never crossed. Rufus, you miss the serenity of the Nooster Woods, of listening to the fiddler play in the clearing and the astounding beauty of the play. Septimus misses his long journeys to Yeohah and Ornasa in the Rose Wood and Kee's Corner. I know this because I have seen him talking to his neighbours and boring them to tears. Don't we also miss the frolics and frivolities that Kee's Corner brought us? There's not much beauty in that small secluded part of our world. The roads are narrower meaning two carriages cannot cross at once, it's too boisterous, they must also build their own fires as the magical element is weakened...'

Bogsley shook his head in disdain. Kee's Corner was still very primitive in its ways. 'Aye, but we miss their ales, do we not?' he finished for Fred.

They all nodded their agreement.

Bogsley observed in wonder as the hint of a tear came to Rufus's eye. Fred's words had struck a chord within them. A nostalgic silence fell in the room as Bogsley thought himself close to hysterics at the mention of their old activities.

Fred, who seemed very much in his element, leaned forward to finish off, a drowsy Hiller almost slipping from his lap.

'The Mimes do not know these friends of ours and will not be looking for them. They seek us. As long as we remain hidden and let these dear friends watch out for us in the world above we shall be fine.'

∾

*B*y the time the trio had climbed back to the wintry welcome of the park the temperature had dropped again. As Sarah poked her head through the opening she gave a squeal.

'It's about to snow,' she announced in an excited whisper.

They would have to find their way out of the park with the sparse lighting. Thankfully there was now a half moon as the clouds had cleared. The weather was changing. As if on cue little specks of white began to fall around them.

Jonathan climbed out last, exclaiming as he looked to the sky. 'It *is* very early this year.'

'It is only a few weeks to Christmas. Here help me with this.' He and Asha covered up the entrance whilst Sarah kept careful watch.

The park was silent as the snow fell to the ground with the moonlight bouncing off it.

'Come on. We'll keep each other warm.' Sarah hooked her arm through Asha's and dragged her along. Asha's heart lurched; it was almost as if nothing had ever happened between them; they had just fallen back into their old routine. Walking along the park with Jonathan, the atmosphere was eerie with the tall trees looming over them. As they trudged on the snow fall became heavier; it was coming down fast around them, covering the ground and building up beneath their feet. Asha was getting worried. They were nowhere near the hole they had used to get in and she feared the snow would cover their exit point.

'We need to hurry,' she urged them, trying to move faster, but Sarah was content to amble along in the snow.

'Relax, Asha. We have no school tomorrow. Nowhere to be. Just enjoy it.'

Asha was not enjoying it though. She found the park hostile. A cry rang out in the air, pained and traumatised. Sarah jumped, pulling heavily on Asha. Jonathan paused in his tracks.

'Someone in pain?' Asha hissed.

'Or being attacked?' Sarah countered.

They listened as the cries continued.

'I think it's an animal,' Jonathan suggested.

'Think? You mean you're not sure?' Asha regretted

bringing them at night. It should have all been done in the day, which was what had been planned, but Sarah had taken longer to come around. Asha was still surprised by the sight of them at her front door; they had not let her down. After all that had happened they were still as reliable and stable as ever.

'Pretty sure it's a fox call. They sound scary as hell,' he said.

Jonathan was the worldliest of the three of them and his reading and study did not stop at the books – he had a liking for nature programmes and wildlife. Asha observed his shoulders relax.

'If you're sure,' she said.

'Pretty sure. We have to keep going or else we'll freeze here. It'll be difficult and slightly embarrassing to explain to the doctor that we got frostbite because we were spooked by a fox call.'

Sarah giggled and Asha sniggered. He was right. The snow was piling around them and fast. The leather shoes they wore were not conducive to the conditions. The weather report had said nothing of snow – or perhaps Asha had simply not checked, her mind so occupied by more important matters these days. They trudged ahead, determined to get themselves out of the cold, feeling the snow breaking down the defences of their shoes and catching their feet. Asha hoped the snow would cease but it only got heavier, reducing their visibility slightly. On any other evening it would have been welcome, but trying to get home after an exhausting day and having to lift your feet higher to gain better ground and speed was tiring her even further. Asha was beginning to struggle.

'Come on. We've got a bit further to go and then we'll

be at your foxhole, Asha,' Jonathan urged as though sensing the slackened speed. He slowed to join them.

Around them heavy snow-covered branches began to creak and snap, penetrating the silence.

'Bit creepy,' Asha heard Sarah whisper with a little giggle.

The snowfall was becoming so heavy that they were forced to quicken their pace. Sarah turned round to check on Jonathan who was now walking a few paces behind.

'Hurry up, Jon.' He did not reply, seeming distracted, his attention caught by something ahead of them.

'What is it?' Asha asked as she and Sarah began to slow down.

'I don't know.' He squinted, his gaze trying to penetrate the rapidly falling snow.

'I could have sworn there was something moving ahead of us.' He paused; they could not see his face but they could make him out in the darkness. They heard his movements and deep breathing as he stared ahead. 'There's someone over there. Someone on a bicycle.'

'Are you sure? The park is all shut now.' Asha screwed up her eyes and looked ahead as they stood there, suddenly uncertain.

The heavy snowfall momentarily eased and they were able make out a lone person on a bicycle cycling slowly through the snow away from them, occasionally making deliberate little circles.

'Round and round it goes,' Jonathan muttered.

A sudden unease moved through Asha. They walked on slowly, each step bringing them closer to the figure. It had a torch in its hand which emitted a dim light as it was flashed along the ground. The snow had settled on its shoulders and the hood that shrouded its features.

'Parks patrol?' Sarah whispered as she squinted in the dark.

'On bicycles with hoods?' Jonathan was not convinced.

The same disquiet he clearly felt had settled on Asha too, but before she could voice her concern he hesitantly called out.

'Hello?'

'No!' Sarah hissed in a low voice. But it was too late. Jonathan's voice although low carried across the heavy night.

The figure, which had moved further into the distance, stopped looking around, its face still hidden by the hood. Something large that hung from its neck also obscured its features. The light from the torch was suddenly put out. Asha and Sarah looked at each other. She felt her friend's fear.

'Hide,' Sarah whispered.

Asha tugged at a confused Jonathan, gesturing for him to be silent.

'The park has only just officially closed, we can't be in any—' But Asha clamped her hand over her startled friend's mouth.

As they climbed over the low wrought-iron fencing that demarcated the restricted area, someone stepped on a dry twig that was not covered by the snow. The loud crack that echoed in the air made them all jump. They hurried into the foliage and picked spots behind large shrubs and trees that hid them from the path, grateful that it was dark. If they could not see this person then they could not be seen themselves. Asha, who could still get a view from her hiding place, peeked through the shrubs; there was no one on the path. She hoped that the person had gone, but then held her finger to her lips; she could see the figure slowly coming along the path. It stopped where they had stood moments before, circling the area slowly on its bicycle. Asha held her breath, cowering behind the shrubbery. She silently signalled to Jonathan, hinting the figure was nearby. Asha saw him looking through the branches and leaves. It was so dark Asha knew he could only make out the figure moving around but nothing else. Then the moon cast a little light onto the figure. Asha got a glimpse of long brown hair peeking out from beneath the hood. It was a female. She could not make anything else out as the hair and hood hid her face. Then she froze as she noticed what hung around the neck, the fear rooting her to the spot. It was a mask. She gesticulated wildly to Jonathan who took a peek. She held her breath but could not observe for too long without being seen.

Asha kept a steady eye on the girl. Even though the figure was female, the way she moved was so calculated that Asha wanted to stay hidden. She hoped Sarah and Jonathan would do the same – the slightest disturbance would betray their hiding places.

The silence was broken when the girl spoke. 'Hello? Who's there?'

Asha stilled, the hairs going up on her skin; she felt her cheeks draining of blood. She didn't know what had caused such an extreme reaction, but the girl's voice sounded confused and scared: there was a clear detachment between her words and deliberate movements as she tried to lure them out. The sound of her voice haunted Asha. She gazed across at Jonathan, making out his outline in the falling snow.

Asha wondered how many of them were around. If it was the same group from a few nights ago, the same that had pushed Yu to the ground, then they travelled in packs it seemed, there was never just the one.

She tensed and held her breath. The girl's voice was soft with no hint of an accent. She paused for what seemed an eternity and then spoke again. 'Can you help me? I'm lost and trying to find my way out of the park.'

Asha shook her head at Jonathan and put her finger to her lips. It was a trap. The girl did not leave though. She peered into the foliage on both sides and looked down at the ground for any signs of a disturbance, but the falling snow was quickly covering their tracks. Then a shrill whistle pierced the air; the girl hesitated and looked towards it with obvious frustration. Looking back to the trees she seemed torn but the whistle was obviously a signal she could not ignore. She walked back to her bicycle, the hood still hiding her eyes. Asha thought she must be leaving. She watched as the girl reached into her saddlebag and found a small object; Asha caught her breath as the object illuminated the path in front of the girl. This was a more powerful torch than the one she had initially used. She and Jonathan were both in dark clothing but Sarah, who was a few yards away, was wearing a bright cherry coat. The girl shone the torch around the snowy area, the light revealing everything in its path. Asha ducked her head, hoping her black hat would help her blend in, cursing Sarah for her clothing choices. They waited, their breaths held, for the moment she would discover them. The adrenaline was beginning to kick in. Asha suspected the rest of the gang were evenly spaced out, combing the park on their bicycles. If the girl located them the friends would have to overpower her quickly before they made their escape. But if the others caught up to them – and she knew they could – then it would not end well and they would be severely injured at least. The dwellers had closed their world to visitors and they would not be allowed back in – the entrance was sealed and hidden.

Asha cowered, closing her eyes for fear of discovery, as the light passed slowly over her hiding place. She prayed her rigid limbs would be able to move quickly. The torch beam had reached the barrier close to where Sarah was hidden when another shrill whistle pierced the air, this time louder, longer and more insistent. It was quickly followed by another. Asha held her breath; it was a signal being given by several of them. She hoped it would provide the distraction they needed.

The girl turned her back to them and switched off her torch. Putting her fingers to her lips she let out a responding whistle, sharp and shrill and startling. Then there was a fourth from the north end of the park. With one final lingering look backwards she mounted her bicycle and cycled off. They waited for what felt like forever, their fingers and toes frozen to the bone but their fear overpowering the cold. Surprisingly, Sarah was the first person to make a move; Asha heard the low rustling as she slowly emerged from her hiding place. She crawled to where Jonathan and Asha were hiding rubbing her hands together. They got up slowly. They chose not to walk on the paths but in silent file walked along beside the wrought-iron fencing that lined the pathways of the park. It was treacherous and not meant for pedestrians; they were tripped up by tree roots and raised flower beds but they bore the pain and frustration silently without a single whimper. It was going to be a very long walk home. Asha believed they had just had their first encounter with Nanette – and it had been terrifying.

CHAPTER 5

*T*he boy walked with a sense of purpose that morning. He felt he had a duty to uphold. He was not one to be so self-righteous but he thought he could approach his employer on a man-to-man basis and discuss what was troubling him. It was not the task of finding the vermin they had been set, that was the least of his worries. The boy knew they were getting closer, although he was now aware the vermin were getting help from someone not of their own world. Who it could be was anyone's guess. There had been no sightings of them in recent days; he would not tell the man that though. It was always best to lie. The man would grow increasingly angry with him if he realised these creatures he hated so much had disappeared from sight. But the boy knew they would resurface. The boy knew how people on the run acted – when all was quiet and they felt a sense of safety they would emerge; he could count on that. The search from the night before had been impeded by the falling snow, which made the routes more difficult to navigate. There were no footprints in the snow to indicate that the vermin had been out and about. They were choosing obscurity, and something or someone was keeping them occupied, but it would not be for long. Whoever they had allied themselves with would realise they were fighting a losing battle against the man and the group. He wanted them all.

The boy's main priority at that point was to keep the group away from his family and his home. They were showing a keen interest in his situation – what he did, where he lived, his family, his younger sister, his mother – almost as though they were trying to form some sort of bond with him. He was worried they were getting terribly close. The girl and the twins, the ones that terrified him, were always there. Yet they remained silent; it was always Tamara asking him the personal questions whilst the others stayed silently by, but he knew they were putting her up to it. They were using her as a funnel to find out what they could about him. Tamara, though, did not frighten him like the others did; she was friendly and prone to violent rages but she was not dangerous, not at all. And that was what he had come to discuss with the man, apart from giving him a report about their activities: the boy felt a duty of care towards Tamara. He supposed it came from having a younger sister who was probably the same age as she was. He also knew Tamara was vulnerable, suffering from some unexplained trauma that was never spoken of, but one truth he could definitely attest to was the lack of violence within her. She was nowhere as unrestrained and psychopathic as the others were. She did not have their dispositions or tendencies towards the macabre. He was supposedly the leader of this band, as the man had instructed from the first, so he hoped the man would respect him enough to listen to what he had to say; after all, it was in his best interest to find the vermin.

The boy stood at the little side entrance to the house. The wrought-iron side gate he was supposed to use, the discreet one that never made any sound, was covered by snow from the night before. It looked so serene and elegantly beautiful but he knew it was a façade. There was nothing serene about the scene; it was morbidly silent. He took a deep breath. It was a momentous task but he would rise to the occasion. He unlatched the gate and walked through the garden. He had long since lost count of how many times he had been there; it was several, but the conditions were always the same and nothing ever changed: the times, the location, the emptiness; it was always consistent. The others were not with him this time, nor were they waiting silently in the private parks around the house. He would not meet them till that evening when they would go on the hunt once more, without the threat of falling snow hindering their search. He walked through the gardens, beautiful as ever but still silent. The hallway beckoned and the large grandfather clock ticked in the corner. Judging from the size of the house he was on the north side of it. A very small part of the house could be viewed from the outside world. The tall brick walls that surrounded the colossal property were spread out for several hundred metres and there was a huge black iron gate at the front of the property, but rather than the beautiful scrollwork the others had, which afforded a look at the house, this one allowed no view past it, the gate and the walls acting as a barricade to the outside world.

The boy had helped with a big job in one of the neighbouring houses a year ago when Gary Robinson, an older friend from his estate, got him a job as a garden landscaper's assistant, if such a role was ever required. It had not lasted long – they came to realise they were doing the job for very little money. However, he knew these houses were always much larger than they appeared and, by his calculations, there would be at least seven bedrooms in the house and it would be separated into wings. He shook his head in disbelief, thinking about the crammed three-bedroomed flat he resided in with his sister and mother where if he moved too quickly and kicked the wall whilst getting out of bed a dent was usually left, where the sounds of the neighbours fighting or watching TV was always heard, while some people lived in houses with wings that they closed off for part of the year.

'These so-and-sos,' Gary Robinson used to say, 'don't you fall for their smiles and pretences. You just keep your nose clean, boy.'

The boy understood and had nodded. It made sense; Gary was eventually sacked for overcharging his clients for supplies and was currently in prison – a short term for benefit fraud. He shook his head. People like them did not get on with people like the man; they were from two different worlds.

He wondered what the man could want all this space for. He clearly was not married, nor did he have a large boisterous family. How many rooms could he possibly need? The boy cast his resentment to the back of his mind and turned the brass handle to the little garden room that led to the grand hall. He moved through the hallway, his trainers barely making a sound on the wooden floor as he trod across. Then an idea struck him. He paused at the large wide stairway with its scrolled banisters; there was a cluster of elegant stained-glass windows above it that let light in from the outside world, casting an ethereal glow across the long room. The boy didn't think about what he would do if he went up the stairs. It was a moment of madness, but he placed his foot on the bottom step and looked up, wondering what was up there, his curiosity getting the better of him. He had been here so many times but this was the first time the need to know had overcome him. Then, with a sudden jolt, he returned to reality. He shook his head. What was he doing? The man would be furious if he found out and he was here for one job and that only, to report to the man and try to get Tamara out. The figures the man was paying him flashed in his mind. It was the most money he had ever earned and was comparable to the figures his peers on the estate were earning working for criminal masterminds.

Cursing under his breath at his clumsiness he made his way down the hall, walking past the firmly shut doors on either side of him and not falling into temptation. They always met in the same room – a large room that looked as if it would have been used for entertainment, probably balls or banquets. The ceiling was high, two large chandeliers hung from the middle, equidistant from each other, many tall windows were spaced equally along the outside wall, the heavy drapes were always held open, but still nothing could be seen of the outside world because of the white voile inner curtains which were always shut, the plants surrounding the house acting as an extra security measure. The boy knew that the gardeners – it could not be just one man doing the job – would be working full time to keep the sprawling greenery flourishing and as the man liked it. He caught his breath. The chair was empty. The desk the man normally sat at with his back to him as he looked out of the window was vacant. The boy was astonished. He stood staring at the leather-covered armchair and the desk, which as always was neatly arranged with nothing out of place. His head filled with doubt; had he got the day wrong? They had been working pretty hard those past few days as the vermin withdrew and perhaps he had muddled the days up. And his sister and mother were at each other's throats a lot of the time and it was up to him to break up the constant arguments; had that confused him?

'You're five minutes early.' The voice in the room made him jump. He turned around. The man was standing behind him. It was the first time he had seen him standing to his full height and although the boy was tall he realised the man was a good six foot five inches – and strong. He walked with a cane, which the boy had never noticed before, but even though he saw the stick, he still felt strength emanate from the man, an insane power that even he with his youth and virility could not topple.

'S-s-orry,' he stuttered. He shut his eyes as he tried to gain control of his speech. The man had caught him unawares; he should have heard him coming with the cane.

'Why do you stutter? Have you done something wrong?'

'No.' The boy shook his head vehemently. 'You just scared me, sir.' He put his hand to his chest hoping his heart rate would return to normal.

The man glided to the large desk, walking elegantly even though supported by a cane, and resumed his seat. He did not turn to face the boy.

'So, I'm sure you bring me good news?' It was more an order than a question. The man *expected* good news.

The boy swallowed as he regained control of his disposition. He stood up straight and inhaled deeply before launching into speech. He told the man about the positive sightings of the vermin, how the team worked well together, how meticulous they had been in avoiding the law. They had tracked the vermin to within a three hundred metre radius in the north side of the park. In a short space of time they would be able to identify a way into their breeding grounds. The boy did not mention finding, and losing, the girl that night but the man would have to know about her appearance. He swallowed. There was a slight problem and he thought it was the man's right to know of it. He watched the hand that supported the man's head as he listened tense suddenly.

'What problem? Why should we be having problems?' His voice was low, the low dangerous snarl which terrified the boy. He still did not turn to face him.

'They are receiving help, sir. From someone.' He licked his lips nervously.

'Help?'

The boy nodded. 'Yes.'

'Who is helping them? One of their own?'

'No, sir. One of *our* own.' The boy swallowed nervously. 'A human. Not vermin.'

The man was still, his hand suspended in mid-air as he contemplated the words. The boy was concerned about what he would say next, not because it would involve watching the vermin – that did not concern him – but because of what that might require. The boy knew all about what could get him arrested and what he could get away with. Stalking strange dwarves that lived underground like rats would never attract police attention, but following a girl would. Judging from her demeanour she was not off the streets, but from somewhere people would care and be waiting for her return; she would probably have a curfew of some kind and a father or at least a mother watching over her. The bike, which he assumed to be hers, propped against the low iron fencing was an expensive one. It was a classic, hand built he estimated somewhere in the north of England with a sprung leather saddle, chrome body in an elegant black, luggage rack, bell; everything about it was lavish, even the tyres and the basket woven in wicker from the West Country.

He began to wish he had been more prudent and regretted telling the man what he had seen that night. He recalled the moment when he had been scouring the park with the others; he'd had an inkling about searching the bushes because these vermin had ways and means. It seemed like a preposterous idea until he heard the mêlée and turned to see one of the others, he was not certain which – they all looked identical – falling back as the girl and two of the vermin scrambled out of the bush. He was taken aback as to how a tall girl could fit into such a small space; it had to be trickery of some kind, perhaps the bush was larger inside than out. He remembered her scream as she caught sight of the mask. He wondered what had terrified her so. Perhaps it had simply been the mask. That would do it. An eerie face appearing before you at night would terrify the life out of anyone. Then he set his jaw grimly; if he could put money on it, it would be the fact that the others had such dark, dead eyes. She had probably seen what he saw when he looked at them. He hadn't believed his good fortune as two of the vermin stood right before them: they finally had them within a hair's breadth. Then they started to run. The boy could not believe it – when they caught up to her the vermin had disappeared, and they still managed to lose her unconscious body after several of the vermin re-emerged. They had given chase but to no avail. They were cunning, slippery creatures. Then he realised it was not such a bad thing – they obviously cared for the girl so she would be an easy way of locating the entry points to their world.

'There is something else?' the man enquired. It was another command but in the form of a question.

The boy was surprised the man had shown restraint over news of a human assisting the vermin. He hesitated then pushed his fears away. He was an inner-city boy and supposed to be tough; the man was wealthy and had probably known wealth and prosperity his whole life, therefore the boy's experiences trounced the man's – or so he thought.

'Yes, sir.'

'Out with it then.'

'It's about the group, sir. You see, there are five of us in total.' *At the moment*, he added to himself. 'But we are not all fit for the task, some of us lack the stomach to do what needs to be done.'

'Oh.' The man paused. 'Who might these people be then?' He sounded almost amused.

'One of them is Tamara. Tamara Lewis. She talks too much, is too jovial and is drawing too much attention to us. I'm afraid she might get us caught or we might come to the attention of the law.' The boy tried to inject as much disdain into his voice as he could. Perhaps if the man considered the young girl a risk he would be willing to get rid of her. It was an underhand ploy but in his eyes he was doing it for her own good. Tamara did not belong with the group and he saw a bright future for her if she could get away from them, and, more importantly, from the clutches of the man who seemed to hold them all spellbound.

'Really?' the man purred.

'Yes. She's too soft and definitely lacks any type of instinct.' The boy continued to twist the dagger. 'There's just no killer instinct in that girl,' he finished, hoping he wasn't laying it on too thick.

'What a fascinating perspective, Mr Ingram.'

The boy nodded in response, satisfied the man found him fascinating.

The man finally turned in his chair and reached for a drawer in his desk. The boy froze, certain he was going to extract a weapon in anger and do him harm. His adrenaline kicked in and he tensed. But all the man produced was a manila envelope.

'Relax, boy. I'm not going to hurt you. Take a look at that.' He slid it across the table where the envelope was stopped by a heavy glass inkwell perched right on the edge.

The boy ventured forward and took the envelope in his hands. The name Tamara Roberta Lewis was etched across it.

'Don't just stand there. Read it,' the man snapped impatiently.

The boy nodded; his hands shook. He opened the file which had just a few sheets of paper bound within it. It was what was written on the papers that scared him. His eyes fervently scanned the pages as he took the information in. Tamara's entire life history was in there and it did not make for easy reading; in fact, it was the most horrific thing he had read in a long time. Even though the boy had friends within the criminal classes, Tamara's atrocities were of a more disturbing nature. They lacked reasoning or the capabilities of a functioning mind.

'If anyone lacks the killer instinct, young man, I would say it was you.' The man's voice had a light mischievous tone to it. If the boy hadn't known better he would think he amused him.

The boy nodded, his hands still shaking with trepidation at what he had just read. He tried to excuse his actions. 'I'm sorry s-s-sir. I w-w-was just trying to make sure e-everyone was doing th-the right thing and working as a team.' He closed his eyes and licked his lips, trying to get his damned stutter under control. It showed up at the most inappropriate and embarrassing of times, making him appear inept and limited.

'Find the girl,' the man instructed.

The boy's heart sank. 'Yes, sir.'

'Will you know how to do that or will you need help?' His voice was mocking.

'No, sir.'

'Go.'

The boy turned on his heel to leave, feeling defeated about being wrong. He was often wrong about things these days.

'One more thing, boy.'

He paused and turned around.

'If you ever look in any direction other than down the hallway towards this room, or if I sense any temptation to go in any direction other than the one instructed, I will make sure you disappear permanently. All of you, your mother and sister included.' The man's tone was light-hearted, as though he was telling an amusing anecdote at a dinner party.

The boy stood rooted to the spot, stunned at the sudden change in the conversation and the alteration in the man's speech. He mumbled a few incoherent words and nodded dumbly, backing out of the room, genuinely afraid to turn his back on the man.

As he cleared out of the property, he realised he was shivering. The man's threats echoed in his head, his words frightened him. If the boy could find the girl and do it quickly, that would make him happy and put him back in the man's good books. The girl could easily be located; she obviously lived in the area, was in her late teens, and was at a private school. It was as simple as waiting in the street where each school was located and searching for someone of her description to emerge. The boy smiled. Finding her would be easy, what to do with her would be difficult but the decision was now out of his hands. The boy was willing to do anything to save his mother and more importantly his precious sister, even if it meant exposing the girl to the rest of the group.

~

*C*larence Mews antiques alley was a little-known London secret. It was where a lot of North London locals went to find old furniture and other artefacts that could not be obtained anywhere else in the vast city. It was a quirky dark winding alleyway that went on for about half a mile, covering many streets and passages in the quaint North London village a stone's throw from were Jonathan Stapleton lived. Unique items from remote corners of the world such as the Comoros Islands to Guatemala could be found there. His mother had acquired her fainting couch from an antique furniture shop a few doors down and it was positioned in a corner of their drawing room, admired by her and everyone else who was into that sort of thing. Why Jonathan found himself there with his two brothers who had just recently returned from university for the Christmas holidays was no mystery. Sam and Tyler had failed to get their mother a Christmas present and knowing her love of antiques had dragged Jonathan out that dreary morning to a little shop that sold rare cups. But Jonathan was bored, the events of the weeks before still weighing heavily upon his mind.

The resurrection of their friendship with Asha,

combined with the new world introduced to them, had been overwhelming. It was now a week and a half since their meeting with the dwellers, a week and a half since they had hidden in the snowy park as the girl had deliberately hunted them. Jonathan had never hidden from a girl his own age before or been as unnerved as he was that night. They had all felt it, crouching in the foliage, that chilling fear as she combed the area with cold-blooded accuracy searching for any sign of life, human or otherwise. When they had arrived home, hours after their curfews, and thoroughly cold, hungry, tired and broken, it was to the ire of their parents. It seemed the local police had been contacted and they had spent time searching for them. Apparently Asha's father had not been as angry as his own father and Sarah's parents. Patrick Saunders had simply been happy to find she had been with old friends and assumedly taking part in activities that normal teenagers indulged in.

Making the promise to help the dwellers that night, in retrospect and in the harsh light of day, had been much easier said than done. Trying to find a hidden world or little people running around London was much harder than they expected. News archives covering the last seven years, tabloid papers and magazines that reported odd stories involving aliens and the supernatural – all had been checked meticulously. Jonathan had even approached psychics, but as suspected they had been shams. Asha and Sarah had no luck in their hunt for the mime masks they had seen and which Asha remembered all too clearly. Costume shops, Halloween stockists, toy stores, tourist shops had been investigated, but no sign of the masks was seen and when the vendors were shown drawings of the masks they did not recall ever selling anything of that nature. They had nothing to show for the past week and a half and he wished Sarah and Asha had not been so hasty in their offer of help to the dwellers. Their hopes had been raised and they had no good news to tell; for someone as exact as Jonathan it felt like a failure.

He found his spirits raised when his brothers returned home for the run-up to Christmas. He had got home late the night before, exhausted and cold after spending an hour and too much money with an East Finchley psychic who claimed to know where the missing Kee's Corner was. It was just a shame he was unable to accurately reveal to them where the first commune, the Unending Canal, was located. After the psychic had a vision of the Unending Canal being somewhere beneath the Tower of London an impatient Jonathan decided it was time to go. Returning home to find his brothers Sam and Tyler home, albeit a week and a half early, had been a pleasant surprise and he had been beside himself with excitement. The boys spent the rest of the night in the drawing room talking and exchanging pleasantries; his brothers had missed the youngest member of the family as much as he missed them. He desperately wanted to tell them what had been going on – the story of the dwellers and how he was trying to help them – but it was not his secret to tell and he had sworn the utmost discretion to them and could not go back on his word.

Sam and Tyler were awake rather early the next morning and had dragged him out with them in their search for a suitable present. He knew they would be headed to Clarence Mews. Jonathan walked down the alley looking at all the little shops huddled side by side resembling quaint little coves. Then he stopped short, mouth agape, at a shop he had never noticed before. The large window was full of masks from the comical to the gruesome. Jonathan could not remember ever noticing such a shop before and wondered if it was new. Clarence Mews rarely ever got new shops – the existing shops were just passed on down the generations or taken over by new owners who continued with the usually successfully model of the previous owners – that was why it was so special. He stood outside the mask shop observing it for a short while, wondering how long it had been there. How could he have missed it in the past? It had such a striking display. He remembered almost every shop in Clarence Mews and this one would surely have clung to his memory. Walking in was more of a surprise than he had expected; the shop was quite dark and devoid of any shoppers. What held his fascination were the wall to wall and ceiling to wall masks; wherever they could be safely placed, there they were. The ceiling was covered and the masks concealed every inch of the walls. He looked around as much as he could but there was so much to take in that he began to get confused; there were different styles from West African to the South Pacific to Western European. He scratched his head, wondering how a mask collector would start a search. The more precious pieces were in glass display boxes, kept behind what Jonathan assumed was the counter. There was no sign of what he was looking for though. There was also no evidence that anyone was actually in the shop or if there was another doorway to a back office.

'Excuse me,' he called out. A surge of excitement ran through him. He tried to ignore it but he couldn't. This was the first potential clue they had received in over a week and it had been beneath their noses the entire time. Someone of this calibre, whoever owned this shop (wherever they might be) would be an expert in this field, would know where the masks used by the Mimes were from, because that was what this shop traded in: the rare and exotic.

'Excuse me,' he called again, twirling around to see if there was a doorway he had missed. The shop could not be unattended.

There was a slight scuffling sound from a vertical row of masks in a display cabinet. Jonathan skirted past a standing display of Venetian masks and moved cautiously towards the sound. He jumped in fright when a man suddenly popped his head around the corner, his face hidden by a particularly hideous wooden mask.

'Hello,' the man said, gingerly taking it off when he saw the look of terror on Jonathan's face. He gazed at Jonathan curiously.

'Sorry. I didn't mean to frighten you.'

'You scared me half to death.'

'Terribly sorry, young man.' He shook his head ruefully. 'I'm sorry but I'm going to have to ask you to leave or I'll have to call the police.'

'What?' Jonathan was taken aback by his change in demeanour and very odd comment. 'May I ask why?'

'I just don't allow young people in here,' he responded sadly, eyeing Jonathan up and down.

'Look, I don't want to cause any trouble. I've been coming to Clarence Mews with my mother for the past few years. I just wanted to find out some information.'

The man gazed at him for several minutes as though weighing him up, then, his mind obviously made up, he nodded.

'I'm sorry. I do get rather carried away. I've had trouble in the past.' He extended his hand. 'Harry Rapier.'

Jonathan accepted the handshake bemusedly, wondering how much trouble a mask collector could have. 'Jonathan Stapleton. Where is that one from?' He gestured to the mask that had caused him to lose his wits a few seconds earlier.

'The Solomon Islands. It—'

'Oh. That's fascinating. I was looking for a particular mask, a mime mask. Rather different to anything you might have here. This one is particularly scary to look at.'

There was a long pause as the man eyeballed him. Then, without a word, Harry Rapier turned his back to Jonathan and began to forage around in some boxes on the floor. Jonathan waited patiently, gazing idly around the shop as the owner continued his search. To his surprise the man brought a few wooden masks out, none which resembled a mime mask.

'Err, Mr Rapier?' Jonathan said. The man turned round to look at him.

'Oh, you're still here?'

'Yes,' Jonathan responded awkwardly. 'I wasn't sure if you heard my question. I asked if you had seen or knew of any mime masks or shops that sell them. These ones are particularly cruelly done and—'

'I'm sorry, old chap, I don't sell mime masks, just antique masks from all over the world. Each one tells a story, you know? Why don't you take a look around? You might find something you like.'

As intrigued as Jonathan was, he didn't have time for stories or mask shopping, Sam and Tyler would be wondering where he had got to. But the man had already started talking about some Venetian masks standing before them and the story each one represented.

Jonathan was deflated and his former excitement dissipated. It had been a waste of time and if Mr Harry Rapier couldn't help them, no one could. Admitting defeat he turned to leave. As he did so he took one last look around and caught sight of a display cabinet on the wall. It was filled with a multitude of scrap paper and newspaper clippings. Jonathan moved towards it to get a better look. There were clippings from as long ago as 1895 about rare masks being found, one about a particular mask of great value being stolen from a member of the Victorian aristocracy. Then his heart began to beat in excitement; there was a clipping dated seven years ago. He peered closer to read the column.

Something peculiar happened to me today. I was exercising Tinker along the Common when I saw the most ghoulish looking person in a mask, the most hideous mime mask I have ever laid eyes on. I was terrified just looking at it. The mask and wearer gave Tinker a good fright as well. I had trouble calming her down after that. Anyway, what was strange was the masked person appeared to be chasing someone, a little person, who then promptly disappeared into some nearby greenery. The masked person, who ignored me in my distress, uttered some words which I dare not mention for fear of appearing less than ladylike.

In that moment Jonathan's world came to a standstill. He glanced dumbly at the words, reading them over and over trying to make sense of them. He paused to look back at the shop proprietor who was still talking, naively assuming Jonathan had stopped to listen. Harry Rapier was now on the topic of West African masks; Jonathan let him talk on and resumed reading the lines again. His heart raced – this person had made mention of mime masks, a chase in a common very similar to the park the dwellers lived in, and a sudden disappearance into greenery. This person would be able to help. It was what they had been looking for for a week and a half. Who would have known a real-life interaction between a dweller and a Mime had been recorded? He

CHAPTER 5 | 155

scoured the small clipping but the rest of it was obscured by another article in the cabinet. Jonathan panicked – the clipping looked rather worn, as though it had been handled several times. What if it was before their time? Harry Rapier was still talking so Jonathan chose the perfect moment to interrupt.

'Excuse me, sir. Can I please take a look at this newspaper clipping?'

The man looked slightly bewildered at Jonathan's request and more than a bit annoyed that he had been interrupted.

'I beg your pardon, young man. I haven't opened that cabinet in years.'

'Please – I just wanted to finish reading the article.'

'A customer could walk in at any moment and I do not want to be faffing around with cabin—'

'Please.' Jonathan felt awkward at having to beg the man but if there were any other details or a name attached they would have their first vital clue. 'My mother is interested in one of your antique Venetian masks for her study. I'm sure she would like to return with me and have a look,' he added desperately. In truth, Jonathan's mother hated masks, but how was Harry Rapier to ever know?

'Well, all right then. I'll look for the key,' he responded gruffly, glancing outside through the only little gap in the window. 'It's a depressing day anyway.'

He walked into his little back room. Jonathan crossed his fingers as he heard him scuttling around. If the key was not found he would have to do the unthinkable and smash the glass when the shop proprietor was not looking. Jonathan had never committed a crime in his life and he was certain, if caught, the charges levied against him would be theft of a newspaper clipping and breaking the glass of a musty old wall cabinet that looked like it was infested with woodworm. He would probably get a severe reprimand but he could not see it going further than that. He had spent enough time with his father to know the ins and outs of the law. The toughest obstacle would not be facing the police, that was the least of his worries; the toughest would be his father, Frederick Stapleton.

'Where is this particular clipping from? What paper?' he asked engagingly, hoping Mr Rapier had not got distracted by something else and forgotten about him.

The man emerged looking momentarily lost; he ambled slowly to where Jonathan stood and looked up at the cabinet. He started fiddling around with a cluster of keys, inserting them one by one in the small lock.

'Well, I do believe that was an entry in a strange encounters journal.' He smiled as the lock clicked open. 'Ah, voilà.' His fingers worked slowly as he gently moved the other clippings out of the way.

Jonathan in a flash of impatience reached up to help him.

'Ah ah, no touching. These are rare.'

Jonathan wondered why they were kept in a woodworm-covered cabinet if they were so rare, but wisely decided to keep his opinion to himself. Mr Rapier picked up the clipping.

'This one?' He held on to it, his eyes going over the article.

Jonathan leant forward. The name beneath the article read Katherine Heathridge.

'I thought it was most peculiar and I cut it out,' Mr Rapier said, scratching his head.

'Yes, but what paper did you get it from? Please try and remember. This is very important.'

'One of the Wimbledon ones I think. Yes, most definitely. She makes mention of the Common, you see. Then again she could mean Clapham Common, or Blackheath Common. Hmm... but seeing as she's a rider and was on a horse at the time she probably meant Wimbledon.'

'Thank you so much,' Jonathan said, committing the name to memory; he would do a search for this *Katherine Heathridge* in the Wimbledon area. She sounded rather elderly and he only hoped she was still around – she was the closest clue they had.

～

*T*he Saunders household was quiet and empty, which Asha preferred. She was in an emotional mood. It was just two weeks to the Christmas holidays, her first without her mother, and she had just received a timely reminder. She had just returned home from school and was settling in for the evening when the doorbell rang. Mrs Redding was not in that day, her father would still be at work, and she was home slightly earlier than normal. Who could be calling at that time? The events of the last few weeks flashed in her mind. It could not be Sarah or Jonathan as she had seen them minutes before when they had gone their separate ways a few streets away. Asha was on her guard after everything that had happened; Jonathan and Sarah were too. The trips to the commune were now few and far between since the night when they had been trapped in the snow and hunted. She shivered as she tentatively walked down the stairs. The doorbell rang again; it was more aggressive this time. Asha stood behind the door and glanced through the peephole. A very annoyed-looking man stood there – a stranger to her.

'Hello?' he called out belligerently, causing her to take a step back. 'I can hear you in there and if this door is not opened the package goes back to the depot and *you* have to pick it up.'

Asha opened the door an inch and was relieved to find out it was a delivery for the Christmas tree her father had ordered.

'Sorry, sweetheart. This is a nine-foot Nordman spruce. I ain't lugging it back and forth,' the delivery man irritably announced as he hauled it into the hallway. Asha made him leave it there. She did not want him coming in any further and ruining her memories. This was the first time the tree had been delivered. The responsibility for tree buying had always been hers and her mother's; her father would return home to a chaotically decorated tree but that tradition, like so many other aspects of Asha's life, was no more.

Although she was reconciled with her two closest friends, things were still tumultuous with her father. She had done her best to avoid him, which was no challenge as he worked so long and so much. However, if she wanted to avoid the ordeal of being roped in to decorate the tree with him, it would mean getting it done before he arrived home. Hauling the tree to the living room she decided she would overcome her trepidation and begin the task of decorating it herself. Her mother was gone and pretending the festive season was not upon them would be preposterous. It was best for Asha to start facing her fears alone.

As she busied herself with setting up the tree in its usual corner by the fireplace and retrieving the baubles and lights, tears pricked at her eyelids as the memories came flooding back.

Loud noises outside as a car screeched to a halt and a door slammed caught her attention. She glanced at the clock on the wall. It could not be her father; if it was he was extraordinarily early. The sound of the front door being opened suddenly caused her to pause, her heart in her mouth, as she wondered who this intrusive visitor was.

'Asha!'

Her fear was tinged with relief and surprise at the sound of her father's voice.

'Dad!'

He walked into the living room looking harried and paused at the sight of the tree. Raising a palm to his forehead he smacked himself hard. 'I'm so sorry, Asha. I thought I would get some sort of notice it was arriving. I came home early to get it set up.' He dropped to a chair disappointedly. 'I didn't want you to do it on your own.'

Asha felt a twinge of guilt at her rush to get it done without her father. 'Decorating it alone wasn't too bad and you can help me finish it off.'

'You've been crying?' He gazed suspiciously at her.

'No,' she responded cheerfully. 'What do you think?'

He stared at the tree for several seconds and with a wide grin remarked, 'It's definitely very festive.' He got to his feet. 'What would you like me to do?'

'Finish off the baubles and I will sort the fairy lights in the garden,' she instructed.

'Aye-aye!' He began to grab baubles and add them to the tree with great concentration, sticking with Asha's chaotic theme. His willingness to just go with the flow disconcerted her; did he ever find displeasure with anything?

She picked up the box of fairy lights and moved to the garden but the motion-activated security light did not come one.

'I don't think the lights in the garden are working.'

'Oh...' He furrowed his brow as he joined her outside, sinking into the thick snow in his work shoes.

Asha kept decorating as he walked past her into the kitchen to retrieve some items, going back moments later in clumpy wellingtons with a ladder. He returned a few minutes later looking puzzled.

'Did you fix it?'

'I'll need to get some new bulbs. It's the strangest thing, but there was no bulb in there. I doubt Mrs Redding would have taken it out.' The tree distracted him again. 'You know, Asha, I'm sure it's entirely possible to see that from a space shuttle.'

'Oh, Dad, you really do exaggerate,' she said with a grin.

'I'll go out and get some bulbs. I'll get us some dinner as well since Mrs Redding isn't here.' He popped out through the front door. Asha finished with the tree and moved outside to put the fairy lights up. It was silent as her foot crunched the hard-packed snow. She was draping the lights on the bushes in the back garden when she became aware of the dark silhouette that stood unmoving in the garden. It tried to blend into the dark but its form was different to everything around it. It was human and it moved slightly in the darkness.

Asha was too petrified to run; she stood there in a terrified silence as the figure remained standing. She could feel its eyes on her in the darkness. A ripple of fear coursed through her as she realised her father was gone from the house and she was alone. If she was going to act, she would have to do so decisively. This was not the time to be frozen by fear, it was one for action – action that would give her the best chances of survival. Then the visitor, as if deciding its job was done, began to retreat into the darkness, melting into the night that surrounded them like some shapeless being. Asha spun on her heel and raced indoors, slamming the garden doors shut behind her and locking them, certain the trespasser would not dare enter. As she struggled to breath she noticed a slip of paper on the little side table by the back door. It was folded. Her name was written across the top in a lazy scrawl. Asha did not recognise the writing, nor did she understand why there would be a note for her there. She reached for the slip of paper. It was smeared in blood; she began to scream.

CHAPTER 6

*J*onathan was excited. The letter he had received in the post that morning had left him feeling amused and somewhat intrigued. It had been written on Conqueror paper in an elegant cursive script. It read:

*K*atherine Heathridge
    The Lock
Cartwright Mews
SW19 4JX
Dear Mr Stapleton,

I was most surprised to receive your letter. It certainly piqued my interest. I would be glad to meet with you to discuss the events of that afternoon upon my return to London. I am currently still at Wellborough until the end of term.

Yours sincerely,
Katherine 'Kitty' Heathridge.

. . .

*T*he name caught his attention and he burst out laughing. She sounded like the prim English teachers he had had at prep school, wholly eccentric and most probably boring. Nevertheless, term would be ending in two days so he would go to the address she had supplied in her letter. He looked at the postcode, which was SW19. 'Wimbledon,' he muttered to himself. Harry Rapier, the mask collector, had been right. Tracking down Katherine Heathridge had been more difficult, though. It turned out there were quite a lot of females in the Greater London area with that surname and Katherine had been a favourite Christian name at some point. They had ended up going through all the London directories, which had taken a fair bit of their time, and written and posted fifty-six letters enquiring for the correct Katherine Heathridge to contact them as they had a matter of the utmost importance to discuss with her regarding her horse ride on the Common that afternoon. They finally had her. She was still alive and, it seemed, teaching.

Walking in through the school gates he saw a friend of his, Charles Bridges. The burly boy came striding over to Jonathan, apparently still excited about a rugby game from a few days before. Jonathan pretended to listen as his friend animatedly rambled on whilst keeping an eye out for Sarah or Asha, who were nowhere to be seen. They shared no lessons in the morning so it was not such a strange occurrence. As the morning progressed, though, his frustration grew and he began to ask around for them. By lunchtime, when they were nowhere to be seen in the dining room, Jonathan knew there was something going on. Sarah was a voracious eater and lunchtime was an important part of her daily schedule. It seemed their fellow pupils had seen them around but no one knew where they were. Suddenly spotting Sarah with a group of friends he called out to her.

'Sarah! Guess what?'

But she walked past him. He gaped after her, momentarily in shock as he watched her athletic form disappear out of the dining room. But he had seen the twitch in her features as he called out to her – Sarah had intentionally ignored him. He looked round to see if anyone had spotted the slight and witnessed a couple of fifth years suddenly lower their heads and fix their concentration on the yogurt pots before them.

At the other end of the dining room Charles Bridges, who was speaking, chose that moment to pause mid-sentence, thus ensuring those who were around spotted Jonathan's humiliation. Never one to let an embarrassing moment pass, Charles guffawed aloud and pointed, laughing hysterically as Jonathan stood there trying to remember at what point he had offended Sarah and what he could have done. Then he spotted Asha walking in behind a group of boys from the lower years. He tried to sidle up to her as discreetly as possible.

'Asha!' His voice was gentle, low enough so that only she would hear him but, like Sarah, she did not say a word, walking past as though he was not there.

Jonathan's face flushed a deep red and a smattering of low laughter ran through the vast dining space. He was joined by Charles and the oafish Terrence.

'Don't worry about them, Jon.' Charles looked at him. 'Sarah is probably just hormonal and Asha, well, she's a bit strange, isn't she? Been like that since her mother died. There was that joke going round about her dad trying to get a refund.'

They all howled with uneasy laughter but Jonathan was

now annoyed, though he was not sure who at. He turned to the twosome in a rare display of temper.

'Well, Sarah wouldn't give you the time of day and I don't think Asha has been quite the same since you tried chatting to her, so no, Charlie, they are definitely not all right.'

He stomped out of the dining room leaving a flustered Charlie with a group of hysterically guffawing boys. The halls were clear of any students, and the sight of Sarah walking towards him again made him grit his teeth in determination.

'Sarah...' he ventured.

'Meet in the courtyard in five minutes. Make sure you're not being followed,' she whispered.

Without breaking her stride she kept moving past him.

'The courtyard? Isn't that a private area?'

But Sarah was gone and the halls were empty once again. Looking around he leaned against the wall, occasionally glancing at his watch. He then made his way to the courtyard, which was a little private garden at the back of the school usually reserved for the headmaster's afternoon teas when he was entertaining at the end of the spring and summer terms, decorated with a little pond. Jonathan had no idea how Sarah would have got the key, as students were strictly forbidden from entering. The cold swamped him as he stepped outside again; the gate to the courtyard was shut. He knocked on it with trepidation, half expecting Mr Critchley, the headmaster, to open it up and grab him by his lapels for having the cheek to try to gain entry. It was quickly opened by Sarah rather than the headmaster, who grabbed him and shut the heavy wooden door behind him. Jonathan straightened his ruffled clothing, glaring at Sarah in shock and annoyance. Then he realised Asha was in there too. She was pacing frantically. She had clearly not had much sleep; her eyes looked tired and dark, and she seemed nervous and jumpy. Sarah went to sit on one of the benches nibbling her fingernails. Something must have gone wrong.

'What's going on?' he asked cautiously, almost afraid of the answer.

Asha, who kept pacing, seemed too wound up to talk so Sarah obliged.

'Yesterday she got a note,' she began.

'What did it say?'

Asha fished in her pocket for it in silence. The note had been read so many times it was in danger of falling apart. As Jonathan unfolded it he saw it had blood smeared across it; he tried to hide his disgust as he pored over its contents.

You think you are trying to help the vermin but you will only make things worse sticking your nose where it don't belong. Keep away from them. We are watching you.

Jonathan mumbled to himself as he read it out. He read it a few more times. 'Oh, they're just trying to warn us off. I think we've scared them slightly.'

'*We've* scared *them?*' Asha glared at him.

'It gets worse, Jon. I stayed over last night after that was delivered. Someone rang Asha's doorbell in the early hours of this morning. Fortunately Asha got to the front door before her father did.' Sarah stopped talking, the look of disgust on her face showing she did not want to say anymore.

'Well, who was at the door?' He looked between the two girls.

She seemed to be carefully trying to pick her words but Asha responded first.

'It was a dead dog. A dog! Who leaves a dead dog on

someone's doorstep? What sort of a sick person does that? I still feel sick thinking about it.' Asha's skin was turning a funny shade. She sat down as though her energy was spent. 'It had been dead a while, though. The blood had congealed.'

'We're not sure how it died but it had been in a lot of pain when it did,' Sarah said quietly. Her skin was turning pale as she recalled the memory. 'There was so much blood on the doorstep when I came downstairs to join Asha.' She shook her head. 'She went down there and then there was silence. I wondered where she was because we had school in a few hours. We had to clean furiously before her dad got up. Blood gets everywhere.' She shuddered.

'It was difficult to get it all off. I can still smell it now.' Asha looked like she was going to be sick.

'Did your dad see or hear anything?'

'No, he barely stirred in his sleep. He's a heavy sleeper anyway so he wouldn't be expecting the doorbell to ring at that time.' Sarah put her arms around Asha's shoulders reassuringly.

'Do you think it was – I mean was – was it Hiller?'

'No, it wasn't. It was a large dog. I couldn't tell the breed.' Sarah swallowed. 'Oh, it was awful. It had been cut open. I couldn't imagine what I would do if someone did that to Troy,' she said.

Jonathan thought back to Dax who would be sitting somewhere in their home, comfortable, warm and sleeping after his morning walk. He could not imagine anything happening to his precious Labrador. The dog was a part of the family and he would never forgive himself if anything happened to him.

Sarah looked despondently at him. 'We can't tell our parents to be careful with our dogs because we would have to tell them exactly what happened this morning, and that would only lead to more questions.' She turned to Asha. 'For the first time ever you should be grateful you don't have a dog and had to give Hiller away. I worry about Kiki too.' Sarah was very protective of her younger sister.

'No, this is our secret,' Jonathan said firmly. 'We won't let these arseholes beat us.'

'Could it be those girls who followed me home when Fred and Bogsley helped me?' Asha looked hopeful at the thought.

'I don't think it's those girls, Asha.' Jonathan shook his head ruefully.

'Well, who else could it be then?' she asked. 'The Mimes don't even know where I live.'

'What if we were followed that night? What if we *were* being watched as we walked out of the park after our visit?' He looked uneasy. 'I hate to say it, guys – they don't just know who we are but they know where you live, Asha.'

Sarah inhaled sharply. 'I had the strangest feeling that night after we saw Asha to her door that we were being followed. I thought it was all in my head,' she said to no one in particular. 'I did turn around a couple of times after I split from Jonathan but the streets had emptied after the snow.'

Asha snapped her fingers as a thought occurred to her. 'That first night when you came to mine, the doorbell rang just before you both arrived but there was no one there. But someone had covered the peephole in dirt. Could it have been them?' There was a deep silence in the courtyard as Asha's words sank in.

'I guess the note and the dog mean that they haven't found the dwellers' hiding place – which is good – but it's still bad because they're getting desperate. They also know we are very much involved now.' He hesitated. Something was wrong with the sequence of events. 'It makes no sense though.'

'How do you figure...?' Asha paused mid-question, sounding bewildered.

Jonathan was confused by the pattern. A blood-smeared note and a dead dog a few hours later was not consistent with the architect of a well-thought-out plan.

'Well, first they leave a note, which sounds like a warning, but then a dead dog a few hours later – they sound entirely unhinged if you ask me. It seems to be separate ways of functioning.'

'How?' Sarah insisted.

Jonathan tried to make himself clearer. 'It looks, to me anyway, that two different people have done this.'

'Yes, but—'

The sound of the bell from the school tower cut Sarah off.

'But we aren't any closer to finding out who these people are, yet they know us and are watching us.' Asha fingered the note in her hand.

Jonathan thought this was the best time to interject with his news. 'I have some good news. We might have made a bit of progress. Remember those letters we sent? Well, I got a letter this morning from a Katherine Heathridge and I think she might be able to help us.' He pulled the folded letter out of his pocket and waved it in the air. 'It arrived just before I left for school.'

Asha grabbed the letter and opened it up as Sarah looked over her shoulder. Jonathan watched their facial expressions change as they took in its contents. Their sour expressions were gone, replaced with hope.

'So she returns to London tomorrow?' Asha said.

'Yes!'

'So we just have to wait to see her tomorrow,' Sarah said brightly, getting to her feet.

Asha hesitated. 'I can't tomorrow, guys.' She looked uncomfortably at them.

'Why not?' Sarah looked perplexed.

'I'm seeing my therapist. There's no escaping her.'

'Is that still happening? After you snuck a look at her file?' Jonathan was surprised. Asha seemed to be on the mend.

'Yes, especially after I snuck a look at the file.'

'Oh, okay. Well, Jonathan and I will go then,' Sarah volunteered. Jonathan groaned. It would be a long journey to Wimbledon and he was not relishing the prospect of spending the afternoon with an old biddy whose mind was slowly dissipating. Would this Katherine Heathridge even recall where she had seen the chase? How much would she be able to remember? Still, he saw how happy the news had made his friends. The worry lines had been chased from their faces, flickers of smiles tugged at their lips and, for the first time in those few weeks of going around in circles chasing their tails, there was hope.

As they made their way out of the courtyard trying to avoid being seen Jonathan asked the question that was baffling him. 'How on earth did you gain entry to the court-yard? This is forbidden territory. I was caught standing outside once in fourth year by Mr Cornwall and given a warning.'

'Two words,' Sarah said with a small smile on her face. 'Prefect's privileges.'

'It means we can talk in there without anyone ever knowing, just in case, you know, they're listening or watch-ing.' The smug smile on Asha's face made Jonathan ponder as Sarah ushered them through the doors. Jonathan seriously doubted the Mimes had any ties to Ark House School. The Mimes' modus operandi, if it was really them, still confused him and left him feeling uneasy – it was as though something did not fit. There was a disconnect in the pattern of behaviour almost as if two different personalities had approached Asha's home that day. Still, he allowed himself to celebrate the good news – at least he had made them smile again and Katherine Heathridge was willing to help them.

~

A surly looking man opened the imposing doors of the townhouse. He looked like he had been woken from his sleep. Jonathan checked the address again. It seemed right. This was The Lock; it was etched in stony letters on a dark plaque by the front gate. It was Cartwright Mews which was a few minutes' walk from the green pastures of the Wimbledon Common. The journey from North West to South West London had taken over an hour on the underground that morning and Jonathan was not in the mood for wrong addresses or any other misinformation. In hindsight he realised staying up all night with his brothers had been a somewhat foolish idea.

'Can I help you?' The man had a strong East End accent which confused Jonathan who stuttered and struggled to form a coherent sentence.

Sarah impatiently interrupted her waffling friend. 'Good afternoon, sir. Does Katherine Heathridge live here?'

'Yes, she does,' the man said, this time with a warm smile, 'she came in from the stables a short while ago bringing her muck in through the house. This way.' He ushered them in.

They stepped into a large hallway where a pair of muddy boots was abandoned on the floor. The man, who still looked out of place in the grand house, directed them into the sitting room. It was filled with antique furniture, the mantelpiece above the fireplace adorned with framed pictures, and the polished floorboards creaked slightly as they walked across them.

'If you wait right here, I'll get her for you. She wasn't expecting guests, only got back from school yesterday.'

'Oh – are you her husband?' Jonathan asked.

The man paused, looking amused. 'No. I am certainly not her husband.'

'Oh, do you work here?' Jonathan forged ahead with his questioning ignoring the strangled sounds emerging from Sarah.

'No,' the man said patiently. He wore a little smile and had a twinkle in his eye. 'I'm her father.'

'Oh...' Jonathan felt the first flush of embarrassment pass through him. 'Oh. Sorry, I thought you worked... her husband... oh crap...'

The man walked out of the room leaving Jonathan mid-stutter. The flustered boy sank into a large leather armchair and Sarah stood over him with a glare on her face.

'What on earth is wrong with you?'

'I'm sorry but I was not expecting an East End geezer to open the door.'

Sarah's dark eyes flashed angrily making him cringe even more. 'Just leave the talking to me. Putting your foot in it seems to be what you do best today. We cannot ruin this. The dwellers are relying on us,' she said.

She walked around the room leaving a disgruntled Jonathan wishing the armchair would swallow him up.

'Come take a look,' she urged mysteriously.

Jonathan got to his feet and went to join her, still kicking himself. The pictures on the wall above the fireplace caught his eye. They were mostly of the same family; a young girl with dark brown hair, an older woman and the man they had just spoken to smiled into the camera.

'I am guessing Katherine is this young girl in the photos, which means she must be our age – not the ancient school teacher you mistook her for,' Sarah said snidely. She was in fine form that morning and Jonathan had not been able to come up with a suitable response to any of her barbs.

They looked like a happy family; the man was not in his current attire of plaid shirt and dirty jeans in any of the pictures but had been cleaned up in a suit. The rest of the pictures showed their daughter's prizes and awards for show jumping, piano and fencing.

'She excels at quite a lot, doesn't she?' Sarah could not contain the sarcasm in her voice. 'She even has awards for recognition of her voluntary work. She sounds like quite the do-gooder.'

'Pretty girl,' Jonathan mumbled.

'Thank you!'

They both jumped as they realised they were no longer alone. The tall burly man had been replaced by a young female.

'Katherine Heathridge. Pleased to meet you.'

The girl extending her hand to Sarah and Jonathan was not the woman he had been expecting to see but a young girl of no more than seventeen. She was pretty in a delicate fashion, the dark brown curls that framed her face giving her a doll-like appearance. She was also porcelain pale, but her cheeks had a bit of blush to them and her lips were very pink.

'You are Katherine? The person who wrote the letter to me?' Jonathan tried to clarify, a puzzled look on his face.

'Indeed. Receiving your letter was a bit of a shock I must admit,' she said with a smile as she shook his hand.

Her hands felt delicate and fragile in his; he blushed slightly, not sure why. Jonathan felt Sarah glancing between him and Katherine. Out of the corner of his eye he spotted the smug smile on her face and wished he could get her to shut up.

'But everyone refers to me as Kitty.'

'Oh. Kitty,' Jonathan muttered shyly before lapsing into an awkward silence.

Sarah stepped forward and took Kitty's hand.

'I'm Sarah. It's lovely to meet you. Sorry – Jonathan is just a bit taken aback by your age. You see, he thought you would be much older. Like, ancient.'

Kitty smiled at him making him look away, blushing even more at her penetrating deep brown eyes. Sarah came to his rescue once more. He found himself unable to speak coherently; excitement coursed through him and whenever Kitty glanced at him a light-headed feeling overcame him, causing weakness in his knees and the pit of his stomach

Sarah got to the point of their visit. 'Kitty, we would like to speak to you about something strange you witnessed a few years ago. The chase you saw when you were riding your horse.'

Kitty motioned for them to have a seat. 'Well, it was all very peculiar,' she said in her soft voice. 'I ride on the Common very regularly and have this particular pathway I enjoy going down...' She paused, suddenly looking unsure of herself.

'Go on,' Sarah coaxed.

'Well, one winter evening it was freezing and the temperature had dropped rather drastically. I'm not accustomed to riding Tinker in the evenings.' Kitty paused again at the puzzled look on Jonathan's face.

'Who's Tinker?' he asked.

The sound of Sarah gritting her teeth caught his attention. Kitty's too. The girl looked amused. It seemed Sarah's irritation with Jonathan had reached tipping point. 'Her horse! Remember?' she hissed at him. 'She wouldn't be riding a bloody ostrich, would she?'

Kitty laughed gaily. 'Yes. She's a great big powerful thing and had not been exercised all that day so riding her was imperative.' She paused, an intense look of concentration on her face as she tried to recall the exact order of events.

'Well, there we were, trotting along happily on one of the paths, when Tinker suddenly went tense. She began to spook. Something had really got to her. That was when I saw it, it was *hideous*.' She looked horrified at the thought, her dark eyes getting darker.

'What was it?' Sarah pressed as Jonathan leant forward in his seat.

'It was a mask. A really hideous mask. It looked so evil. I know I sound like I'm grossly exaggerating but it gave me the chills. It was a mime mask, but an evil mime mask.' She fidgeted uncomfortably. 'It was being worn by someone on a bicycle who appeared to be chasing after a child who had just run past. Only when I looked closer it wasn't a child but appeared to be a little man. The little man disappeared very quickly causing the person in the mask, who was male, to swear most explicitly. Something about his manner was frighteningly violent. Needless to say I didn't want to wait to find out. I can't explain it but I didn't feel safe even on a strapping great horse like Tinker. I was finding it difficult enough to keep her under control and was in danger of being unseated so I rode off very quickly.'

'You say you didn't feel safe? What exactly do you mean?' Jonathan asked. For the first time during the visit she avoided his gaze.

'Well, this person could have just been a teenager that was up to no good, but there was something deeper and darker within him that terrified me.' She paused then added with emphasis, 'And Tinker. That horse still won't go down that stretch by the water trough.'

The grandfather clock in the room marked the hour, the tones resonating around the room breaking them out of their reverie. It was quite a story.

'But where are my manners – would you like some tea? We also have a batch of cookies I baked warm out of the oven.'

Jonathan found himself nodding before Sarah could say anything. Kitty smiled and got to her feet. 'Please excuse me.'

When she had left the room Jonathan winced and Sarah turned to glare at him. 'You fake. You don't even like tea.'

'I drink tea – sometimes.' He tried to sound convinced.

'Name one brand of tea.'

He racked his head to recall what his parents drank in the morning. 'Builders' tea?'

'Oh, don't give me that. One thing you certainly do like is Miss Kitty Heathridge, even though it is against your better judgement.' She snorted and he squirmed in his seat once more.

When he spoke his mouth was dry. 'You assume the

silliest things, Sarah. I most certainly do not like her. I find her eccentric and weird.'

'Really?'

'Yes!'

'Well, it's a good thing we'll never have to see her again after we leave. After all, there's no reason to.'

'Ah, but that's where you're wrong.' He wore a little grin on his face. 'Because we need her to show us where this all happened – I mean a point-by-point description.'

The atmosphere between them turned serious once more.

'That story sounds so similar to what we've experienced – the masks, the bicycles,' Sarah stated.

'Definitely. Also a bit terrifying. However, it does mean that these Mimes were so hellbent on finding the dwellers that they were willing to come across London,' he mused. The more they looked into the workings of the Mimes the less sense it made.

'We need to find out what the dwellers know. I know they're hiding something from us.'

Their conversation was suddenly cut short when Kitty came back in with a tray laden with cookies and an assortment of teacups, saucers and teapots. Jonathan sprang to his feet to help her, narrowly missing Sarah who had also stood up to help. Kitty, who was oblivious to what was going on around her, began to pour the tea.

'Kitty, if you're not too busy could you possibly show us where this happened?' Sarah ventured.

'I know it will be difficult for you to go back there but it's imperative we know where it happened,' Jonathan explained, wanting to be as honest as possible without revealing too much.

'Of course. Right after tea and biscuits,' Kitty said with a warm smile.

Jonathan and Sarah smiled back. Jonathan wondered why she hadn't yet questioned their motives.

Twenty minutes after the tea and biscuits had satisfied them they set off for the vast Common in silence. They were walking along the road about to cross over to the grounds when Sarah shot Jonathan an evil look.

'I think Jonathan might have mistaken your father for a tradesman,' she said mischievously.

Jonathan cringed, mortified that Sarah would bring up a past error. There was no way he could have known who Mr Heathridge was; he sounded like a tradesman. He expected Kitty to show disdain at such a slight but she shrugged nonchalantly.

'That's fine. My father is a plumber by trade. He met my mother when was hired to do some building work on her family home. My mother saw him and says she fell instantly in love.' She laughed. 'It took my father time to fall for my mother – he was expecting a spoilt little princess and he's a tough lad from the East End, as he always likes to remind everyone.'

Kitty directed them into a quieter, darker part of the Common. There was a winding path with thick trees and shrubbery on either side which meant they could never see further than a few feet ahead until they turned the corner.

'Tinker and I always take this path at the slowest walk you have probably ever seen. Do either of you ride?'

They both shook their heads.

'I prefer to appreciate horses from a distance,' Sarah replied.

'She thinks she once got chased by a pregnant mare when we were kids,' Jonathan added with glee, ducking the blow that Sarah threw in his direction and glad his wits had returned.

Kitty seemed oblivious to the war of words between them as she led the way. They walked deeper down the path. The silence was accentuated by the sound of their feet on the muddy path.

'So where is your mother now?' Jonathan asked, wanting to make as much conversation as possible and build a bond with the delightful creature. He thought that the more he knew of her, the more he would know her.

'She died several years ago when I was seven. She was very ill. My father was distraught. I have very few memories of her, sadly.'

'I'm sorry to hear that.' Jonathan gritted his teeth, resigning himself to a humiliating silence for the rest of their time with Kitty.

'Don't be. It was a long time ago.' She stopped as the path suddenly widened into a small clearing.

The part of the Common they were in was so dense that the trees overhead blocked out most of the drizzling snow. There was a large stone object at the end.

'This is where it all happened, that's the water trough over there.' She pointed, and her hand had a slight tremor to it. Her pace quickened as she started to recollect the events. 'I first noticed them – here...' She turned around to point in the direction they had come from where the path had become narrow and winding. 'He just seemed to disappear somewhere there. I daresay I was relieved the little man got away. The person in the mask stopped here and started swearing. He looked around, even got off his bicycle, he never took his mask off though. I had stopped to get Tinker under control. I'm not sure why I didn't just let her run off.

It would have been at breakneck speed, but the Common is surrounded by roads...' Her voice tailed off.

Jonathan sensed something in her speech; she was holding back. 'And?' he pressed her, breaking his vow of silence.

'And he turned around and noticed me looking at him. He started to ride back slowly to where Tinker and I were standing and in a muffled voice said if I told anyone what I had seen he would kill me. He said he knew me well, even mentioned the house in which I lived. He couldn't come any closer as Tinker was rearing by now. We rode off at speed down there past the water trough. As soon as we'd left the area that evil feeling was gone and Tinker just returned to normal.' Kitty's voice shook slightly. 'The only person who knows of this encounter was the writer who I told the story to. I never told anyone close to me, not even my father. It was a few days before I would get on Tinker again and I had to go out with a group of riders.' She looked past Jonathan and Sarah in the direction they had just come. 'That mask was the most terrifying thing I had ever seen. I stopped riding along here after I heard there were some other riders who had stopped coming along this path because of strange events—'

'What strange events?' Sarah's voice was sharp.

'Well,' Kitty continued grudgingly. 'There were other riders who got threatened too. Jane Thompson's horse spooked so badly whilst she was down here that she was thrown off and trampled upon. She died from her injuries a few weeks later. Once I heard the Common was even on fire.' She began to amble back the way they had come.

Sarah and Jonathan lingered behind, hastily making mental notes. 'Can we remember the route fairly easily if we need to?' Jonathan asked, slipping a little notepad and pen out of his pocket.

Sarah nodded. 'Yes, definitely. The water trough is the landmark. Even if we get lost we just locate the water troughs on the Common and we're sure to find this one. There'll be local maps too.'

Kitty was still talking.

'So, you see, this bit of the Common got a reputation for being cursed over the years. Too much happening, normally obedient horses suddenly becoming agitated, a few deaths, a fire, threats being made... people started to actively avoid it.'

'A *few* deaths?' Jonathan asked shortly.

'Yes. I left for Wellborough shortly after Jane Thompson's death – it had been my mother's wish. I know another rider was killed here – no one was aware until the horse was found wandering the Common a day later – and an elderly jogger had a heart attack. It proved to be fatal. Then the fire broke out. My father knows a bit about it though. Would you like to ask him?' She looked at them.

'Err, probably not. We're trying to keep this quiet.' Jonathan was hesitant.

'Well, a friend of ours has been threatened too,' Sarah admitted.

'Jonathan, Sarah. I know you wonder why I don't question why you're taking so much interest in the musings of a young girl. I've come to realise there are a lot of strange things going on. Things that you and I will never understand and I'm fine with that. I know you want to return to take a closer look at this place and that's fine. Some secrets must be kept.'

Jonathan and Sarah exchanged a glance. He was impressed and pleasantly surprised by Katherine. Although she seemed slightly precious and affected in behaviour she was obviously very intelligent, and certainly beautiful.

'Look, if you really want to know more about the events after my departure to Wellborough I'll ask my father. Don't worry, I won't let on that it has anything to do with you. I'll simply say, oh, I don't know, an article in the paper piqued my interest.' She looked at them both. 'I have to leave you now. My father gets nervous when I'm away for too long.'

'Thank you. We can find our way from here,' Jonathan said, his voice reassuringly confident even though they had no idea how to get out of the Common.

'Oh, splendid. I will let you know as soon as Father tells me anything.'

'Thank you, and be careful,' Jonathan called as she walked off. Kitty gave a delicate wave and walked towards her home which was in view from the Common. They watched her walk away for a moment before Sarah began to pull her friend along.

'What a vault of information that girl is,' Sarah exclaimed.

Jonathan nodded and got onto his hands and knees, scoping the ground for any clues.

'Jonathan,' Sarah urged. 'We've done what we came to do today. Let's pace ourselves and return early for a search.'

Jonathan knew Sarah was right even though he wanted to stay, but he was tired and very cold. It was now late afternoon and it would be dark by four. Time was against them and they had to make the journey back to North London. He could not be late for dinner either. His father was keeping strict tabs on his comings and goings.

'Come, Jonathan. We'll see her again.' Sarah tugged on his arm.

'How do you know?' He was morose.

'Because we need to find out what happened. If we know what happened here we can better understand what's happening in our part of London. To understand all that we're going to need Kitty's help – she's lived here all her life and would have seen incidents she didn't think or know were important. So don't you worry.'

'Okay.' Jonathan allowed himself to be pulled away by Sarah. 'At least we know they're alive.'

She nodded in response. Huddling together they walked through the snow. Sarah put her arm through his, pulling him along at a quicker pace as they hurried through the winter cold. Jonathan's heart was warmed not just by his friend's words of comfort and support but by the knowledge that Kee's Corner was somewhere down below, safe and waiting.

~

Sarah emerged from Hampstead station with Jonathan in tow and walked with him the short distance to his home. She was slightly concerned for her friend. He seemed so committed to finding Kee's Corner, putting every minute of his day into the expedition; she cared for Jonathan and didn't want him to be disappointed. It was obvious why he was investing so much time in the search: he was avoiding his father and the pressure he was putting on him about his future.

As they entered his home, Jonathan's mother, Irene, was waiting with a message she had written dutifully on a piece of paper. Sarah grinned at the look of elation on Jonathan's face as he calmly read the message his mother had scribbled down. He broke into a wide smile.

'Kitty called half an hour ago,' he exclaimed, eyes wide,

'which means she would have spoken to her father as soon as we left.'

Sarah had not seen Jonathan this excited in a long time and it warmed her heart. The search for Kee's Corner, and now Kitty, was giving him a boyish lease of life she had not seen for many years. She was happy for him.

'That was rather quick.' Her voice was dry but amused. She gently prodded him as they walked to the kitchen but he was completely engrossed in the message, reading it again.

'Keep an eye and ear out for Sam or Tyler,' he cautioned. 'They ruin everything.' He reached for the phone.

Sarah guffawed. Jonathan's older brothers realising their younger, more studious brother was interested in a girl would certainly be a cause for celebration and mayhem in the household. She moved to the kitchen door but the house was silent.

'Your brothers are either out or fast asleep, but I hear nothing.' She inched back to where Jonathan had taken a seat at the kitchen table with the telephone in his grip.

Jonathan dialled Kitty's number and turned away from Sarah who was watching him intently. Sarah did not gather much from listening to the conversation; Jonathan simply nodded a lot, his voice monotonous. He reached for a pen and scribbled further notes on the slip of paper.

'Well, I'll see you soon. Thank you,' he said as he put the receiver down. He sounded a bit sad. When he looked up he appeared even more confused.

'What is it?' Sarah was cautious and prepared for bad news.

Jonathan fell silent and stared at the scrap of paper. Sarah looked over his shoulder. It was an unintelligible collection of hastily scribbled words only Jonathan could decipher. He looked up at her and she saw a spark in his eyes.

'Kitty says the person responsible for the fires in Wimbledon was a local troubled youth called Billy Bragg. He came from one of the surrounding council estates. He had an accomplice with him called Dante Silva. She says they are both very violent and that her dad looked curious when she asked but she explained it was all a bit of history from the local paper. Her father didn't want to talk about the people who were tragically killed.'

'Why not?' she asked.

Jonathan shrugged. 'She said he was getting frustrated.'

'Interesting. Well, at least we know who is tormenting Asha,' Sarah concluded, noting that Jonathan still looked confused. 'What is it?' She tried to hide the worry in her voice.

'Well, first of all he sounds like trouble, this Billy Bragg. Second, he must be very determined to come all the way across London to torment the residents of the Unending Canal after trying at Kee's Corner, and third he would have to be seven years older now so why would he want to keep pursuing the dwellers? What has he got to gain?' Jonathan looked puzzled.

'It doesn't matter. We know it's him. We have a name and we can let the police know so they can handle it and, hey presto, he stops tormenting Asha with the notes and dead animals. It means we're in the clear too and most importantly we can find Kee's Corner and figure out a way of sending the dwellers back to their time.' Sarah sighed in frustration. Jonathan did not look convinced by her words.

'Billy is obviously very troubled to pursue them with such determination, but there are some things we will never understand. Let the police try to figure him out while we help the dwellers.' Sarah nudged him gently. 'Come on, let's go and see Asha and tell her the good news. She's probably been at home scared out of her wits all day.'

~

*J*onathan baulked at the sight of Asha when she opened the front door. He shot Sarah a glance and was glad to see she looked just as horrified at their friend's appearance. Her braided hair had lint stuck to it, her eyes had dark circles around them, and she was wearing a stained dressing gown and looked on edge and strained. A mug of coffee she held on to looked like it had gone cold hours ago.

'Goodness, Asha, when did you last sleep?' Sarah exclaimed.

Jonathan ushered them in and shut the door behind them.

Asha looked at them as if she was trying to formulate her thoughts but couldn't. She was jittery, her lack of sleep and coffee intake had clearly upset her state of mind. They shut the door behind them and watched her walk back into the living room.

'I'm going to make some hot drinks. You speak to her,' Sarah urged, making her way to the kitchen.

Jonathan followed Asha into the living room, which was a mess. Several half cups of coffee lined the tables and the floor. There were milk bottles positioned beneath each windowsill.

'In case anyone tries to break in,' she explained as Jonathan stared at them, mouth agape.

'Asha, that's what the alarm system is for.' He gazed at

her, worried. He wondered if helping the dwellers was worth Asha losing her mind.

'My dad's away on business for two nights and Mrs Redding is not in for the next few days so I'm home alone. I've been staying awake.' She stood in the middle of the room clutching the mug in a death grip. 'The coffee is helping.'

'What are you staying awake for?' Jonathan asked, perplexed.

'Them. In case they come,' Asha said, walking to the window to glance outside.

'You need to get some sleep, Asha,' Jonathan urged.

'I can't – they'll get me.'

'Has anyone sent you anything else?'

'No. Not really.' Asha's eyes darted between Jonathan and the window, which looked out to the driveway.

'So what is it?'

'Someone has been following me, been here watching me. They haven't left me alone,' she whispered, wrapping her arms around herself as though cold. Jonathan glanced anxiously at the door awaiting Sarah's return. Asha needed to calm down.

Sarah walked back in with three mugs of hot chocolate. She placed one in front of Asha and firmly moving away her cold mug of coffee. She looked at Jonathan and he shook his head abruptly. Jonathan was now concerned and wanted to keep the news they had from Asha until the facts were verified. She was in a strange state and he worried false hope might tip her over the edge.

'Sarah...' he began.

'We've got very good news, Asha,' Sarah began. Jonathan thought it considerate that she was desperate to share the news and alleviate their friends suffering but he had become uncertain. He shot Sarah a warning look which she ignored.

Asha looked expectantly from Jonathan to Sarah with dark, staring eyes, but Jonathan hesitated, not happy with telling Asha the news until the police had been informed and they knew the whereabouts of these Billy Bragg and Dante Silva characters. Sarah continued, regardless.

'I know who has been doing this – we both do. The visit to Kitty Heathridge was worthwhile and we learnt so much.' She gestured to Jonathan who flinched. He didn't want to be included in the conversation.

He walked to the window and gazed out, feeling Asha's eyes on him.

'Go on,' Asha whispered.

'Jonathan thought we should wait but I don't agree.'

He glowered at Sarah from the corner, wondering why she was so impetuous at times.

Asha patiently waited for the answer that might make her demons go away.

'His name is Billy Bragg. He has a friend, a Dante Silva. We've just come over from Wimbledon where we met this girl Kitty who was threatened by Billy Bragg. He was wearing that same mask seven years ago. He was chasing a dweller at the time. We think. It all fits.'

Asha sat back in her seat, pondering this new information. A look crossed her delicate dark features; Jonathan recognised it as relief.

'Thank goodness.' She put her head in her hands. 'So what happens now?'

'We're going to let the police know about it. He sounds really dangerous. We just thought we should tell you first.'

Jonathan thought it was best to chime in before Sarah got carried away. '*If* the police can do anything about it. We have no evidence that Billy or Dante did anything here and even if they did the police are going to be looking for evidence of some sort.'

Sarah's eyes widened. 'The note?' She turned to Asha who began to jump up and down excitedly. Jonathan was surprised she had the energy to do so.

'I still have it,' she screamed excitedly, shattering the quietness of the house.

'Oh – you and Jon are the best friends anyone could wish for.' Asha hugged Sarah tightly.

Snippets of their conversation drifted back to Jonathan who gazed idly out of the window in discontent, sipping his hot chocolate. He gritted his teeth. He was annoyed with Sarah; she had always been so impulsive, so spirited. As he glowered he noticed the lone figure standing a few doors down across the street, by the lamp post outside number twenty-five. It did not try to hide itself, nor did it move when it realised Jonathan had caught sight of it. In fact, it moved beneath the full beam of the light. Jonathan calmly sipped from his cup. It was a boy with dark brown hair with an athletic frame and wearing dark clothing. In his hand was a partially obscured mask of alabaster white. Jonathan wondered what it meant. Was showing up and letting himself be seen a warning to them to keep away? Then a flash of anger went through him. How dare he think he could turn up and intimidate Asha and the rest of them? Sarah was right; the sooner the police were informed, the better. Jonathan glanced up and noticed the darkness slowly gathering in the skies; a snowstorm was on the way. When he looked back down he saw the figure was gone and the street was empty once more. He realised he might have just caught his first unhindered glimpse of one of the Mimes, but that did not fill him with any satisfaction.

CHAPTER 7

*B*ogsley knew he'd been grumpy of late. He took no satisfaction from his famous soups, which were rather popular down below, nor did he enjoy his fishing trips with Fred and Hiller. Darkness surrounded him and penetrated his heart. It was night-time and he briefly considered going for a long walk in the world above where the snow was beginning to fall once more. But he remembered what he had promised Asha, Jonathan and Sarah – the dwellers were to remain out of their world whilst they searched for Kee's Corner. This was proving a rather difficult task for Bogsley; he did not wish to see his fellow dwellers nor did he want to converse with them. The atmosphere between him and the rest of his immediate community had grown increasingly strained in the past few days and Fred was doing his best to build bridges between them all. The cheery greeting that came from the Hootch family next door was no longer welcome or reciprocated. He had also rejected invitations to tea and cake from Emily – and everyone knew she was one of the finest bakers around. Bogsley's discontent with his people stemmed from

news received when Asha had paid them a visit, unbe-
known to her friends.

That last visit from Asha had been brief but revelatory.
She had come alone and, with a glimmer in her eye, told
them the others had important business to attend to in a
part of London referred to as Wimbledon. Although she
came with good news her demeanour showed much had
happened in her world. There was a tiredness and fatigue to
the young girl he had not seen before. She had aged before
his eyes. Yet she spoke happily, telling a tale that sounded
familiar. The others crowed with delight at the news that
they were a step closer to Kee's Corner, cried with alarm
when she recited the story of the Mime chasing the dweller,
and looked impressed when informed the dweller vanished
into thin air, wondering with great interest which one of the
residents that would have been. Then with bated breath she
gave them a name – the name of a Mime. Billy Bragg. It was
a male name Bogsley did not recall but the news did not fill
him with cheer. All were excited with the exception of
Rufus, but nothing ever seemed to cheer Rufus up these
days. It had been many years since they had seen him smile.

But when the rest of the party cleared and they were
left alone, Bogsley had pulled Asha aside and talked to her,
keen to discover what was haunting her, why she looked like
she had been avoiding sleep and had lost her peace of mind.

'It's nothing,' she'd said, a wry smile on her lips.

Bogsley, although the most jovial of his circle, was not to
be put off that easily. 'Please, Asha. What troubles you? I
sense a darkness surrounding you.'

The girl had looked around and, ensuring they were out
of earshot of anyone else, revealed to him the most
disturbing story of what had occurred in the past few weeks.
Bogsley faltered, troubled that those who had chosen to

help them were coming under attack themselves. Was this not what they hoped to prevent? The Mimes would be so busy looking for the dwellers that they would fail to notice the human element in their world. Their new friends were supposed to be impermeable to the wills and follies of the Mimes. They were supposed to help find Kee's Corner and that would be it. Now, by aiding the dwellers in their search for Kee's Corner they found themselves hounded and targeted in ways no creature should have to endure, dweller or human. It was on the tip of Bogsley's tongue to call the counsel back to the square and tell them what had befallen those who had come to their aid, those who were supposedly never to have come to the attention of the Mimes but Asha, the kind sweet girl, had stopped him.

'Look, Bogsley. What's done is done. The Mimes targeting me has nothing to do with you or the others or even my friends. That is simply what they do and who they are. They're a bunch of bored teenagers who have nothing better to do. We're a step ahead of them, however. Now we have a name we'll let the local constabulary know what's happening. We have evidence,' she announced more cheerfully.

He thought Asha so brave to speak the way she did. His mind returned to Hiller and how he and Fred would be in pieces if the young pup was ever presented to them in such a grotesque manner as the cadaver of the deceased dog had been to Asha. However much he felt she and her friends suffered for the dwellers' plight, Asha implored him to be silent and not reveal the truth to the others; she thought they would be disappointed and more than likely terrified. So he had carried the secret with him those past days but, like most burdens, it affected his physical wellbeing and Bogsley grew sullen and detached.

He was ambling along Ooons Alley late that evening, feeling morose, when he felt himself gain an unwanted companion. He turned. It was Fred. Bogsley turned back and kept walking, hoping Fred would leave him be.

'Bogsley,' Fred said in a low voice. 'What ails you, my friend?'

'Leave me.' Bogsley, although usually of a cheerful disposition, felt anything but and he had his brethren to thank for that.

'What pains you so?' Fred continued, trailing him as Hiller paced behind him, lingering to sniff at whatever he could. He was still without a collar and lead.

Bogsley slowed to a halt and spun around. Fred should be the last person he was speaking to.

'You ask what troubles me...' He faltered. A promise had been made to Asha and he could not break it. Bogsley, although aggrieved, would never be the one to betray a confidence.

Fred glanced at him with a steady eye. 'Forgive me, friend, for I should not have asked such a foolish question of you. I know what saddens you and it troubles me too.'

'How could you possibly know?' Bogsley asked, then he stopped. Fred himself had been quiet those past few days. Could it be that he knew?

'You worry about the people who undertake this perilous task for us because they themselves have come under the scrutiny of the Mimes.'

Bogsley's jaw hung as Fred continued. He had no idea his friend was so astute.

'I saw it in the girl when she came. They hunt her like they do us. Her eyes, her movements are those of someone who is being watched. She came without her trusted companions because she didn't want them to know she was making the journey here alone to see us because they would fear for her safety. After all, it's these very woods the Mimes stalk in their search for the entrance to our world. The girl did not have to say she was being hounded. I could see it in her.'

Bogsley heaved a sigh of relief, glad that he was not the one to reveal his thoughts but he had instead been read – and very easily too.

'If the Mimes hound her, Fred, then surely for their own safety we must tell them to stop their search for Kee's Corner and carry on ourselves.'

'Yes, that would be the noble approach, but I fear now they will not listen. They are too involved and they have made more progress in a few weeks than we have made all these years. They have another name, Bogsley,' Fred said imploringly.

Bogsley understood his friend's frustration – to have come so far and be so close to finding Greenbottom, Flydro and the rest of the inhabitants of Kee's Corner only to advise the search be called off seemed impulsive at best. Fred was correct when he stated he did not see Asha or her friends abandoning it.

'When they return – since we have been forbidden from going above – I shall be the one to tell them what we know.'

'Of the girl? Of Nanette?'

'Yes. Hopefully the knowledge they will then possess will keep them safe.'

'Everything?' Bogsley was adamant there were to be no conditions.

'Everything,' Fred responded ruefully. 'The good and the bad, so shall it come.' He looked up at Bogsley with his dark eyes and when he spoke again his voice was grave.

'However, one thing we must remember is that the revelation of what we know might put them in even more danger than they are now.'

'How so?' Bogsley asked. Asha, Jonathan and Sarah were smart and he trusted them to be careful with what was divulged to them in confidence. 'They have brains, Fred. They'll know how to handle such matters.'

'I do not doubt they are intellectually gifted, Bogsley, but what happens when we tell all we know? The knowledge will only make them want them to enquire further and that will take them to that place, the one we never speak of. What do you think will become of them then?'

Bogsley nodded sombrely. He understood Fred's words but his mind was resolved to revealing the truth. They owed them that much.

'We have underplayed how dangerous the Mimes are for our friends' own benefit so they don't feel fear and can go about their business with ease, but the more they know the more entangled they'll become.'

Bogsley looked his friend steadily in the eye. 'Do we tell them the reason why the runners were after us?'

'Heavens, no.' Fred shrank back. 'That sort of knowledge is dangerous and would ensure we were never left alone again.'

Fred's sentiments were understood. The humans would only be told what they needed to know to keep them safe. The circumstances that had led to the dwellers' pursuit by the runners would be taken to their graves.

≈

*A*lthough Jonathan was nervous he felt confident about what he was going to say. He was in his father's study because he felt that making the call from there would give him the strength and coherence he so desperately needed. He picked up the handset and dialled the number, his heart skipping a beat as it began to ring. He swivelled the chair around so he was looking out of the window, watching the snow which had begun to fall again. A woman answered.

'St John's Wood police station?' She sounded gruff and a bit irritable.

'Hi. My name is Jonathan Stapleton. I live on The Bluefields in Hampstead and I wish to file a report please.' He held his breath. She sounded bored when she spoke again.

'What is the nature of your query?'

'My friend is being threatened by an individual.' He doubted the dog's corpse would still be fresh but they had the note with the blood smears and that had to be enough. 'They also put a dead dog's corpse on her doorstep.' He added for extra measure.

'Please hold,' the woman said. Jonathan finally breathed normally again, glad she did not end the call.

There was a brief silence and then a man came on the phone.

'Hello. Is this Mr Stapleton?'

'Yes.'

'I am Sergeant King. You say your friend is being threatened and she had a dead dog left on her doorstep?'

'Yes – it was a dead dog that had been mutilated.' Jonathan gave a quick thank you to the Stapleton home library for enabling him to have such an extensive vocabulary. 'And yes. We have an idea who the person might be.'

'Oh...'

Sergeant King sounded interested and Jonathan could tell he was taking notes. He wondered if it was normal practice for the police to take random callers with such wild claims seriously. Delighted he had the sergeant's ear, he continued.

'Yes, I strongly suspect it may be a Billy Bragg of Wimbledon. He will have an accomplice known as Dante Silva.' He held his breath as he heard the man taking notes. 'The other day – Saturday morning – I went to see the friend who was being subjected to their threats and saw someone I thought might be Billy Bragg watching us from across the street. He just stood there bold as brass. Apparently they've been following and watching my friend's home for a while now.' Jonathan realised it might have been Billy or Dante but decided to go with the former.

'Hmm... This is something that will have to be discussed in person. Where do you live?'

'Hampstead, sir.'

'I can send an officer round—'

'It might be best for me to come in to the station,' said Jonathan quickly, imagining the terrifying situation of police officers and his father coming into contact. 'We are constantly in and out of the house due to Christmas preparations.'

'Okay – can you come in to the station as soon as possible? I'm away from this evening for the Christmas break.'

'Yes, as soon as I can. I'll try to be there within the hour.' Jonathan felt oddly jubilant that he had got a chance to speak to someone at sergeant level and instantly disregarded his reservations. He put the receiver back in the cradle, almost doing a little jig.

His brother Sam was putting his jacket on in the hallway when Jonathan walked out.

'Are you heading out?' He glanced quizzically at Jonathan's heavy coat through dark brown eyes.

'Yeah, St John's Wood.'

'Oh – how is Asha these days? Are you all good now? I hear the cold war is over.'

'Yes. She's good, thanks. But I'm going to the police station first before popping over to hers.'

As soon as the words were out of Jonathan's mouth he bit his lip, cursing himself for being so careless. Sam paused, a look of warning on his face.

'Why? What's happened?'

'Nothing.' Jonathan groaned inwardly – why couldn't he have made a good excuse?

'If you're in trouble you'd better tell me. Dad would kill you if you did anything stupid.' Jonathan never forgot the reason they were all so cautious. His father was the reason: a prominent lawyer, very well known and respected. He had a reputation for being ruthless in the courtroom but treated his family the same way. Jonathan had never known where Frederick Stapleton the lawyer ended and his father began. He had always been very frank on the topic of disgrace being brought on the family, once kicking Tyler, the oldest, out for being caught smoking on school grounds. The Stapleton boys at ages seventeen, nineteen and twenty were terrified of their father with Sam and Tyler only returning home for the holidays from university when their mother pleaded with them. Tyler, who had initially regarded university as a chore, now viewed it as an escape from their domineering father. Their mother had been demoralised and browbeaten years before Tyler was even born so always kept silent when any family discussions or disputes were taking place. To appease Sam, who was looking ever more nervous by the minute, Jonathan laughed out loud.

'I witnessed a car accident and have to go and give them some information.'

Sam still looked unsure. He opened the door and they both stepped out into the falling snow.

'Where are *you* going?' Jonathan tried to distract his brother.

It worked.

'The high street – I'm still gift hunting for Mum. Tyler gave me a great idea for a gift.'

'Don't you mean you stole Tyler's idea?'

'The exact details are all very blurry.' Sam had a wide grin on his face. 'Well, good luck getting to The Wood – the bus services have been stopped for now and there's no way anyone is going to drive down the hill in these conditions.' With a laugh he jogged in the opposite direction, skilfully dodging the snow that Jonathan kicked in his wake. Jonathan swore under his breath; he would have to walk. Clenching his jaw determinedly he began the cold journey, anxious to speak to Sergeant King and put the Mimes to rest once and for all.

By the time he had reached the police station he was cold, shivering, exhausted and thoroughly sick of the snow that was now holding the city to ransom. If Jonathan had been given a chance to go head to head with Billy Bragg and Dante Silva at that moment he would have given it a go. The station, like the rest of the buildings around it, was dark, foreboding and built in the late 1800s. Outside, an iron plaque with the word 'Police' written across it in white lettering on a blue background was hanging above the doorway and swinging slightly in the light wind as the falling snow gently buffeted it. There was a tall street lamp glowing as dusk settled, giving the doorway a ghostly feel. Jonathan shivered as he looked through the dark doors but couldn't quite make anything out. He walked up the steps and entered the building cautiously. There was a small, dim waiting area and a woman at a reception desk; the solitary light in the room was the lamp on her desk. He reckoned it was probably the same woman he had spoken to earlier. He approached the desk.

'Good evening.' He waited for her to look up at him but she was engrossed in her magazine. 'Is Sergeant King available?'

Lifting her head she appraised him with great curiosity.

'Who are ya?'

'Err, Jonathan Stapleton. I called earlier and spoke to him, just over an hour ago, and he asked me to come in.' He doubted anyone else but himself would have been desperate enough to call into this particular police station – the place seemed abandoned. She scraped her chair back across the linoleum floor, which caused the hairs to rise on Jonathan's neck. She got to her feet and disappeared around the corner. A minute later she returned.

'Sergeant King will be with you in a second, so if you just wait...' She ducked her head behind the desk to resume her light reading, leaving Jonathan to amuse himself.

He was content just to stare at the walls of the pokey station but did not have a long wait. The sound of heavy feet caught his attention and he saw someone he assumed to be Sergeant King approaching. He was a very tall, broad-shouldered man and had a steely glint in his eyes.

'Outside, please, Mr Stapleton.' His voice was curt with a hint of barely restrained anger. The receptionist, clearly trying to eavesdrop, had cocked her head in their direction.

She wore a slightly disappointed look as Jonathan stepped outside with the sergeant. He walked down the steps to stand in the snow whilst Sergeant King remained on the final step giving him an extra threatening look. Jonathan was tall himself, but Sergeant King was just that much taller, a throwback to the days when police officers had towering height requirements, forcing him to look up at him like a child. To add to his discomfort the wind had picked up.

'When I asked you to come over, Mr Stapleton, I thought you had a valid complaint to make.'

'But I do, sir. It is valid. Threatening notes handed to my friend and dead filthy animals left on her doorstep. She would be here but she hasn't been quite herself of late,' Jonathan said, trying to sound as convincing as possible, but deep down he knew something was wrong.

'Really? And you say this was done by Billy Bragg and Dante Silva?'

'Yes, yes! Absolutely certain. I saw him with my own eyes.' Jonathan did not bother explaining which of the two he meant; they were probably just as culpable as each other.

'The same Billy Bragg of Pemberton Estate in Earlsfield?'

'Yes. I assume so.' Jonathan thought it through. There could not be that many Billy Braggs in trouble with the law, so he nodded. 'Yes, it must be. The same chap who was threatening people on the Common a few years ago.'

'According to our records Dante Silva has been at Greystone for the last four years.'

'Where is that?' Jonathan was puzzled, trying to understand what the sergeant was saying. He had heard of Greystone but could not remember where or in what context.

Sergeant King sighed irritably.

'Greystone is a Category A prison on the Lincolnshire borders.' The sergeant's voice took on the tone of someone speaking to a person who lacked a great deal of understanding. 'He is there for the next ten years then he will be due for release.'

'W-what's he in for? What is the nature of his crime?' Jonathan asked, head reeling furiously. Prison! He tried to understand but he was too confused. Sergeant King was still talking.

'Beat someone to death.'

Jonathan came back to reality with a start.

'B-b-but we were so sure Dante was involved,' he insisted.

There was a brief silence between them.

'Prison!' he exclaimed aloud. 'Billy Bragg is working with others then. We've seen them together, combing the parks – heard them.' He was adamant the sergeant listen to him, but he was looking more enraged as the seconds passed.

Sergeant King rolled his eyes. 'Look, I'm going to assume that you really didn't know and you are genuinely not trying to waste police time. But before you go pointing fingers at people, make sure it really is them. Now – do you want to file a report for this friend of yours...'

The sergeant's voice sounded distant again. Jonathan thought hard, realising he was out of his depth and wishing Sarah or Asha had come along with him for support. It was his fault – he'd been insistent on coming on his own. Christmas Eve was a week away and everyone was in the midst of preparations for the season and suddenly busy. Jonathan wondered what Asha would want him to say if she were here. He could no longer say that people in masks were after them, could he? He would sound a bit unhinged if he gave the sergeant the entire spiel. He could not conveniently refer to the Mimes without bringing up the dwellers. How could he explain he and his friends being in the park out of opening hours? Didn't that act alone count as trespassing? The irritated police officer was slowly and surely taking his story apart.

'Is your father Frederick Stapleton, the lawyer?'

The mention of his father's name brought Jonathan back to reality.

'Yes, he is,' he responded; his chest went cold.

The decision had been made for him. He would have to remain silent. If the sergeant knew of his father they had been in contact at some point and the last thing he needed was the concerned police officer speaking to him about Jonathan's comings and goings.

'Ah, I thought so. Your father is a great asset to the legal system in this country.' Sergeant King came down from the final step and held his face mere inches from Jonathan's. 'I do urge you to be careful, Mr Stapleton. I'm not sure how a young man like yourself has come to be involved with the Billy Braggs and Dante Silvas of this world but you need to tread very carefully. Those are dangerous and corrupting influences.'

The meaning behind those words was ominous, and they hung in the air between them. Jonathan knew he was being warned off. But there was still one question left unanswered.

'Okay, sir, so Dante has been in Greystone all these years and could not possibly have committed any crimes.' Jonathan idly wondered if it would be possible to break out of prison but shook the silly thought out of his head. If he was going to be taken seriously, he would have to maintain an air of maturity and common sense.

'Exactly.' The steely glint returned to the sergeant's eye.

'But how about Billy Bragg?' Jonathan made one last attempt. Why was Sergeant King being so difficult? If it could not have been Dante following Asha it must have been Billy.

'Billy died in a fire seven years ago.'

CHAPTER 8

*R*eading about the premature death of Billy Bragg made for a very depressing afternoon in the public library. There was an abundance of literature concerning the young man in the Wimbledon papers – he seemed to have become something of a local anti-hero. Born into a large family in Earlsfield to clearly unfit parents, his family were no strangers to the police and social workers who were always making visits to their cramped little flat. By age seven he had been taken away from his parents because of concerns for his safety and placed into foster care. By the time Billy was ten he had been arrested more times than he could count; his reading and writing was poor for a boy his age and he thus fell behind at school. After launching a particularly vicious assault on a fellow student he was permanently excluded from the system, eventually resurfacing at a special school. A decent future did not appear to be on the cards for Billy because he kept getting arrested. His foster parents eventually decided that he was too much of a risk to the rest of the children in their care and, for reasons no one could explain, he was returned to his biological parents and his old home, the place where it seemed most of his torment stemmed from. It all came to a head one night when police were called to Earlsfield by a concerned neighbour and arrived to find the boy badly beaten by his own mother. After being examined in hospital Billy was taken away by the police rather than social services, but the newspaper articles made no mention of where he ended up.

His sad life took a more positive tone a few years later, according to the articles: by age twelve, Billy Bragg had finally stabilised under local mentorship schemes which exposed him to role models that helped him come to terms with his anger and abandonment issues, giving him a future as a responsible young man. There were pictures of him in the local paper, hailed as a success story at age fifteen, standing with some of the local judges and magistrates and others who Asha assumed had been part of the mentoring process. The next story about Billy Bragg was almost three years later and was given just three column inches in the paper, stating he had died from first degree burns while committing arson. It seemed a welcome relief to the residents of Wimbledon Common whom, if it was to be believed, he had terrorised for almost a year. The circumstances surrounding his decline were murky with the blame laid on drugs and alcohol.

Billy's friend and close companion Dante Silva's story was sadly similar. His father had died when he was very young, and his mother had brought him over from the West Indies at age five. He had been very angry from his youth. He and Billy had both attended the same special school which was where they had become firm friends. It seemed Dante's mother had been as incapable as Billy's parents according to a few lines in the paper stating she was known to police for offences ranging from prostitution to drug dealing as well as beating her young son. Billy and Dante had both had a change in fortune with the mentorship schemes which were implemented but both, it appeared, had fallen apart shortly after.

Asha read the articles with a mixture of disbelief and sadness. She was saddened that anyone should be failed by their parents – yet felt a heavy blow after all the expectation; Billy was not the person following her or behind the carcass and frightening note. She was sitting with Sarah and Jonathan in the reading rooms of their local library. It was full for a weekend. Asha had been naive enough to begin the search in the Ark House School library but was sharply informed by the librarian that newspaper article searches not linked to education would not be found within its walls.

What she had now found, though, left her morose.

'I don't understand. They weren't bad their entire lives. Billy changed – they both did. They actually had a future.' Asha's voice tailed off. She was miserable; she sat upright on the chair in the archives library. It was bad enough that their only link to the Mimes was gone but the story surrounding the boys' lives was heartbreaking. She gazed at Sarah; they were both at a loss to explain what they had just read. Billy had started off with a life that would have been a nightmare for anyone, had been put into a system that was clearly overburdened and could not cope with an extra child, and then had his life changed by people who cared enough about giving him a bright future. So why had he thrown it all away?

Asha sat back and gazed across the table, lost for words and truly despondent. Jonathan was opposite her with his head on the desk. Her heart went out to him. Whilst she was at home being terrorised he had been running around trying to find out what was going on and to what end, but all he had done was to draw the attention of the local constabulary as well as that of his father who was beginning to ask questions about his movements.

Sarah, seeing she was saddened by the turn of events, put her arm around her shoulders. 'Best not to dwell on it, Asha. They did what they did.' Her voice was brusque. 'It is sad and unappreciative of them to throw so many opportunities away.'

Sarah glanced at Asha then Jonathan and then, as though deciding it was best to leave them to their despair, started gathering the papers together. Asha got to her feet and began to help her.

'I'm sorry. I guess I shouldn't be so down about all this but it's so odd, isn't it? There must have been something that sent them both off track. They weren't always bad.' Asha knew it was trying of her to keep going on about the two boys but, as Jonathan had divulged after his humiliating conversation with the sergeant, Dante was behind bars for very violent reasons.

'Come on, Jonathan. We might as well leave. We're not going to find out much else and this place is getting me down,' Sarah said jovially. She disappeared into the aisle.

Asha watched Jonathan reluctantly get to his feet and begin putting the papers away. They all played different roles in their friendship circle and balanced the slew of personalities that being in a friendship group involved. Asha liked to think they could be rated on a scale of brazenness with Sarah being at the far end, while she came somewhere in the middle and Jonathan was at the opposite end of the scale. He was the most restrained of the group; whilst Sarah and Asha were impulsive, Jonathan was cool and level headed. There was something else she could not fathom about her friend, though; his demeanour had changed and she suspected it was not just the disappointing news about the Mimes that ailed him.

Sarah returned to join them and Asha motioned her to the side.

'What's wrong with Jonathan? I've never seen him so down.'

Sarah shrugged, brushing it off in her candid manner. 'He will be. Jonathan feels he's failed us all even though that's preposterous.'

'That's ridiculous. None of this is his fault.' Asha cursed inwardly, blaming the day they became entangled with the Mimes.

'He probably also misses that girl, Kitty. It's been a week since he's seen her,' Sarah mused.

Asha had heard quite a lot about Kitty. She knew Sarah had found her peculiar but it was that same peculiarity that had drawn Jonathan to her. She snapped back to reality, continuing to return the borrowed material to the shelves. When they were done they paused for a moment of clarity as the dust settled around them.

'What shall we do now? We're no closer to finding out what's happening,' Sarah said.

Asha sighed in frustration, kicking at the carpet with her shoe. 'I know. We're at a bit of a dead end and I don't know what to do. We haven't got anything to tell the dwellers now.'

Jonathan nodded in agreement. 'We just carry on until we have something concrete from Kee's Corner.'

'Well, what strikes me now is we don't know who is after me – we thought it was Billy and Dante but clearly not. We have another name from the dwellers, Nanette, but there's no mention of anyone like that in any of the papers and I've done a search. We're no closer to discovering who these Mimes are,' Sarah added.

Asha chose to look on the bright side. There was good news amongst all the doom and gloom. 'We might not know where the Mimes are but we do know we've found Kee's Corner somewhere below the expansive region that is Wimbledon Common. Once we send the dwellers back to their world in 1821, the Mimes will have nothing to chase after and perhaps they will simply return to terrorising people on the streets and leave us be.' To her it was all very simple.

Jonathan nodded. He pulled her to one side. 'I should tell you something.'

Asha stilled. She knew from her friend's tone it was going to be information she would not like. 'What is it?' she asked, her voice catching in her throat. Sarah shuffled away and disappeared from view as though expecting a storm.

'Jonathan?' Asha probed. 'Tell me.' She had never seen the usually confident boy look so uncomfortable.

'That day we came to yours to give you the news after we saw Kitty Heathridge and she later called to give us the names...'

'Yes, yes.' Asha nodded impatiently. Jonathan was being intentionally slow. 'Just spit it out.'

'I saw him waiting outside your house. A boy about my height, dark brown hair, dark eyes – he was holding a mask. We saw each other but not once did he try to hide.'

'What? Why didn't you tell me? We could have given chase or followed him,' she yelped.

'I know but I thought we had their names. I thought it was all sorted since we knew who they were, but as it turns out we were... I was wrong.' Jonathan swallowed, wincing as she shot him a sharp look.

'So they aren't even afraid to show up outside my home and be seen?' she cried, attracting annoyed glances from the other library users. Asha's concern and fear grew.

Jonathan faltered. There was something else at the tip of his tongue. Asha was worried.

'What is it?' she asked wearily.

'He didn't look... I don't know... he didn't seem dangerous. He looked normal.'

Asha gazed at him in stupefaction. 'They aren't exactly going to go around wielding axes, are they? If you'd told Sarah and I we could have let someone, perhaps the police, know we were being watched.'

'Yes, but we agreed with Fred and Bog—'

'I know what was agreed. I made the agreement, after all, but this would have nothing to do with them. It was about someone following me and watching my home.' She shuddered at the thought. 'What do you think it means? He didn't try to hide his face,' she wondered.

Jonathan shrugged. Asha was suddenly remorseful about her flash of anger towards him. Jonathan was only trying his best and she was behaving as if even that was not good enough. Sarah, apparently sensing the storm was over, strolled over to join them. Asha was surprised she was handling all the bad news so well.

'It could mean anything, Asha. We'll never know unless we ask him,' Sarah remarked pointedly.

'I'm really sorry, Asha,' Jonathan said. 'If I could have done things differently I would.'

As they headed out of the building Asha's head was riddled with conflicting and confusing thoughts. Who was the boy standing outside her house? Why did he choose not to wear his mask? Why was he not concerned with revealing his identity? Jonathan, who was normally a good judge of character, had tried to reassure her with the rather bizarre explanation that the boy looked normal. What was normal? The problem concerning Asha the most was the rabble that was terrifying the dwellers. Just who were the Mimes and what were they capable of?

~

*T*he boy was having a difficult time. His mother was being burdensome. It had begun when he had returned home late that night, tired, cold and thoroughly dissatisfied with himself. Although he had been wholly unsuccessful with the hunt that day he was getting closer – he could feel it – even the man could see that. Whereas the boy had found the task harmless enough at first, it now disturbed him and he wanted to be done with it; the quicker he finished it the less contact he would have with the man and the rest of the group.

What troubled the boy was not the tracking of the vermin, that was to be expected, rather it was the order the man had given at their last meeting which he had followed almost slavishly. His own actions hounded him. The ruthless manner in which he'd been told to go after the girl who was friends with the vermin, who was aiding them, disturbed him. He wondered what he was becoming. The thought of emulating the rest of the group because of the time spent together was terrifying. They were monsters and he was not. He was just a normal human being trying to survive. *And they aren't?* he thought.

He was confused and needed guidance but none was forthcoming. Lowering his head he rubbed at his temple, agonising over decisions made over the last few days and all at the behest of the man who had disingenuously learned about the girl from him. Quite a lot had been discovered about her. Her name was Asha Saunders, she was adopted, had been a sociable student until a few months ago when her mother passed; however, recently she seemed to have come out of her shell. Her fellow Ark House pupils could not understand what had caused her to break her vow of silence; the boy knew exactly what it was and he was determined to stop it. He gleaned most of his information from hanging around the school gates and jumping into conversation with different groups of students from the school. He had also learned of her two closest friends, Jonathan and Sarah. The rest, he was ashamed to say, had been derived from breaking into the house. The boy watched enough to know the movements of the household. Asha and her father made it so easy for him to learn so much. Their lives were lived in the open even though they would not see it that way; the large bay windows were never shuttered, the drapes always pulled open, meaning their movements could be tracked and with ease. Her father, who was a work addict, was gone early in the morning and appeared later at night, sometimes holing up in his study as he went through paperwork and tomes of hardback literature that surrounded his desk. The man was a partner in a prestigious law firm in the City of London, a role the boy imagined would be moneyed as well as demanding. Asha spent most of her evenings alone playing the piano or being visited by friends, two others he had noticed before.

The afternoon he had spent rooting around the house was when he had come perilously close to getting caught. The housekeeper suddenly arrived and he was forced to spend the next few minutes avoiding her in the house. He finally managed to make a break for it and let himself out of the front door when she was carrying out chores upstairs.

Leaving the evidence for Asha to find the next day was easy for him to do. The man's words echoed in his mind as he had prepared it all, the workflow hindered by the flow of blood staining the paper. The boy worried about leaving evidence behind but realised there was nothing about him on any police database so there was no way anything could be traced back to him or his family.

The boy felt so bad about his actions and the potential fallout from them that he agonised over the next few days. Deciding to return to see if she was all right would alleviate his fears but he found her in a poor state, pacing the house and staring out of the window several times during the day. Then her friends had appeared suddenly and he watched them calming her in the front room. A flash of guilt passed through him. He was responsible for it all. Her friend, Jonathan, the boy who attended the same school as her, was standing at the window to her front room and staring out with a mug in his hand. He looked grim. The boy wondered what troubled him. Then their eyes met and they observed each other. The boy felt a wave of revulsion as Jonathan stood there watching him silently, not bothering to alert the others to the intruder's presence. There was so much contempt in his eyes. The boy understood the sentiment but he was under threat too and could not have his family life jeopardised.

The boy returned to the tall grey tower block he called home that evening exhausted, the thin layer he was wearing still not doing much to fight off the bitter cold. The lift was still not working, which he expected. It was the fourth month in a row, so he hauled his bicycle up six flights of stairs as he normally did, eternally grateful that he was not going anywhere the next day. Avoiding the pool of sick in the corridor he wheeled his bicycle to the tiny poky flat they called home. He left the bike outside and walked into the flat. The smell of burnt food filled the air; he wrinkled his nose in disgust as he moved towards the small kitchen. There was barely enough room in there for two people. He thought about Asha Saunders's vast kitchen with large window, luxury amenities and the beautiful units that lined the walls. Shaking his head grimly he experienced a rush of envy – they would never understand how the rest of them lived.

'Boyce.'

His name. A voice floated out of the kitchen. He walked in. His sister, thirteen-year-old Rebecca, was in there. She looked up on his arrival holding an oven tray upon which were the charred remains of an unidentifiable mound of food.

'I didn't burn this, Boyce. I was in my room and smelt something burning. I came out, *she* was passed out on the sofa and the kitchen was almost on fire.' He could see she had been crying. He quietened her gently and gave her a comforting hug.

'I know how hard you work to bring money in but she ain't done nothing in years.' Rebecca's voice wavered in a mixture of anger and frustration. Her dark eyes began to spill with more tears.

'Hey, don't you dare cry or else you'll set me off too,' he said. He grabbed the oven tray and emptied the contents into the bin, worried that his mother had still not woken up and their council flat had been almost on fire.

The entire block would have been ablaze by now if Rebecca hadn't been home.

'Go to your room and relax for a while. I'll stir something up.'

'Why can't I help?'

'Because the kitchen is too tiny for the both of us,' he retorted and she giggled because it was true. He watched her walk past the sofa where their sleeping mother lay and into her bedroom. He waited for a few minutes and then with a deep, shaky breath walked into the small dingy parlour; he hated confrontations. Their mother was snoring quietly, an empty bottle of gin on the floor beside her. He shook her gently but firmly awake.

'Mum, Mum!' His voice was soft yet determined. She stirred awake, eyes bloodshot, looking disgruntled at being woken from her deep slumber.

'What is it?' she snapped irritably.

'Mum, your dinner was burning.'

'Oh.' Her eyes widened for a second then she let out a snigger. 'Good thing you came along then, son.' He did not like her calling him son. He never had but could never come up with a good enough reason to ask her to stop in case it caused another argument. He sighed in frustration as he got to his feet. She was still drunk. He walked into the kitchen wondering what he could fix for himself and Rebecca, doubting his mother would be able to keep anything down. He threw some chips onto the oven tray and pushed it into the oven. The small freezer was laden with frozen food; he grabbed some iced-up vegetables feeling slightly guilty. He had watched one of those programmes last week about children surviving on frozen meals, and he was trying hard to ensure they ate healthily.

'Ma, why didn't you buy some fresh vegetables?' he whined to no one in particular.

But his mum was standing behind him getting stability from the doorway.

'We don't need all that stuff.' Her breath stank of alcohol, her face looked haggard, her hair was stringy. 'It will all be off by the time Christmas is over anyway.'

'Yeah, but perhaps a little at a time would help.' He was doing his best to be diplomatic.

'Don't talk to me like I don't know what I am doing,' she sneered. 'I brought you two up without the help of your father.'

'Dragged us up more like.' Rebecca had emerged from her room in a flash; he couldn't blame her for hearing every word – the walls were ridiculously thin. 'Always drunk, ungrateful, sneering—'

'Shut up!' her mother shot back.

Boyce tried to calm Rebecca down, his head beginning to throb. This was the sort of argument he was always trying to avoid and he just wanted a quiet night after the week he had experienced. It seemed waiting around in the cold, no matter how many layers you wore, would have a detrimental effect on your health.

He clenched his jaw firmly. The sudden appearance of the Asha Saunders and her friends had thrown things into disarray, and he now found himself with two tasks rather than just the one. He wondered what would happen if she did not do as he wanted and leave the vermin alone. What would the man's instructions be then? So far the others had been left out of their plans and he hadn't let on what he was doing, not because he was afraid of them but more because he was concerned about what they might do to her if their attentions became focused on her. So, rather than using the resources of the others and watching Asha's home and school in shifts, he had taken it all upon himself and the result was the heinous cold he could feel coming upon him. He returned to his kitchen as the argument raged on.

Rebecca, his feisty younger sister, was talking and it seemed giving as good as she got.

'You ain't even got a job, you just sit on the sofa and complain about everything. It's never your fault, is it? Tell me when exactly you last had a proper job, Ma?'

'That's it – get out.' His mother pointed, but she was so drunk she was pointing in the wrong direction.

'I am not leaving. This poxy little flat belongs to the council, not you, and apart from your little hand-me-down income which ain't fit for a dog, *he*,' Rebecca gestured vehemently at Boyce, 'is the one bringing in the money and I go where he goes.' Her eyes flashed.

'Enough. I'll sort it out.' He tried to regain control of the situation and grasped Rebecca by the shoulders.

'I don't like the way she treats you. Why don't you ever tell her the truth?' His sister was almost on the verge of tears, a little girl once more as he gently steered her towards the box room that was filled up by a single bed. He stroked her dark unruly hair.

'We have to try and help her – she's our mother.' He opened the door to her bedroom. 'I don't want you focusing on her. You're only thirteen and have a long way to go. I don't want you ending up like her filled with all that anger, hate and remorse. I don't want you ending up a deadbeat like me being someone's dirty errand boy. I want you to finish school.' He looked back in the direction of the kitchen where his mother was slumped against the door frame groaning to herself. 'I want you to be all right and not end up like Dad, Mum or me.'

Rebecca was crying again, which broke his heart.

'There's nothing wrong with ending up like you, Boyce.' She hugged him and then he ruffled her hair and, in a gruff voice that hid the lump in his throat, pushed her into her room.

'Now get in there before I set her on you.'

Her giggle and smile as the door was shut behind her lightened his mood considerably, so that when he turned to speak to his mother and found her collapsed on the floor in her own sick it did little to dampen his spirits.

CHAPTER 9

DECEMBER 25TH

*C*hristmas dawned on London bringing with it a fresh blanket of snow, covering the city. Whilst the snow quickly turned to sludge in the more central parts of the city, North West London remained very white, very cold and very still.

Asha watched her father's face as he pulled an antique hardback copy of a book she knew he had always wanted out of its wrapping. The look of delight and surprise on his face pleased her.

'My goodness, Asha, how did you manage to lay your hands on this?' He gazed at it in a childlike fashion. 'It's a first edition and worth its weight in gold.' He didn't wait for her to answer and kept talking, delicately holding on to the large leather-bound book. 'It's been so well preserved.' He got up from his chair, still looking stunned, and embraced Asha in a tight hug. She hugged him in return, inhaling the pleasant smell of his aftershave and for that brief second everything was all right. There was no threat from the Mimes and her relationship with her father was as normal as it had ever been. The feeling lasted a very short while – he let her go and returned to scrutinising the book.

'This means a lot to me, Asha,' he muttered absent-mindedly.

She was glad he had not pressed her on its origins. She didn't know what *The Pilgrim's Progress* was about but she had heard it mentioned on more than a few occasions. Spotting it on Bogsley's bookshelf was a rare opportunity; she had asked if he had a spare, knowing her father's love for old books.

Bogsley gave her the most curious look. 'A spare?' He looked slightly affronted that she should think he would have a spare of the book. 'That is a most rare book.'

'I'm sorry.' Asha apologised, believing she had offended him. 'My father likes old books and I've been thinking of a Christmas present for him.'

Bogsley had pushed it into her hands, wanting her to have it as a gift.

Asha cleared her throat and looked at her father. 'Sorry I only got you the one gift. If Mum were here you would have got at least two.' She smiled wanly.

'One gift.' Her father sounded choked. 'This is a lot more than one gift. I have wanted this since I was a little boy. Your mother tried to bid on a copy for me at an auction once but there was too much interest in it.'

Asha smiled and turned to the two small boxes she had in her hand. Gently ripping the light purple wrapping paper off she found it contained a small box. It was too small to be anything other than jewellery. Within it lay a jewellery box with a slim gold watch inside it. Her father was watching her closely.

'It was your mother's. She had set it aside for you to

have for Christmas this year.' He sighed. 'She never got to wrap it though.'

Asha blinked back tears as she gently lifted it out of the box and placed it on her wrist.

'Thank you. It's beautiful.' The second box was larger; it was from her father and contained a bracelet with a message inscribed. *To my dear Asha*, it read, with the date inscribed.

Asha swallowed the lump in her throat, a well of emotion rising within her. There were so many question she wanted to ask him. In the last ten months they had barely spoken and she thought she no longer knew her father. It seemed the perfect moment to rid herself of the angst that had built up between them in the intervening months. She wanted to ask him about Aunt Grace and the telephone conversation she had overheard. She wanted to ask why he had not defended her when her aunt made such horrible comments about her. She wanted to cry and ask why her father had chosen to work almost twelve hours a day since her mother's passing. Asha, most importantly, wanted to ask whether he thought he had made a mistake. Did he have any regrets about choosing her when there were hundreds of other children waiting? Lots more children who looked just like he did. Asha wanted to ask so many questions but remained silent because she was afraid of the answers.

The afternoon was a quiet one in their household, spent fielding calls from relatives and friends who they could not see, joking with each other like they had done in Christmases past – it seemed nothing had changed yet so much was lost. Asha kept the yearly tradition of speaking to Sarah and Jonathan; now they had formed a new bond she was desperate to keep it and not lose them again. She called both of them halfway through the day. Their respective Christmases were the same as ever: in the Stapleton household Jonathan's oldest brother, Tyler, had got into another argument with their father. They had discussed Jonathan's university choices; his father was pushing for Cambridge, his alma mater, although Asha knew Jonathan favoured a gap year. Sam, just two years older than Jonathan, had managed to avoid an inquisition; for once being the middle child had its benefits. The Collidge household seemed balanced and normal – Sarah and her dad had helped her sister Kiki set up her new steam train so it ran through her bedroom whilst her mother had some work to do and had retired to her study halfway through the day.

The final few days in the run-up to Christmas Day had been quiet for Asha. There had been no nasty surprises awaiting her and when she caught up on her sleep she found she was not as nervy or jumpy. She was also certain she was no longer being followed. The realisation that they had reached a dead end was disappointing but there was nothing they could do now; London was at deadlock and, being snowed in, the most they had managed to do was leave Bogsley and Fred a little present which they hoped would not be completely hidden by the snow – or discovered by anyone else.

Asha and her father were looking through his new book in the early evening. Darkness had already descended when Asha felt it. They were being watched. She looked past the French doors into the darkness, but the darkness stared right back at her. She could not see them but they could see her. Her father had noticed her stiffen.

'Are you cold, dear?' She could not possibly be cold – the house was very warm and she had a jumper on but she couldn't tell her father that they were being watched.

'No. I-I'm fine. I just thought I heard something.'

'I didn't hear anything. I'm very old though, my hearing has completely abandoned me.' He chuckled at his frail joke.

'What were you saying about this paragraph?' Asha tried to divert his attention back to the book.

He looked back at the line he was trying to explain. So far he was being very precious with the book and to Asha's amusement was not allowing her to touch it for fear she might damage it. She wished she could tell him that it had been generously gifted to her from folk who lived several hundred feet underground, and had been sitting on an old wooden bookshelf at risk of flood, fire and damp – just to see his reaction. She watched him pore over it with fascination, his dark head moving over the text, his lips moving almost in a whisper as he explained some of the text to Asha.

'Well, these next few lines are particularly poignant – they highlight the need for deliverance—'

The loud anguished wail that pierced the air and filled the room made them both jump; her heart skipped a beat.

'What on earth was that?' Her father was startled to his feet. 'It sounds like some sort of animal,' he said, looking a bit pale, 'in terrible pain.'

Asha jumped to her feet and ran to the French doors, trying to look out of the windows. With a burst of adrenaline she decided to run out and challenge whoever it was watching them, but there was an extra lock on the door and the key was missing. She gazed at it in surprise, wondering when it had appeared.

'Dad. I need to get out,' she said, desperately fiddling with the lock. He looked at her from across the room as if she had lost her mind.

'Asha, I am not letting you out. We have no idea what that thing is.' He walked over to stand beside her as she pressed her nose up against the doors. 'I've had the doors reinforced and an extra lock put in. Some blasted person keeps tampering with the security lights so they don't come on. Or perhaps it's the snow affecting them. Goodness knows we haven't had it this cold.'

Asha kept looking out into the black garden. It was not the snow affecting the security lights; they were being deliberately tampered with and she knew exactly by whom. It was the boy – it had to be. The same one Jonathan had seen, the same one she now knew had made enquiries about her at Ark House School. She knew he was there watching her, she could feel him; the sight of her and her father together had clearly disturbed him. Her father, completely oblivious to her tension, had returned to his precious book.

~

Kitty Heathridge woke up to a snow-filled morning. Gazing out her bedroom window overlooking the Common she chuckled with glee. Tinker loved nothing more than a gallop in the snow. However, more pressing matters needed attending to like breakfast and her father. She jumped out of bed and prepared herself for the day ahead: she donned her riding attire of jodhpurs, warm socks and a thick waxed riding jacket. A lovely breakfast, which her father had made especially for her, was waiting downstairs. Most importantly, Mrs Wimpole, the housekeeper and her former nanny, who had lived with them since she was a baby, had come down to join them. She was suffering from flu and was frail, but she managed to make it out of her room that morning to have breakfast. The house was tastefully decorated, and the warm fireplace had been roaring all morning giving the front room a cosy warm feel. They were expecting some other family members to join them for Christmas lunch. At exactly noon the doorbell rang and their friends and family poured in – an odd mix of people, some of her mother's friends who had become friendly with her father over the years and some of her father's family, all enjoying the day together. They had a lovely, filling lunch, then the serious talk started which was when Kitty excused herself.

Tinker had been in the stables all morning; there was no groom to tend to the horse that day so Kitty would have to deal with her. Pulling her yard boots on she walked out into the surrounding whiteness. The stables were a short walk away and as her boots made large indentations in the snow she looked back the way she had come, feeling almost guilty for disturbing the snow. She let herself in through the large iron gates with her brass key. Some of the horses poked their heads out of their stables as she walked past, looking expectant. Fishing the apples she had brought with her out of her pocket she gave one to each horse, greeting each one by name. Tinker was in the last stall, one of the largest, which Kitty had secured for her. She let herself into the stall. Her father, ever obliging and diligent, had already cleaned, watered and fed Tinker that morning. It must have been rather early. She tacked up and led the horse out into the forecourt of the stables. Tinker snorted contentedly as Kitty mounted and, with a gentle squeeze, walked her out and down the quiet road which would lead to the vast Common.

It was very quiet; not a single person was in sight. No dog walkers or children playing in the snow. Katherine remembered how paranoid the local residents became after the Billy Bragg terror years and then there was that great fire. She cantered Tinker into the snow and the horse gave an excited little kick. Her excitement made her grin to herself; it seemed snow could bring out the child in anyone. They continued down the quiet path, Tinker leaving a trail and snorting excitedly due to the much-needed exercise she was getting. There were bits of snow falling from the tree branches as they passed underneath. Kitty giggled as they landed on Tinker and herself. They rounded the corner to continue down another path. Usually they would ride it on a clear sunny morning but the route was now impassable. The heavy snow had caused the trees to bend over at awkward angles that would make it difficult to ride through. She looked to the path that led to the right, knowing where it would go, and her heart began to beat rapidly. In that moment Kitty realised she would have to come to a difficult decision and it was one she did not favour. She knew she could not let Tinker feed off her fear, she had to be brave for both of them, and the only way to do that was to go down the path to the right. The same one where the incident had happened all those years ago, the same one they had both actively avoided. Grinding her jaw determinedly she turned a reluctant Tinker in that direction. It took all her strength as the heavy sixteen-hand mare resisted, but Kitty was decided and pushed her on firmly, using as much of her legs as she could and turning in the direction she wanted to go.

'Come on, Tinker,' she said out loud, trying to alleviate her fears. Nothing could or would happen now – Billy was dead. Jonathan had spoken to the police sergeant who had confirmed it. Discomfort stirred within her at the thought of Billy Bragg and the intensity with which he had gone after the little man all those years ago. Then she thought of Jonathan, who would be returning soon, and was comforted, a warmth spreading through her. She knew they would be coming back to continue their search. The last time they'd spoken she found him rather downcast and knew he found the news of Billy Bragg's demise disappointing.

As she and Tinker ploughed on into the snow, Kitty kept her eyes forward, trying to focus on what she could see ahead. But as they got closer to the winding path with the water trough at the end, Tinker started to slow and try to turn around, ears pinned back, body tense. It took all of Kitty's strength to keep her going ahead whilst keeping her own nerves under control. After a while it became too difficult even for Kitty; the melancholy that surrounded them, the air of sadness, the dark feeling was too much to ignore. The residents were right to have avoided this place: it was most certainly haunted. Billy Bragg's presence could still be felt here, even now he was dead. Yet there was another presence she could not explain. Was it the souls of the unfortunate people who had lost their lives at this spot? The riding accidents, the sudden heart attacks – perhaps the area had suffered too much trauma and the ghosts of the lives lost still lingered. Tinker began to grow agitated once more and Kitty made the best decision for both of them.

'No, Tinker. We are going to deal with this.' Her voice was firm.

With a strength she did not know she possessed she pushed Tinker on, feeling elated as the horse seamlessly moved from a clumsy trot to a graceful canter. Then the water trough came into view at the end of the path and Kitty felt Tinker's energy changing. She knew a buck was coming before it did and she tried to counter the force by bracing herself, but her petite body was no match for a strapping horse like Tinker, however sweet and mild. Kitty found herself flying through the air, the cold wind shocking her into action – she made herself limp as she crashed into the snow, grateful it was there to act as a cushion. Kitty lay there for a moment then anger coursed through her. She blamed herself. She was the rider and Tinker should never have reacted the way she did. The horse should have taken her cue from her.

Getting to her feet suddenly she brushed herself off. 'You blasted fool. There is nothing to be frightened of.'

But although she blamed the horse for her fall Kitty knew it was not Tinker's fault. As she stood there she sensed them, the whispering ghosts clamouring and calling for her attention. Tinker took a step back and to pacify her Kitty held on to her reins, scared the horse would run off. She gave her a quick reassuring pat as she led her down the path, deciding to walk rather than force Tinker. Something had happened here; Billy Bragg had been trying to hurt someone and it had got out of control. It was obviously the little person he had been chasing who disappeared, the one Jonathan and his friends were searching for. She remembered the violence in Billy's reaction as his quarry got away: it was a murderous rage. It had happened here, but she could not imagine where the little person could have disappeared to in the chase. The shrubs and trees had not changed much in seven years. They had been damaged in the fire but the great oaks still stood. Then Kitty had an idea. She turned to the tense horse.

'You have to be patient with me, Tinker. I'm looking for something.' She poked her head into the undergrowth, craning her neck around to get a better look in the darkness, but the snow had covered everything up and there was hardly any sunlight in that stretch of the Common; the trees blocked out any light, giving it an eerie feel. Tinker began to pull at the reins making the search more difficult. But Kitty kept looking; instinct told her something was here – another presence. She got on her hands and knees, crawling beside her horse, feeling the crunchy coldness of the snow through her gloves. But she kept at it, poking around for several minutes and moving deeper into the brambles and thorns where the little person had disappeared. Then she caught her breath as she spotted a dark spot several metres ahead that the snow had failed to cover.

'There you are,' she whispered. Kitty was not certain if it was something important or nothing at all, but it was revelatory. No riders had come down the trail in years and the only other users of the path were occasional dog walkers who would stride ahead, leaving their companion to sniff contentedly at the dark spot.

It was very well hidden but she managed to get her head through the brambles and tough branches and shrubbery without doing herself much damage. She realised the area *had* changed – a lot of the tall trees had gone. They had been here all those years ago, protecting the entryway, if that was what it was, which was why no one had ever spotted it. The trees that should have lined the path had been removed by some force – she presumed they were destroyed in the fire. A sense of satisfaction tinged with slight worry filled her. She desperately wanted to get through to Jonathan and pass on this most urgent message, hoping it would gladden his spirits. This was a result. It was true Billy Bragg was long gone but she hoped this news would make up for the failure Jonathan was feeling. She quietened Tinker, who was getting agitated again, and walked her to the end of the path. Once the horse became amenable she mounted her, riding her all the way back to the other end of the Common. This meant having to lead her back along the road but Kitty was prepared to take the risk. She decided to return home as quickly as she could; the information gleaned from her morning ride was time sensitive and lives depended on it.

~

*D*own below, the dwellers were happy; they had not experienced such joy in a long time but they were determined to enjoy the day regardless of their troubles. There was much fiddling, dancing and games as they did their best to celebrate as they would have done in their own time. The celebrations in the Unending Canal were being held in the large market square and many dwellers had started their journey early on in the day to be part of the festivities.

The younger dwellers ran through the pathways along the dark waters of the canal, dodging and weaving in and out of the alleyways as they played hide and seek with their dogs. There was a huge Christmas tree suspended over the canal decorated as festively as possible, the muted fairy lights twinkling gently. It glowed in their dim underground home, conveying an enchanting mood.

Inside Bogsley's cottage were his close friends and some family. It was an arduous time for Bogsley who also had family residing in Kee's Corner and the Rose Wood, family not seen in nearly seven years. Yet for all the pain he felt, the dweller tried to push aside his uncertainties and enjoy the day. They were talking excitedly amongst themselves, trying to remain cheerful as the fire crackled in the fireplace. For once Fred and Hiller were nowhere to be seen, having gone off on Fred's Christmas rounds, poking their heads in through the various doors. Hiller would be hoping for as many treats as possible and Fred would be his usual nosy self, whilst bringing seasonal cheer and well wishes.

Bogsley looked down at the basket that had been left for him and Fred; it was covered in a red cloth. It had been discovered the evening before by Perry who, whilst carrying out his rounds, spotted the basket conveniently hidden a distance away. Thinking it a conveniently placed trap they waited for several hours, eventually sending Macintosh to another entrance they knew could be accessed through a large rabbit hole. Watching Macintosh retrieve the basket, they waited with bated breath for the ambush, but none came. When the basket was eventually opened they realised it was a gift from the world above. The note on top of basket read 'To Fred, Bogsley and Hiller. From all of us. S. A. J.' Sarah, Asha and Jonathan. Bogsley lifted the red checked cloth for the umpteenth time and peeked into the basket. It was filled with food: slabs of meat, dried milk, sweets and bottles of ale amongst other things. They had even included a few treats for Hiller. He smiled to himself as he placed the cloth back in its place and slid the basket under the table.

He was distracted by the sight of Rufus shuffling into his cottage looking decidedly the worse for wear. The older dweller was slurring his speech.

'Rufus, it's good to see you looking so relaxed,' Bogsley said with a smile as he got up to meet his old friend. But Rufus looked miserable. 'Cheer up, old friend. It's Christmas. Where's your spirit?'

Rufus simply looked back at him and slumped against the doorway, looking as if he was on the verge of being sick.

'Shall I escort him back to his cottage?' Titus got to his feet looking slightly miffed. He was the youngest in the room so it was only polite for him to volunteer.

'No, you rest up, Titus. You've been keeping watch for the past few days. I'll see to Rufus.'

Bogsley tactfully ignored the relieved look on Titus's face as he put a strong arm on Rufus's shoulder.

'Come now, Rufus,' he said, steering him out of the cottage. 'We'll see you put to bed, old chap.'

They both walked out of the vibrant cottage, Bogsley steadying Rufus who suddenly felt very heavy. It would not be a long walk back to Rufus's cottage. The older dweller lived only half a mile away. Bogsley would be back at the ale in no time.

As they walked they were accosted by jolly dwellers who lined the streets, the smell of strong ale in the air; some of them called out to Rufus and Bogsley. The latter was all smiles but Rufus was his usual surly self. It seemed even with the disinhibiting effects of alcohol Rufus was still unhappy.

'I wish you would put on a smile, Rufus. At least for everybody else. We're having a rather miserable time of late and need all the cheer we can get. Think, before we know it we will be united with Kee's Corner and back in our own time. There will be so much to be thankful for.'

Rufus ignored him as they stumbled onwards, letting out burps every so often and mumbling incoherently to himself. It was unclear what he was saying but Rufus was tormented and the knowledge than an old friend was not at peace pained Bogsley. He tried to engage Rufus in conversation once more as he walked alongside him but to no avail. Rufus was not in the mood to converse. The paths split in different directions as they got closer to the narrow lane where Rufus's crooked cottage was located. Suddenly Edith came running along one of them at speed, almost knocking the two over.

'Careful will you, Edith,' Bogsley called in haste as he narrowly avoided her.

A moment later Binkers came running after Edith, chasing her with what looked like a pail of water. Bogsley rolled his eyes; sometimes the dwellers got quite boisterous at Christmas time. The two walked on for a while longer, taking in Christmas down below in all its eccentric splendour, avoiding the dogs running around with their Christmas hats dangling from their heads. The path they had chosen inclined upwards and when they were high enough the dark still mass of water that was the Unending Canal came into view from above. Some of the dwellers were sitting in the brightly coloured boats sailing quietly down the canal, telling stories. Bogsley paused to watch as a young one stooped over the edge of the canal and placed a boat on the calm waters, pulling it along with a little rope and chuckling with glee as the boat sailed alongside him. Bogsley walked parallel to the child from up high with Rufus a few feet ahead of him.

'Ay, that's a lovely gift you have there, young one.'

The boy looked around to see where the voice had come from.

'I'm up here,' Bogsley called out.

The child looked up at him and smiled shyly.

'What journey is your vessel on?' Bogsley called down to him with a smile.

The boy looked up, still with a smile on his dirty face.

'To freedom. My vessel is going where it can be free.'

Rufus had paused at the boy's words; his head drooped lower, his hat almost upended.

'But we *are* free.' Bogsley tried to put as much conviction into his voice as he could.

'Then why do we always run and hide? Messrs Perry, Macintosh and Titus are always guarding our world.'

Bogsley did not have a suitable response to the question

and was staggered by the gravity of the child's tone. As Rufus began to walk off again with his head hanging lower, Bogsley caught up with him, afraid the damage was already done. They rounded the corner together in silence. Rufus paused outside his door and turned to look at him.

'Thank you, Bogsley. I can manage on my own now.'

'Rufus. Why do you wish to spend Christmas alone?'

Rufus's face suddenly contorted. 'I have been truly terrible, Bogsley. I am an evil person.'

'What could you have done that is so bad?'

'I have hurt you all. I have betrayed you and it pains me.' He broke down on his doorstep, sobbing into his hands, his bottle of ale dropping to the ground.

'Come now, Rufus.' Bogsley led him indoors and helped him sink into his armchair. 'I think you have had too much to drink.' He sat opposite him on a little stool, watching his friend sob with a sinking heart. 'Tell me, Rufus. Pray, tell me.'

But Rufus vehemently shook his head, his body racked with sobs as he put his head in his hands.

Bogsley leant forward and put a hand on his friend's shoulder.

'Get out of here,' Rufus snarled suddenly, catching him off guard; he threw Bogley's arm off.

'What is it that haunts you, Rufus? You act like you're crazed.'

'Devil take you, Bogsley.'

A shocked silence settled between them. Bogsley saw instant regret in Rufus's eyes but he was not to be so easily appeased. Rufus had to learn there were consequences to his actions.

'Bogsley, I—'

But Bogsley, normally good natured, turned on his heel,

astounded by the darkness his friend exhibited, but Rufus had been that way for too long. He tried to remember when Rufus's dark moods had begun – he couldn't recall the older dweller ever being so dark back in their own time. Yes, Rufus was surly but was always kind-hearted. This Rufus of late was consumed by a blackness that could not be shifted no matter what news came their way, even that of Kee's Corner. Without another word he left Rufus's cottage, determined to enjoy the rest of the day. Outside he walked with a group of carollers who were going from one cottage to the next, wisely avoiding Rufus's. Bogsley was not sure how much more of his dark moods the residents of the Unending Canal could handle.

~

It was six o'clock in the evening on Christmas Day. Boyce walked past his mother who was on the sofa once more, fast asleep, still clutching the bottle she had saved for herself for the special day. She had stayed awake long enough to wish everyone a Merry Christmas and enjoy the roast that Boyce had made. It was slightly overdone but he was so proud of himself; he had read the different recipes and bought the ingredients. It had been a simple honey-glazed roast with potatoes. He had decided to forego the turkey as he thought he might be taking too much on and the cost was rather excessive. Most of the income coming from the man was being saved for the future. There would be many more Christmases and festive occasions to come. Rebecca had tasted her first turkey a few Christmases ago and did not particularly like it so it was all very well. It was his first Christmas making the dinner; their grand-mother had always been in charge of it since his mother was always incapable and inebriated. But his grandmother had passed away a year ago, her flat a few floors below taken over by new tenants, leaving him lost and alone. The thought of his mother not being able to cope with Rebecca had caused him to stop feeling sorry for himself and he had snapped into reality, taking on his new role which was to keep Rebecca out of the type of trouble that the young girls in his dreary part of London were accustomed to. He cleared the rest of the dishes to the kitchen. He remembered a Christmas many years ago when Rebecca had just been born. His parents had left the dirty dishes to fester for days, the kitchen had begun to stink and the garbage had piled up. The smell had driven him to the brink of insanity so Boyce had cleared it all up the only way a five-year-old knew how, putting the dirty dishes into bin bags and dragging the rubbish to the industrial bins downstairs. Quite what the rubbish collectors had thought of all the plates in the bin he had no idea. He had learnt responsibility early on and was grateful for that.

Rebecca walked into the kitchen and began to help him clear up, her green paper hat sliding to the side of her head.

'No, Rebecca, sit down and watch some telly.'

'No, Boyce. I want to wash up. You can't do everything, you know, you have to let me help.'

He chuckled.

'Okay, you win. I'm going to pop outside for a minute.' He opened the front door and walked out into the cold air, relieved to see his bicycle still chained up to the balcony outside. The estate was surprisingly quiet for this time of the year but the police crackdown in the last few months had been so severe that it was no surprise. The angry voices coming from the flat next door signalled the start of a fight, but Boyce wasn't worried; the Moriarty boys a few doors down would break it up as they always did. He dodged the few wet spots on the stairs and pushed open the secure door that had been unsecured for so long. He was not sure why but he wanted to be alone; he did not want to be in the flat because he found the sight of his mother sometimes upset him even after all these years.

He sat on a small cement block outside looking up at the night sky. The dim lighting all around him made the stars shine brighter, not detracting from their beauty in the least. He could not remember the last time he had done this – probably as a child, on one of the many occasions he had waited for his father to come home on his release days from prison. The day his father had stopped returning home was the same day Boyce had stopped expecting him to return. He had also stopped looking at the night sky. That had been almost eleven years ago. The estate had changed a lot since then; some of the less salubrious characters had been moved along or arrested or, in some cases extreme cases, killed. There had been a lot of premature deaths; some of the children who had been forgotten had been taken in by social services, a fate Boyce had heard was sometimes terrible.

Somehow, he, Rebecca and his mother struggled on, his mother and sister never getting along and Boyce trying to keep everything and everyone together for the sake of survival and, more importantly, to avoid social services. Rebecca's attendance at school was to be exemplary. There could be no days off school without good reason. Boyce at seventeen was under no legal obligation to attend education. They could not attract the attention of the authorities. They needed to live with their mother since the flat was in her name. They were also both underage – Rebecca was thirteen and he just turned seventeen. He could not apply for aid yet and he wanted a safe environment for his sister, regardless of his mother's antics, because he had seen what happened in unstable families: there was chaos, pain and then eventually the children were taken away. If Rebecca was ever taken it would mark the beginning of the end for her. She was too rebellious, too spirited. She needed to remain with him. He was good at keeping her grounded.

Boyce was unsure why he had no faith in the system but he thought it had something to do with the Queenies and his once best friend Dale, who had a little sister, Charlotte. Boyce usually brought her name up in conversation when-ever his sister mentioned a boy at school but Rebecca always just grimaced and stuck her tongue out in response, which made him laugh. Rebecca would never understand how hard he worked to keep them all together. The Queenies had not been so lucky and chaos ensued once the social workers and police began calling at the residence. Then one day the social workers returned for the last time – for Char-lotte Queenie. Dale was arrested for his role in a robbery a few weeks later. Boyce sighed.

'Wow, Dale, it's been ages,' he whispered out loud. He was not sure when Dale was supposed to be released but he had almost served his time, Boyce was certain of that. He had mixed feelings about seeing his friend again. Very mixed feelings. They would not be able to just carry on as though nothing had happened; they had gone on two very different paths which were very hard to reconcile. Boyce had not seen Charlotte or Dale Queenie in five years, but they were deep fixtures from his childhood.

He caught his breath sharply as slim arms wrapped around his torso from behind. Jumping to his feet he got into a fighting stance. It was his sister, Rebecca. She watched him apprehensively and he laughed nervously.

'Christ, Becca. I almost had a heart attack.' His

breathing steadied. The others had not found him. He was safe. He looked around the estate; his building was hidden from view and he could not see anyone watching them. It was Christmas Day, after all, and he wondered where the others would be. Did they have family? Lives? Homes? He knew nothing of their personal lives and that suited him. Aware his sister was watching him he forced a smile to his face.

'You must get in, Becca. It's freezing out here.' *Act normally*, he urged himself.

'You were out here for so long,' she said softly. 'I heard you mention Dale's name.' He wondered how long she had been standing there. 'Come back in.' He recognised the tone in her voice. She was worried about him. Scared to leave him alone with his thoughts in case... He didn't know what Rebecca feared but he knew she was anxious for him sometimes, scared that one day all the pressure he was under would become too much for him and she would never see him again.

'I will in a minute. Just trying to get some fresh air.'

'I love you, Boyce,' she said, moving forward and clutching him very tightly.

He swallowed. 'I love you too.' Suddenly his throat hurt.

'Come in soon so we can watch a movie. I circled all the good ones in the TV guide,' she said softly as she let him go.

He watched her walk back into the filthy building, glad she hadn't noticed the tears that were lining his eyes. He wiped his eyes with his hands, inhaling deeply to compose himself as he got to his feet. He never wanted Rebecca to see him cry. Looking back up to the sky he jammed his hands into the pockets of his sweatshirt as he walked into the building.

CHAPTER 10

The snow-covered trees flashed past as the car sped down the silent road. London appeared deserted but retained its magnificent beauty under the blanket of snow. Whiteness descended around them, lending a heaviness and peace that showed no signs of abating in the frosty chill that held the city captive. Although it was a holiday the paths and roads had finally been cleared making travel possible, yet the warning of black ice on the roads remained. The beauty was as enchanting as it was deadly, so the car travelling through the isolated roads maintained a low speed, making the journey longer than normal for its occupants. Several accidents were spotted along the way as cars ditched and plunged off the road. The inside of the car was silent and no one spoke. It had been that way for the past thirty minutes: absolute silence with the radio switched off. Mr Stapleton stated he preferred to think on car journeys rather than taint the peace with incoherent babble, or so he called it.

It was Boxing Day and the trio, Asha, Sarah and Jonathan had got a lift with Jonathan's father. Jonathan was

246 | THE DWELLERS BENEATH THE ARCHES

sitting in the front passenger seat whilst his father drove. Sarah and Asha sat in the back seat and were glad for it, particularly when Jonathan's father began to grill him. Asha gazed out of the window, trying to distance herself from the conversation. Becoming involved in Stapleton family conversations was not always a good thing and served no purpose other than to have Mr Stapleton compare his youngest son's achievements to everyone else's. Asha had been witness to those conversations time and time again and she detested watching her normally witty and intelligent friend maligned and put down by his overbearing father, and reduced to a babbling child. Asha usually thought her father was bad, but would then spend time with the Stapletons and recall why she was so grateful to have been picked all those years ago by her parents, the differences between her father and herself aside. So she gazed intently at the passing lamp posts, trees, post boxes, falling snow from trees, scenery – anything. But try as she might to block them out, the words from their conversation kept filtering back to her and infiltrating her thoughts.

'I didn't know you had friends in Wimbledon,' Mr Stapleton pressed.

Asha realised her father had not bothered asking her where she was off to that day. He knew it was with Sarah and Jonathan and was just glad that their differences were cast aside and she was emerging from her period of isolation and depression. He must have seen it as evidence of life after Esther Saunders, a sign that perhaps if his daughter could begin to manifest living and happiness after her mother's death then maybe it was possible he could start to come to terms with his wife's death – to him it symbolised hope for the future rather than the dismal end they had both been anticipating.

'Just one or two, Dad.' Jonathan was trying to be as evasive and vague as possible whilst answering his father's questions.

Asha found the line of questioning rather inane. Surely Jonathan could have friends across London. They would not all be consigned to within a three-mile radius of Ark House School.

'Oh, well I doubt they would go to Ark House, because that would be a bit of a journey, wouldn't it?' Mr Stapleton persistently prodded but Jonathan remained tight lipped.

Asha gritted her teeth and gave her friend a cursory glance. Jonathan was in a mood; she knew he had been kept awake the previous night by his older brothers who had invited friends around for a Christmas night gathering. They would have been loud and boisterous but the Stapleton family home was large enough for their parents not to be affected. Jonathan would not have got any sleep and would have stayed up with his beloved older brothers even though a momentous task lay ahead of them that day. Asha and Sarah had been invited to the Stapleton gathering but it would have been cruel for her to leave her father behind. It was their first Christmas together since her mother had passed and she knew he felt the strain just as she did.

However, receiving a last-minute frantic call from an excitable Jonathan late on Christmas night had been thrilling; it seemed Kee's Corner had been found – or at least he thought so. Kitty Heathridge, who she was yet to meet, had called him moments before to say she had located an entrance that was not part of the Common. It was not very clear what sort of entrance it was or where it led or even if it *was* an entrance, and could he please go to Wimbledon the next day. Asha had sensed something else in his voice as they excitedly made plans and he spoke at great length about Kitty and her find, but she could not fathom what it was; either way he seemed enamoured with the girl. Asha was not a jealous person by any means but she felt a flicker of resentment stirring within her at the thought of this Katherine Heathridge and the new role she was to possibly play in their lives. She realised it had taken her so long to get her friends back, their quest to save the dwellers being the force that brought them together, and she did not want anything else coming between them, Kitty or otherwise. She snapped back to the present when she realised Sarah was frantically gesturing towards her.

'I'm sorry, what?' she stuttered in confusion.

'How did you come to meet this Katherine girl?' Mr Stapleton had turned his interrogation to her.

Asha realised Jonathan had used her name in a little fib to his father about how the mysterious girl from Wimbledon had come to be in his life. It was a good point to intervene before his father got any more aggressive with his questioning and would give some Jonathan some much-needed respite; perhaps they would once more settle into the uncomfortable silence of moments before which was much preferred.

'Oh, Kitty. She's a girl.' Asha realised it was not enough. 'Who is a friend of mine. I introduced her to Jonathan and Sarah.' She tried to lighten the mood as Jonathan was reduced to unintelligible grunts, distractedly looked out of the window. Asha hoped his father would not emerge from the car to meet Kitty, otherwise it would be a most uncomfortable conversation and she did not like looking silly.

'Ah, I see.' Mr Stapleton glanced at Asha in the rear-view mirror. His dark eyes showed he did not believe her story. 'Just make sure your school work is unaffected, Jonathan. It's the wrong time to be making new friends.'

It seemed her explanation was not good enough. She wondered if there ever was a right time to make friends. Mr Stapleton worked in a different way to the rest of the human race; he was a man of very little emotion.

Asha sat back in her seat and lapsed into silence, wondering why she had chosen to come along. Being in the same space as Jonathan and his father was always an uncomfortable experience and she usually emerged from it feeling even sorrier for her friend. Sarah gazed fixedly out of the window as though the conversation was not happening, probably regretting her decision to enter into the inquisitory cell that was Jonathan's father's car. They could have taken the underground but Mr Stapleton was giving them a lift to Wimbledon as he was on his way to a lunch with a client in Putney. Although it was against their better judgement Jonathan had thought it best to accept the lift. This decision had not been made lightly; it was not just to save time and avoid the half day's journey across London in the snow. It was also to ensure they were not being followed. After Jonathan's encounter with Sergeant King and what he had learnt they were all being extra vigilant. The Mimes were no strangers to violence, prison or experiences that were out of Asha and her friends' purview. Although Billy Bragg was dead and Dante Silva under lock and key, the rest of the Mimes still walked free and appeared as dangerous and unhinged as the others. Her thoughts returned to the boy with dark brown hair who watched her.

Peace settled in the car once more as Mr Stapleton, Jonathan and Sarah followed her suit and fell into silence, glancing out of the windows as though transfixed and hoping for a swift and painless end to the journey.

Wimbledon was fast approaching, the city having been left far behind, and with that their imminent arrival at the commune. For that good news alone they felt grateful, all their woes suddenly worth that moment when they would reveal to Rufus, Bogsley and the others that they had found their missing friends. She imagined the look on old Rufus's face in that moment when he realised he was wrong about them and they had bested him. A frisson of excitement ran through her. She could feel the apprehension from Sarah and Jonathan. Asha smiled smugly. It was their secret, one Mr Stapleton could not cross examine them about or sully with his cynicism – they and they alone would be aiding the dwellers and they would not need any help in their task.

As the car began to slow to adjust to the narrower village roads Asha gazed excitedly at Sarah and grinned broadly. She was getting ahead of herself and daydreaming of trumping the results of the day with further good news. Perhaps the third part of the commune would be found just as easily, she dared to hope. How difficult could it be? Jonathan locating Kitty had been fairly straightforward, so what if they followed the same trail and looked for similar clues? Even if Kitty's discovery turned out to be nothing there would have been sightings of the dwellers across the vast city, however bizarre the witnesses' interpretations. No one would have been believed it if they reported it; a claim to have seen olden-day dwarves in local woodland would usually get the informant put into the back of an ambulance before being driven to the nearest psychiatric hospital. The dwellers were fairly skilled at hiding themselves and they had not let her see them until they trusted her and were ready. The underground creatures had had a lifetime of practice at hiding themselves; they had done it with the runners in

1821 so would have no trouble concealing themselves now.

Still wrapped up in her happy state of mind she turned her thoughts to how they would go about uniting both worlds with them being so many miles apart and with so few places to hide. Then she realised the fact they were alive and well would be enough for them to know, and they could be reunited back in 1800s London. As Fred had mysteriously informed her, there were ways and means. Asha nervously wondered how much time they would have to themselves before they had to meet Jonathan's father for their lift back to North London. Although the persistent snow fall had stopped, a fresh batch of snow was due that night and they would only have a few hours with Kitty and the commune before they had to meet up with Mr Stapleton again. It was early afternoon already, meaning it would be dark in just a few hours.

Asha felt the car slowing and focused. She pressed her nose up against the glass excitedly. The outline of Wimbledon Common loomed as they approached. The willow trees stood tall under heavy coverings of snow almost transformed, their leaves and branches altered as the snow formed deep trenches around them. The streets were empty; nothing stirred.

'Where do you want to be dropped off?' Mr Stapleton asked, breaking their reverie.

'Anywhere along the Common is great, Dad.' Jonathan's voice had gone from being gruff and unresponsive to light-hearted, but he sounded apprehensive.

Asha exchanged a glance with Sarah in the back seat. She leant over.

'How are you feeling?' Sarah whispered.

'All right. Excited – but I feel like I want to be sick.'

'Yeah, me too.' Sarah sounded grim. Her perception seemed different to Asha's.

'What's wrong?'

'Nothing. Just a feeling.' Sarah shrugged, looking pointedly to the driving seat where Mr Stapleton was glancing at them in the rear-view mirror, his dark eyes narrowed.

Asha did not feel whatever Sarah did – instead she felt optimism. When Jonathan had spoken to Kitty on Christmas night he said she sounded confidently positive. She believed she had found something of magnitude; it was right next to the spot where the dweller had disappeared and Billy Bragg had stopped in confusion thinking his prey had vanished into thin air. Apparently it had not been a clever vanishing act, but rather a very well-concealed entrance, or so Kitty thought. London had not had heavy snow in over ten years and Asha believed the presence of the commune was what had exposed the dark spot Kitty had seen. Regardless of Sarah's misgivings Asha was resplendent with joy. Kee's Corner after much agonising was discovered.

≈

Sarah was not one for negativity but she felt an ominous presence she could not shake off. It had begun all those weeks before when Yu had been pushed to the ground. Asha had shared the same anxieties. Now Asha was full of positivity and enthusiasm and when Sarah mentioned her misgivings to Asha, her friend was quick to push them aside.

'Sarah, you've never been this cautious. We're getting somewhere, it's good news. We've found the missing commune. Well, Kitty has, anyway.' Asha's voice was snide.

Sarah noticed the way her friend waspishly pronounced Kitty's name; there was a hint of grudge, betraying the obvious envy Asha felt about Kitty joining their friendship group just when they were becoming reacquainted.

Now she gave her old friend a sideways glance. Asha had dedicated the last few months to helping the dwellers; it had become her sole purpose. School work, activities, even their social lives had been set aside in her quest to do what was right by them, but Sarah secretly wondered why she was so fixed on Fred, Bogsley and the others. It was true that they were in a quandary and being hounded by forces unknown to them. Their stories of 1821 London were terrifying to hear and she felt for them and would do whatever she could to help, but Sarah still felt resentment towards Asha and it refused to go away. No sooner would her friend mention the dwellers than she would recall Asha returning to them that cold winter afternoon pleading with them to help her and these new creatures who had come into her life. And for that reason Sarah felt used. It was not a feeling she had expressed openly but one she endured alone. Jonathan would not understand – he was just glad to have his old friends back – anything was better than having to spend the evenings and weekends after school at home with his mother and father. Sarah flinched as the venom in her thoughts hit her. When had she become so miserable, so bitter and taciturn? She shook her head to clear it, refocusing her gaze out of the window as she tried to plan for the task ahead. How could she be of any help to the others and the dwellers if she was in such an irascible mood?

Her home life was just as painful as Jonathan's and she was still tired from the day before. Although her family was just as tedious to have around as Jonathan's, she still had to celebrate the day with them and they had hosted grandparents, uncles, aunts and a few of her annoying cousins till late. Her mother had conveniently disappeared, citing work and the legal system as reasons for not taking a day off. It was freezing outside and roaming through the cold with Kitty on a wild goose chase was not Sarah's idea of fun. She hoped Kitty was right about her hunch, otherwise they would have wasted an entire day driving across to Wimbledon only to return empty handed and irritable, and that would be devastating.

The car turned towards the Common and her tension returned. Sarah was still angry with her friend. There was still so much she wanted to say to Asha; she wanted to scream at her and shake her and release her anger about the way she had treated them over the past nine months. It had been embarrassing having to explain to her parents that Asha had just suddenly stopped talking to them, and then the rumours began at school about why the friendship had suddenly ceased. No one linked it to Asha's mother's death because they would never have expected her to isolate herself in such an extreme manner. At the back of her mind, Sarah wondered what would happen once the dwellers were reunited – for how long would this strange chapter in their lives continue? And when the dwellers were returned would their new friendship cease once more? They had never discussed the rules and had simply welcomed her back into their fold with open arms. Sarah gave her friend a sneaky look. Jonathan did not seem to care and was keen to let Asha continue being involved, but she was not prepared to give Asha an easy time of it. So when Asha leant over to ask her how she felt, Sarah showed her misgivings for the task ahead. There was no excitement, no trepidation, no trembling hands at the thought of discovering Kee's Corner and walking into another commune with new dwellers and explaining to them over cups of tea and a warm fire that they had found their long-lost friends. There would be none of that.

There was another feeling tugging at Sarah; it was disturbing and she could not rid herself of it. As the car stopped, she paused to glance at Kitty who was making her way across the snowy road. Kitty as usual was dressed like a grown-up lady of the manor – all tweeds and leather boots with brass accents. Sarah idly wondered if she spent most of her time at her wardrobe or whether Kitty's appearance was always so effortless. She gazed fondly at Jonathan, watching as he stiffened when Katherine came into view. He hid his excitement well from his father.

Grasping frantically at the handle she opened the door and stepped out of the vehicle, the fresh air filling her lungs, the biting cold snapping at her exposed face. She shuddered and pulled her coat tighter around her torso. Looking up to greet Kitty with a smile she froze as she saw it in the background: the silent Common. The place felt dead and a horror dawned on her; dread rose within her but she could not stifle it. Something was horribly wrong. How could they all be experiencing different emotions? Asha, Jonathan and even Kitty were excited, but all she felt at that moment was dread.

'Is that her?' Asha whispered excitedly to her as she came round the car.

Sarah gazed at her for a moment before she responded. 'Yes.'

'She looks like—'

'Something out of a turn of the century novel. Yeah, tell me about it,' Sarah said with a forced laugh. 'Jonathan is besotted with her though.'

She turned as Jonathan emerged from the car, reluctant to say any more until Mr Stapleton was out of earshot.

'Thanks, Mr Stapleton.'

They waved as he drove off, watching his car disappear in to the vast whiteness.

'I've never seen London like this before,' she muttered to herself.

'No, nor me. The snow normally starts turning to slush by now and it gets all ugly,' Asha agreed. 'It's been beautiful for so long. It's a sign of what's to come.'

Sarah stopped talking about the weather long enough to grab Asha by the shoulders and steer her in Kitty's direction. She was standing with Jonathan by her side.

'Asha, this is Kitty Heathridge. Kitty, meet Asha Saunders. Our oldest friend.'

'Pleased to meet you, Asha.' Kitty flashed pearly white teeth as she took Asha's hands and shook them warmly.

'Did you have a good Christmas?' Sarah asked, indulging in pointless conversation to fill the odd silence. Asha had gone quiet and Jonathan seemed lost for words.

'Yes and no. Yes, because it was lovely. I had family here. No, because... I might have found something, which is why I thought it best Jonathan came.' She smiled apologetically. 'I didn't mean for you all to have to come together, especially on Boxing Day, but the last time I spoke to you, you said it was urgent so I decided to waste no time and call Jonathan yesterday. I thought it might be best to have a look today when everyone is still recovering from Christmas festivities and snowed under, rather than when the Common gets busy again with dogs, horses and walkers.'

There was that sweet smile again.

'Of course,' Sarah said, taking control as no one else seemed to know what to do, 'let's walk across then.' Bracing themselves for a bit of exercise after a day of indulgence they followed Kitty across the abandoned road into the clearer part of the Common, their heavy boots making indentations in the snow. Asha stayed back with Sarah whilst Jonathan walked alongside Kitty ahead of them, ever attentive, his eyes never leaving her.

'How did you find this place?' Jonathan asked.

'I was exercising Tinker yesterday,' Kitty began. Her voice was melodic and quaint and she sounded like she was about to burst into song.

'Tinker?' Asha whispered to Sarah, eyebrows raised and a curious look on her face.

'My horse.' Kitty had very good hearing.

'Oh!'

Sarah noticed her friend's slight discomfort but she could not fathom why. She wondered if it was due to Kitty's presence, which was absurd. The girl was nice enough, polite, well-mannered, albeit a bit pretentious, but there was nothing malicious about her. Jonathan had clearly warmed to her and hung on to her every word. There was the added advantage of Kitty finding the commune for them which was a great help – if it was the commune. Either way they owed her a debt of gratitude for trying. Asha did not have a right to feel anything but indebted to Kitty.

'Tinker and I found something,' Kitty explained, as though the horse had been part of the search effort.

Sarah raised her eyes, catching Asha's astonished gaze, and tried to hide a snort – which made it louder and more pronounced. Jonathan glared at both of them, his gaze demanding they be quiet and listen. Kitty did not seem to have noticed their amusement and carried on.

'I can't explain it too well but it was a hiding place, some sort of entryway. The snow fall was so heavy that it toppled off the trees and bent some of the branches, exposing it.'

Asha edged closer to Sarah to avoid being heard.

'Shouldn't the entrance have been protected and hidden? Isn't that what keeps them safe? Why would they leave it to be exposed by a freak snowstorm?'

It was a puzzling question. The Unending Canal was guarded and annoyingly difficult to find unless the dwellers were expecting them. Sarah shrugged – she did not have the answers. It was best to wait till they found the commune and gained entry. For all they knew the entrance could now be protected and they might never find them.

They were quiet as they continued into the trees.

After a long pause Kitty spoke again. 'I felt that dreadful feeling again, you know, during the ride, and Tinker wasn't comfortable either. She senses something here and I think it has to do with that patch of darkness. Don't forget – there's the presence of Billy Bragg, Jane Thompson and all the others who have died at that spot.'

A shudder passed through Sarah as Kitty's words reverberated around the small enclosure they'd paused in, everything around them suddenly hostile and cold.

'Do you think it's haunted, Kitty?' It was the first direct question Asha had asked her. She sounded incredulous at the thought.

'I don't know. I do believe in the energy of a place and it is troubled here. There is certainly a disturbance in that part of the Common, something evil. I know I sound strange but how do you explain normally obedient horses spooking and throwing experienced riders to injury or death? There have been so many accidents here over the years. So many experienced riders dying or meeting misfortune in the most ridiculous accidents. Something is going on and it's all happening along that stretch of the Common – the one I rode down yesterday. I tell you it's cursed.' She halted. Sarah held her breath. There was more.

'Tinker bucked me off yesterday. She's never done that before. You might think me foolish, even fanciful, Asha, but animals do not lie. They sense evil.'

Sarah exchanged a wary look with Asha and Jonathan. Kitty was not joking and certainly sounded anxious.

'The sooner we find out what is in that hole then perhaps we'll get to the cause of who these people are hounding your friends. We need to look in and around that area where the dark spot is. I can help you and my dad has all sorts of tools in the house,' Kitty continued.

They walked a few more metres. The part of the Common they approached was quieter than everywhere else; it was a heavy, burdening silence that did not feel normal. Kitty slowed before stopping at a spot with the large water trough just a few metres away at the bottom of the narrow trail.

'Just down there,' Kitty whispered, pointing ahead of them.

Jonathan, who had been strangely quiet for the journey, looked around as if expecting something to emerge from the thick trees that surrounded them. Asha stuck behind Sarah as though she would protect her from this curse Kitty spoke of, whatever it was.

Sarah had to admit the snowy atmosphere, looming trees and stillness added a dramatic air to the already tense mood. She grinned inwardly, trying to think of a gentle way to tell them to compose themselves.

Then she felt it too, the same feeling Kitty had just described to them, the one she had experienced as she got out of the car minutes before. The feeling of imminent dread; although the Common was quiet the area was deathly silent, but it was no longer just the quiet that was chilling, there was also melancholy in the air.

Sarah did not voice her emotions as they walked behind Kitty, moving closer to the path leading to the water trough. The snow had barely been disturbed in this part but the sadness persisted. She and Asha linked hands as though what was present could not divide them if they were physically connected.

'It's here.' Kitty went off the path to the right where it was thick with bushes and shrubbery and pointed her finger.

Getting down on her hands and knees she gestured to the others who held back nervously. Sarah and Asha glanced at Jonathan who gave them a suspicious look.

'If there was ever a time to impress her, Jonathan...' Asha whispered with a wan smile. He shot her a dark look and muttered something under his breath.

It was supposed to be a joke to lighten the mood but did nothing for the ambience.

Jonathan crouched down to where Kitty was, almost having to press his body against the snow to get a look. Sarah shivered as she watched them.

'Do you see that? That dark bit...'

'Yes, it's very well hidden,' Jonathan said as he peered down beside her. 'I wonder what it is.'

Sarah stood back from them to see if she could get a better look without having to get down on all fours. She moved as far back as she could into the foliage, dustings of snow falling over her head and shoulders as she disturbed the bushes and smaller branches, before catching a glimpse it. The heavy snowfall had pushed down on the bushes, leaving the area slightly exposed. From the short distance it looked like a large dark circle but to find out she would have to get on her hands and knees and under the hedgerow with them. Sarah was claustrophobic enough without having to subject herself to enclosed spaces in miserable conditions.

'What do you think it is?' Asha had come to join her; she leant as far back as possible, her hair getting caught in the bramble. She no longer sounded so certain.

'I don't think any dwellers live here,' Sarah whispered to her.

The look of disappointment on Asha's face was profound.

'That's a shame,' she said. 'I really hoped this would be it, you know.'

'We might as well see what's down there though. Wimbledon Common is old – why would there be a covering down there? There's no drainage, no lights, nothing man-made here, so it does seem strange,' said Sarah.

'They might have installed something,' Jonathan quipped from down below.

'It makes no sense. I read up about it and it's just a Common there would be no need for anything to be installed in the ground,' Sarah said. The dread persisted.

Asha nodded in agreement.

Jonathan got to his feet and helped Kitty up. He brushed himself off then stopped as though it was pointless.

'Okay, Kitty, you stay here with Asha. Sarah and I will check it out,' he said, not seeming to notice the deflated look on her face.

Sarah grimaced. Someone had to do the dirty work but why did she have to go in there. He knew she would be the last person to go down a mysterious dark hole. She glanced at him expectantly.

'Ah Jon, my coat is brand new. It's pure wool. I only got

it yesterday—' she began, but before she could finish Kitty interjected.

'If I may be so bold perhaps it's best for me to help you. Asha and Sarah might be better off staying together. I know the areas and history of the Common quite well. I'm also wearing my riding clothes,' she added, giving Sarah a pleasant smile.

Asha let out a noise that was something between a snort and a cough.

Kitty was anything but dishevelled and her clothing did not look as if she had been anywhere near horses that day, but Sarah glanced at her with relief, cursing Jonathan for suggesting she go down there.

'Great. Asha and I will keep watch here then.' Sarah happily finalised their roles.

'Hardly anyone will come down this path anyway. Not on Boxing Day. I'm just going to head home and bring some tools that we might need and flasks of tea to warm us up,' Kitty said with her cheery smile.

'I'll come with you,' Sarah hastily volunteered, still grateful she had been spared going down a hole.

'We'll be a few minutes at most,' Kitty said, turning to Asha and Jonathan with a smile.

Sarah looked back at her friends as she walked off with Kitty. The sight of Asha and Jonathan standing there watching them go was strange. Asha, in her dark brown coat, her braided head covered in a thick woolly snug hat, looked excited at the prospect of the task ahead of them and Jonathan, standing there in his dark navy coat, pristine as ever, dark brown curls blowing in the wind, dark eyes lighting up with glee at the thought of an afternoon with his friends and Kitty, however cold it was.

Then Sarah felt it again, the dread that stirred within

her moments before had returned and was now taking hold of her body. With a dawning realisation she worked out it was a sign of things to come – her inner self was trying to warn her but she seemed to be the only one feeling this way. Her friends were relaxed and excited about what the day was to bring. But all she felt was alarm. She wanted to yell at them to run away and she would go with them, they would wait for their ride back to North London where it was safe and not look back, but the words refused to come. Instead she said nothing but smiled at her friends, the smile not reaching her panicked eyes. She must have been looking at them oddly because Asha raised her hands and gave a little reassuring wave and Jonathan awkwardly raised his hands in a half-hearted attempt at humour. For Sarah it felt like the beginning of the end; events were only going to get worse, but she did not know why and would not be able to properly explain her reasoning and, for the normally eloquent Sarah, that made her sad.

CHAPTER 11

*J*onathan watched as Kitty and Sarah trudged purposefully through the snow. When they had disappeared he went to sit by Asha who had found a comfortable spot on an exposed low-hanging branch. She wrapped her arms around herself to keep warm. They were both silent for a while, basking in the peace of the space, Jonathan more than a little curious about what might be in the hole.

'Wouldn't it be funny if we saw an actual dweller now?' he asked, eyes flashing excitedly.

'That would be great,' Asha said with a smile. 'It would stop us having to go down a strange hole.'

'You mean Kitty and I having to go down a strange hole,' he teased.

'Well, you like her so I guess it does help. She can hold your hand when you get terrified,' Asha retorted.

Jonathan laughed a little as he gazed at her out of the corner of his eye. The happenings of the last few weeks did not seem to have diminished her but rather had strengthened her resolve. They had Asha back, but for how long?

He decided to plunge in and ask the question that was uppermost on his mind. If it scared her away then their friendship was not to be.

'So how was your first Christmas with just you and your dad?'

'Strangely nostalgic.' Asha hesitated.

Jonathan knew she wanted to talk about her mother but was uncertain if it was going to be all right with him.

'Because of your mum?' he asked.

Asha nodded and swallowed. She looked pained. 'I miss her so much. She would have made us all sing out of tune whilst she played the piano. The tree also didn't feel the same without her touch. I don't know – everything is still so messed up.'

'But getting better, right?'

'Yes, but very slowly.'

'You're still mourning her so it's understandable. My mum said it never goes away but you learn to live with it.'

Jonathan sensed she was holding something back. There was something else she wanted to say but was apprehensive about it.

'What is it?'

She inhaled deeply, her hands trembled and her voice shook as she spoke.

'We had a visitor...'

'What do you mean a *visitor*?' His eyes widened, his heartbeat accelerated – if she'd had one he wondered if they had come to his home too. The Stapleton family had the large Bluebell Woods opposite their home and any uninvited visitors would have been able to hide without being seen.

'Well, yesterday I was home with Dad, reading. We were being watched and then the most ear-shattering howl came from the back garden.' She wrapped her arms around herself again. 'The security lights as usual failed to come on because they'd been tampered with. Dad didn't suspect anything, though. He thought it was an animal.'

'Wow.' Jonathan exhaled. 'That sounds scary. Was it all of them watching or just one?'

'No idea. When we heard the cry it sounded like one person.'

'Yes, but I suppose they're all different, aren't they? They must be.'

'Why do you think they did that? Why would they howl and attract attention to themselves?' She looked at him curiously as though he had the answers.

'I really don't know, Asha. What I do know is Sergeant King said they were very dangerous – well, he said Dante and Billy were – so I suppose the rest of them must be just as deranged.'

'I wonder if my father and I could be in danger.' She didn't mince her words.

Jonathan understood her thinking. If these people were so bold as to watch whilst her father was present then they didn't fear him enough to keep away.

'Do you think they could try to come in?'

'No – they may be unhinged but they aren't stupid. They'll know the law and we have the right to protect ourselves in our homes, right?'

Asha didn't look too certain about what action one could take in one's own home but Jonathan wanted to do his best to alleviate any fears she had about the Mimes gaining entry.

'Who knows – this might solve the puzzle once and for all.' He motioned to the mystery circle.

Asha nodded emphatically. 'Yes, I hope so too. We find

the missing commune and send the dwellers back – somehow – and the Mimes leave us alone.' She made it sound so simple.

'But at the same time… I somehow don't want this to be over.'

'Why?' Asha sounded confused.

'Because a part of me thinks we'll go back to where we were just a few months ago – you not talking to us and me wondering what I'd done wrong.'

'You didn't do anything wrong, Jonathan. It was just me. I thought I could control everything by not speaking after Mum died. The thought of me, you and Sarah together would be too normal. Things were far from that though. It would be real, but Mum wouldn't be around anymore and I just got scared.' She looked at him; her voice was a little wobbly. He knew she was close to tears but chose to turn his head. 'It was the only part of my life I had control over. I couldn't control who around me lived or died but I could control who I spoke to, who I saw.'

'So you thought you would push us all away instead?' He kept his gaze fixed on the snow.

Asha nodded mutely.

'Everyone suffered at some point, you know. I really needed you back in March. I called your house and your father said you were busy. I knew he didn't have the heart to tell me you didn't want to speak to me or anyone else.' Jonathan's voice wavered slightly. 'Charlie and the rest of the rugby lads are hardly the ones to speak to.'

Asha turned to look at him; she placed a gentle hand on his.

'What happened?'

'Sam was in a bad skiing accident and disappeared for several hours. They couldn't find him anywhere. Tyler was still trying to get back from university. Mum was in Paris at the time and, well, you know Dad, not the most emotional person, but he took the next flight out. Sam had had a bad fall when he went off-piste on his own like a complete idiot. It was the longest night of my life.' He couldn't look Asha in the face. 'When they found him he was delirious, very broken and suffering from hypothermia. Luckily he had survived because he took sandwiches out with him, you know what he's like with food, and a whisky flask. I called you because Sarah's grandmother had just passed away. I wanted to talk to you because I could hardly call her to burden her. I wanted to see you.'

There was a long heavy silence as they sat there; the snow and woodland surrounding them seemed surreal.

'S-Sarah's grandmother passed away?' Asha blinked in disbelief. The shock in her voice echoed in the clearing.

'Yes. She did. Dead and buried for quite a while now.' Jonathan did not mean to sound callous but it was time Asha discovered the hard truth. Life went on without her.

He gazed languidly at her; he had been right about everything. Sarah's grandmother had passed away, so much had happened and Asha had not even known about it. Asha had sleepwalked through the past year, failing to notice the grief and turmoil in their lives because she had been so busy with hers. Why hadn't her father told her about all this? Patrick Saunders was at the funeral. When enquiries had been made about Asha's whereabout he had said she was down with the flu. Jonathan wondered what had happened in the Saunders household for the past nine months, what had life been like for father, daughter and housekeeper. It would have been a strange experience.

When Asha finally spoke she seemed to be struggling to get her words across. Her voice kept catching in her throat and she sounded stilted. Jonathan gazed at her in concern and when she looked up at him again he saw something he had never seen before: contrition.

'I'm so sorry, Jon. I'm sorry I wasn't there for you. I'm also sorry you had to go through that on your own. Letting you two back into my life meant I had to acknowledge my mum was gone and never coming back.'

Jonathan couldn't look at her; he found himself overcome with emotion. She wrapped her arms around him and gave him a hug.

'It won't happen again. I promise.'

'I thought I was never going to see Sam again. Suddenly everything that twit had ever done to annoy me when we were kids seemed like a gift.' When he turned to look at Asha his face was racked with emotion. 'When you leave people the way you did, Asha, it leaves them feeling confused. I still think I did something wrong and so does Sarah, even though she pretends she doesn't. You have to mourn your mother, Asha, it's part of the process, but you can't push people away and expect them to hang around.'

'I know. I'm sorry.'

'I'll also tell you this now. Sarah is still very angry with you although she hasn't shown it yet – but she will. You know how close she was to Grammy Collidge.' He was warning her. Jonathan had seen the pain Sarah had carried around for months and he knew she was still a long way from resolved about her grandmother's death.

'Thank you for letting me know,' Asha said, hugging him as they sat waiting for Kitty and Sarah to return.

It wasn't a long wait before they heard voices in the distance, then Kitty and Sarah appeared pushing a wheelbarrow.

'Don't you two just look absolutely miserable. Like two street urchins.' Sarah threw a large backpack to the ground.

'I'm sorry we were longer than expected. My father was asking us a lot of questions,' Kitty said.

'He wants Kitty back in an hour because we're due to get more snow and we haven't got much daylight left,' Sarah added, grimacing.

Jonathan abruptly got to his feet and squared his shoulders.

'Don't worry, Kitty, we don't have too long either. My dad is our lift back home. Besides, the snow is supposed to start at about four o'clock so we have a couple of hours.'

'Yes, but there's an entire world down there,' Sarah cautioned him. 'It could take days to find them.'

'So we pace ourselves and come back if we have to. It'll be fun.'

Sarah mumbled something unintelligible under her breath. She reached into the wheelbarrow and threw some overalls at him.

'Here – they belong to Kitty's dad. They're spares.'

Jonathan pulled a face as he donned the musty overalls. The others stifled laughs as he looked down at himself.

'Still charming, Jonathan,' Asha said with a wink.

'This is a bit pungent,' he moaned.

'Oh hush – it'll keep your coat clean,' Sarah said.

～

*A*sha stood back as they covered up their tailored clothing with overalls and gloves and as much protection as one would need to go down below London. The melancholy and sadness of the last hour was gone, replaced instead by promise, expectation and excitement.

She stood by as Jonathan complained about the smell of his overalls and Kitty and Sarah teased him mercilessly. This was what it was about, this camaraderie, the friendship, the selflessness – even Kitty who knew nothing about them and had never met the dwellers was helping with supplies and volunteering herself to go down below.

Asha was not sure how long it would take to find them. If Kee's Corner was anything like the Unending Canal then it would be a walk of at least a mile before they discovered any civilisation. She recalled Fred's description of Kee's Corner – the antiquated commune that was a small frag-ment of their world with its tiny winding streets, low ceil-ings, no fairy lights, and rather unsophisticated way of life, the magical element not as strong as the Unending Canal. 'Like a rabbit warren,' he'd sniffed as he sipped some tea with Hiller at his feet. 'Why they do not reside somewhere more beautiful I have no idea. However, we do have good friends and some family there and goodness knows you never leave them behind or let them suffer alone.' Now, as Asha stood there amongst the readying group on the verge of discovering Kee's Corner, Fred's words reverberated in her head; that remark about friends and family had stuck with her. That was what Jonathan and Sarah were to her and so were the dwellers, yet here she was being precious about going down below and scurrying around in a bit of darkness to find the entrance to Kee's Corner. The dwellers had saved her from the Mimes when they had no reason to and her friends had come to her aid despite her failings of the past year. Kitty should not be made to scrabble precari-ously down below – it would have to be up to her. She had made her promise to the dwellers and would carry it out.

Asha decided then and there. She placed a firm hand on Kitty's shoulder. Jonathan and Sarah paused uncertainly at her action. 'Kitty. I'll go down below. You wait here with Sarah.'

'But...' Kitty began.

'It's fine. I can handle a bit of claustrophobia and this is about friendship, after all.'

Kitty nodded in understanding and a smile stretched across her delicate features. Jonathan and Sarah were grinning broadly too.

'Besides, if you break an arm or something down below Jonathan will never forgive me,' Asha added cheekily.

'Well, look at you being all noble. What's brought this on then?' Sarah teased.

'Just something Fred said to me,' Asha responded, deliberately cryptic. She swallowed apprehensively, almost wanting the adventure not to end and knowing if it did the dwellers would be gone, returned to their world in Georgian London. Asha would return to her old life, plunged into the desperation of the months before with no focus, and her life would be once more about school and family – only now there was no longer a family. She swallowed painfully. Her nerves began playing up. Jonathan was watching her; she felt his eyes on her. He turned around to make sure Sarah and Kitty were out of earshot before turning back to her.

'It's okay. It'll all be fine,' he said reassuringly. 'It'll be fine down there.'

'I'm not worried about going down there. I'm more concerned with what happens when they're gone.'

'Yes. When they're gone – the dwellers – you'll have Sarah and I, I promise. It won't be all silent.'

'Are you sure?' she asked.

'We'll always have each other,' Jonathan assured her.

'How about Kitty?' she ventured. 'I know you really like her and she's your friend,' she said. 'What if you end up spending time with her and Sarah spends all her time with Yu.' Asha felt the panic rising in her throat as she struggled to speak.

'Remember, we wouldn't have come to help you out if we didn't care,' Jonathan responded with a genuine smile.

Asha took deep breaths as she composed herself and reminded herself that she was not alone. She did have friends, good friends, and even though the dwellers would be gone she would not be alone.

'Thank you. All of you,' she added looking around, including Sarah and Kitty who were standing a distance away.

Kitty smiled, a palm to her chest. 'This is so sweet. You're all such good friends to each other. I wish I had that – I mean, I used to have a good friend...' Her voice trailed off as she choked on her words.

'Oh lord,' Sarah said with a begrudging smile. 'Why is everyone getting sentimental? Can we please get down below so we can at least get some warm tea by a roaring fire before heading home?'

They all nodded in agreement.

'Oh yes,' Asha exclaimed pulling her overalls on, suddenly motivated by the thought of a warm fire. She wrinkled her nose. Jonathan had been right. The overalls were musty. 'I do hope this *is* Kee's Corner,' she muttered under her breath.

'It is going to be one of two situations down there,' Sarah surmised. 'Either this will lead to a commune and an enchanted world down below – Kee's Corner – where we will regale the dwellers with our adventures over cups of tea and freshly baked cookies, or,' she paused dramatically, 'you and Jonathan will end up in the sewers being chased by huge rats.'

They all descended into peals of laughter. Asha was comforted by Sara's comedy. It soothed the moment and calmed her nerves. The laughter filled the wintry air chasing the apprehension away.

'I wish we could savour this moment a bit longer,' Jonathan mused.

Kitty looked up with concern. 'That will be impossible I'm afraid.' She motioned towards the sky. Darkness loomed in the distance. 'The snow will be arriving soon. We must begin.' Her words had a finality to them.

Jonathan looked at her, his eyes wide with excitement. 'Well, this is it.' He exhaled shakily, but could not deny the frisson of excitement he shared with the others.

ABOUT THE AUTHOR

Oyinda Aro is an author of novels. This is her fifth published book. She lives in London with her two dogs and can be contacted on her Facebook page, her website or Instagram Oyinda_Aro

To get your free ebook sign up below

www.oyindaaro.com/subscribe

author@oyindaaro.com

THE DWELLERS BENEATH THE ARCHES

Browning House (Book 2)

The Longest Night (Book 3)

COATS

Black Coats (Coats series Book 1)

The Fall of the Reds (Coats series Book 2)

My Brother's Keeper (Coats series Book 3)